Sir Alan Herbert was born in 1890 and educated at Winchester and Oxford. Having achieved a first in Jurisprudence, he then joined the Royal Navy and served both at Gallipoli and in France during the First World War. He was called to the Bar in 1918, and went on to become a Member of Parliament for Oxford University from 1935 to 1950.

Throughout his life A P Herbert was a prolific writer, delighting his many readers with his witty observations and social satires in the columns of *Punch*. He was the creator of a host of colourful characters – notably Topsy, Albert Haddock and Mr Honeybubble – and wrote novels, poems, musicals, essays, sketches and articles. He was also a tireless campaigner for reform, a denouncer of injustice and a dedicated conserver of the Thames.

By the time of his death in 1971, he had gained a considerable following and was highly regarded in literary circles. J M Barrie, Hilaire Belloc, Rudyard Kipling and John Galsworthy all delighted in his work, and H G Wells applauded him saying, 'You are the greatest of great men. You can raise delightful laughter and that is the only sort of writing that has real power over people like me.'

TO MY DEAR WIFE

CONTENTS

Explanation   1

THE TENS

The Last Teen   7
Twitting The Turk   8
The Cure   9
On the March   (1) Lost Leader   11
               (2) The Road to Oonoesware   12
The Coming of Peace   14
Spring Cleaning   16

THE TWENTIES

A Criminal Type   19
Gin and Mixed   24
Topsy: The Noble Animal   25
Equality etc.: or Clause Four   29
Topsy: Reducing   30
'Twas at the Pictures, Child, We Met   34
Topsy: The Fresh Mind   37
'It May Be Life…'   41
Mr Mafferty Has a Hair-cut   43
Why Doesn't She Come?   47
The Wash: or, Dawn in Hospital   49
Mr Mafferty Takes a Lady Out   54
Love in the National Gallery   58

I Told You So: The Smellies 60
Mr Mafferty and The Oppressed Races 61
The Daily Seventeen 65
Topsy Goes Hunting 70

THE THIRTIES

Helen 75
The Reasonable Man 77
'Mr Speaker, Sir… ': Maiden Speech 82
'Nothing's Been the Same' 83
Free Speech – Why? 85
A Nice Cup of Tea 89
Scene Seventeen 91
Ninth Wicket 94
Other People's Babies 97
'Not Catchy' 99
The Common Cold 104
Love Lies Bleeding 107
Mullion 116
'Mr Speaker, Sir… ': Royal Commissions 118
Do You Say 'Dorn'? 120
'Mr Speaker, Sir… ': Tuberculous Beverages 123
Song of Sport 125
Why Is The House of Lords? 127
I Told You So: 'A H' 131

THE FORTIES

'Mr Speaker, Sir… ': Books Tax 133
Invasion 135
To WSC 135
We Were The First… 135
'Less Nonsense' 136
Blow the Blues! 137
Monty the 'Martinet' 139
Morning Paper 142

'The Change' 143
The Lords 144
Big Ben 145
My Big Moment 148
From the Russian: The Dawn 149
Doomed 150
The 'Deposit' 151
In A Garden 151
Anywhere 151
'Mr Speaker, Sir…': Double Summer Time 152
From the Chinese: The Traveller 155
Spelling – and Mr Shaw 156
'Mr Speaker, Sir…': Swan Song 160

THE FIFTIES

What Can You Do if Your Mum's Not a Psychiatrist? 163
London River Men 165
Vital Statistics (1) 168
(2) 169
'No Fine on Fun' 170
The Way Out 172
Protest 172
The Christmas Stars 173
Ballad of Ballistics 173
What's My Whine? 175
'Delouse the Treasury!' 177
Robert Burns 181
'I Told You So': Clause Four (1) 183
Clause Four (2) 186
The Pools Case 187
'Is it Cricket?' 191
Is That the Face…? 194
'Let Me Go Down the Mine, Daddy' 195
From the Russian: Confessional 196
From the Chinese: The Ambassador 199

The Missing Show   202
From the Chinese: Consolation   206
From the Chinese: A Woman's Work   207
Matrons and Molls   210
The School for Saints   212

THE SIXTIES

The Sunday Bosom   217
Harnessing Hell   219
Birds Don't Want Wings   223
Ode: The American Constitution   226
'Old Iron': or, 'What About the Tides?'   230
Annual Dinner   236
The Blue Sea   239

My grateful acknowledgments and salutes to *Punch*, who have printed and suffered me for fifty years, and to any other editor represented here: to Messrs Ernest Benn Ltd for permitting me to re-publish fourteen pieces from *A Book of Ballads* and *The Topsy Omnibus*: to the Controller of Her Majesty's Stationery Office for permission to quote from *Hansard*; and to Miss Deirdre Handcock for her excellent and patient labours.

APH

EXPLANATION

This is not the 'Definitive Collection of Herbert's Miscellaneous Works'. That, if anyone bothered about it, would fill the fattest bomb. No, this is a kind of birthday present from my kindly publisher, Mr Alan White of Methuen's. He said: 'On September 24, they tell me, you will be 70. You will also – just – have been writing for *Punch* for fifty years. Why not go back through all the decades and make a sort of birthday jumble book? You may find a lot of things that you have forgotten – and some the young folk never knew.' So here we are.

I must have been born with some lyrical bug in my blood, for very early I was committing rhymes. At about the age of 10 I lost my amateur status at Bognor (it was not 'Regis' then). A small variety company at the end of the pier offered a prize for a new refrain to one of their songs. The refrain was:

'If I was – – Somebody or Other
I would – I would'

I forget what followed, but I won the prize and was given that melting book *Black Beauty*.

Very early I became a Gilbert and Sullivan lover, and did violence to them on the piano, instead of practising my prescribed exercises and 'pieces'. At Winchester a kindly prefect introduced me to C S Calverley (do schoolboys read him now?) and I was doomed. I published my first book of verse in my last

1

year at school. I cannot pretend that it was good. At about the age of 16 I had begun a regular bombardment of *Punch*, and, after three years, in 1910, scored one or two hits at last. Again, except for dogged pertinacity, I can find small virtue in them now.

But do not think that I was a frivolous boy. In 1908 I won the Maltby Prize for Latin Verse (subject – The San Francisco Earthquake) and in 1909 the King's Gold Medal for English Verse (subject – the Messina Earthquake). Earthquakes, beloved by the masters, are not my favourite theme. My Messina was an odious composition – 200 lines of tosh. But it won the Gold Medal.

Punch, in those days, was run by two men, Owen Seaman, and his Assistant Editor, Charles Graves (I do not believe there was a female secretary behind them). Sir Owen Seaman, apart from other high qualities, must have been the most painstaking editor in history. Every weekend he took away with him a despatch-case full of 'contributions'. He was not, when he saw any promise, content to reject. He wrote in long-hand, with a 'stylo' pen, elaborate letters of correction, suggestion, and encouragement – even to a schoolboy of 16 years. 'I don't like this or that rhyme' – 'Verse three, logically, conflicts with verse one,' etc. For three years he nursed and stimulated me thus. Often I would send back an amended version of the same piece two or three times. I have never ceased to marvel at the trouble he took.

A fine light poet himself, be was very strict about the rules of the difficult art. His discipline, to my detriment in the theatre,* has remained with me ever since.

At Oxford I wrote much for the *Isis*, and, blow me, published another little collection, *Play Hours with Pegasus*.

In the 1914 War, in the rare spare moments of an infantry officer, I scribbled away, and sent some pieces back to *Punch*.

* See "Do You Say 'Dorn'?" page 120.

Two more 'slim volumes' followed, *Half Hours at Helles* and *The Bomber Gipsy*.

After the war I became a 'regular' contributor to *Punch* and in 1924 was invited to the Table, the weekly gathering at which the political cartoons are discussed and settled. This was, and is, an honour and a delight. It is highly exciting for a new boy to carve his humble initials on the famous Table, not far from those of Thackeray, Tenniel, Phil May, Charles Keene. In those days we dined: today it is lunch. Long clay pipes lay on the Table at my first dinner, but were not much used. My arrival made the full company thirteen, but nobody seemed to mind.

I can see them now – Phil Agnew, proprietor and host, at one end, where he had sat since 1891, Owen Seaman at the other – Raven-Hill and E V Knox on his right, my humble – and I felt very humble – self on his left. Next to Agnew were Bernard Partridge, senior cartoonist, and E V Lucas, charming essayist and lovable man. Then there were Charles Graves, W A Locker, Ernest Shepard, George Morrow, Frank Reynolds, art editor, and young Ewan Agnew.

Only two others, E V Knox and Ernest Shepard, are alive today.

I do not remember that we were very merry, but there were some very robust arguments. The sparks flew many times between Raven-Hill, who was a strong Conservative, and E V Knox, who was not.

In the Twenties my long practice of light verse led me to the theatre, and 'light opera', as we called 'a musical' then. I began in 1924 with a play, *King of the Castle*, for William Armstrong, that fine, delightful fellow, at the Playhouse, Liverpool. Dennis Arundell did the music. Angela Baddeley was Principal Boy. Then my neighbour Nigel Playfair rang me up, and there began five happy, but not very remunerative, years at the Lyric, Hammersmith – *Riverside Nights* (music by Frederick Austin and Alfred Reynolds), *La Vie Parisienne* (Offenbach), *Two Gentlemen of Soho*, *Plain Jane* (Richard Austin), *Tantivy Towers*

(T F Dunhill), *Derby Day* (Alfred Reynolds). I wish that someone would give the last two a full-scale production. The music of both is just as 'good' as that of some of the foreign works performed at Sadlers Wells; and *Tantivy Towers* is real 'light opera', with no spoken dialogue.

In 1931 the great C B Cochran summoned me to the West End to do *Helen* (La *Belle Hélène* – Offenbach – Reinhardt – Evelyn Laye – George Robey – Oliver Messel) a wonderful production. For a short time *Derby Day* and *Helen* were running together, and with *The White Witch* at the Haymarket (a lamentable flop) I was on three play-bills. In all I did eight musical shows for Cochran – *Streamline* (a revue – with Ronald Jeans and Vivian Ellis), *Home and Beauty* (Binnie Hale, Nelson Keyes), *Mother of Pearl* (Oscar Straus – Alice Delysia), *Paganini* (Lehar – Evelyn Laye, Richard Tauber), *Big Ben*, *Bless the Bride*, and *Tough at the Top* (all Vivian Ellis). I loved Cochran and the work: but I hankered often for the humbler days at the little Lyric. I was fortunate indeed to find favour with two such fine men of the theatre, each in his way a creative artist, as Playfair and 'C B'.

In 1935 I was elected to the House of Commons, and my threads began to tangle. While my 'Marriage Bill' was in Standing Committee, Cochran's *Home and Beauty* was rehearsed across the river and produced at the Adelphi. At the end of a big speech on a Government Bill (Population Statistics) which was said to have reduced the Bill to a shadow, I recited nine stanzas of verse which had appeared in *Punch*.

I forget when I began to write after-dinner speeches in verse, but I have done six or seven – one in alternate English and Spanish couplets to the Argentinian Authors at Buenos Aires. This is a great labour, but the diners seem to like it. I have two or three times succeeded, to my surprise, in delivering these orations without reference to the text. The use of wine has not yet, I am thankful to say, proved fatal to the memory.

4

Not even the Second Great War could mute my voluble Muse. I was still a Member of Parliament and fairly active there. But, as well, all the war, I had the honour to command a very small patrol-boat (of the Royal Naval Auxiliary Patrol) in London River, with a beat of sixty miles from Teddington, west of London, to Southend, near the mouth. Also, I did my best to comfort and hearten my countrymen with brief verses in a Sunday paper. I began these weekly lays on February 4, 1940, and all the war, I am rather proud to say, I never missed a week (except when visiting Newfoundland). But the Navy came before the Muse. In the six months of the Big Blitz, 1940–1941, our little vessel (eighteen horse-power) steamed 6,000 miles up and down the river from Chelsea to Sea Reach, forty-five miles, six or seven days a week, fair tide or foul. Between sirens, at the end of a long Friday, I would creep into the nearest pub and cogitate and scribble in a corner while the sailors banged the piano or played a talkative game of darts. Sometimes the Muse would do a little preliminary work at the wheel while we steamed up the river, or wandered vainly about on patrol under the Battle of Britain that raged in the blue sky over Southend and the Shellhaven oil. Sometimes the Muse had to wait till the Petty-Officer-in-charge *Water Gipsy* was between his blankets with a midnight tot of rum, sometimes even till breakfast-time on Saturday. Then, very often, there was the problem of getting the stuff to the paper. When our journey's end was somewhere in London it was generally easy, though not if we were in distant dockland. But many a Saturday would find us at the bottom of the river, at Gravesend or Holehaven. Sometimes after the night's blitz the telephone line would be cut, often it was feeble and intermittent. And everybody wanted to use it – bargemen and tug-captains seeking orders or due to report, sailors anxious for relatives in London. How often have I stood in that dark hole behind the bar at The Lobster Smack yelling my poetical works into the crackling instrument, lighting a match from time to time to see what they were, while fishermen and sailors with baleful mutterings waited for their turn. 'How is the old Top Wop…?' I would yell. 'What's that? Sorry. The line's very faint. They hit a main.' 'TOP – T – O – P! WOP – W – O – P! "W" for William – "O" for Orange – "P" for Percy – WOP! The Top Wop! Mussolini! Surely you've heard of *him*!' 'Sorry, the line's very faint. I've got "How is the old – What – – What" ' 'Is that right?' Worse still would be the public telephone-box, where, often about every verse, a cold voice would remark, 'Three minutes up. Please insert another one shilling and fourpence,' and the angry bargemen glared through the glass wall, or sometimes opened the door to enquire if the poet was aware 'that there was a war on'. Homer, perhaps, but few other bards, had more trouble in getting their works to the public.

But it all began with *Punch*, fifty years ago, and to that great paper I offer my salutes and thanks. I have sat at the Table under two proprietors – Phil Agnew, his nephew Alan. Peter Agnew, of the next generation, is now managing director; the Agnews have been in it for nearly 100 years, and Bradbury and Agnew have been the owners since 1872. This long and faithful family tradition on the bridge must be good for the ship. There have been five editors in that time – Owen Seaman, E V Knox, Kenneth Bird (Fougasse), Malcolm Muggeridge, and, today, Bernard Hollowood. Each has been different, and left a little of himself behind. But the ship rides on still much the same, and still, I think, pretty good. I, at least, am proud to have been so long a member of the crew.

A P HERBERT

THE TENS

THE LAST TEEN

(Yes, there were teen-agers then. But, it seems, we didn't mind.)

When I was merely 'M or N',
   I wanted more than peace and plenty,
When I was six, when I was ten,
I thirsted for the moment when
I should achieve the years of men
   And reach the glorious age of twenty.

Nor had my ardour lessened yet
   When I discarded G A HENTY,
Learned to indulge without regret
The humours of the cigarette,
And, in a word, contrived to get
   Most of the faults that come at twenty.

But, be the years approaching lean
   Or be they fat (*deo volente*),
They will not be as this has been,
This last and most delightful teen;
And I shall make a sad, sad scene
   On Friday next, when I am twenty.

Punch – September 21, 1910

A P HERBERT

TWITTING THE TURK

(Strange episode at the Dardanelles)

With faces flushed and eyes like wine
The men sat mute along the line,
And some polemical design
    Was palpably in view;
A flare soared sudden through the murk;
They turned unflinching toward the Turk
    And shouted all they knew.

No ordered cheer, but each man cried
The sound on which he most relied,
Or just invoked the Soccer side
    Of which he once was proud;
A milkman happily 'Milk-o'd',
Myself I simply said, 'Well rowed!'
    But said it very loud.

A wilder din you will not meet;
It hit the hills, it shocked the Fleet,
And many a brave heart dropped a beat
    To hear the hideous choir,
While the pale Turk, with lips tight set,
Peered out across the parapet
    And opened Rapid Fire.

For it was clear the Christian cur
Intended something sinister,
And Pashas hastened to confer
    On that hypothesis;
Stout souls, they felt prepared to cope
With stratagems within their scope,
    But, Allah, what was this?

Far down the lines the Faithful heard
And had no notion what occurred,
But plied their triggers, undeterred
    By trifles such as that;
From sea to sea the tumult spread,
Nor could a single man have said
    What he was shooting at.

Then spoke the guns, and gave it hot
To the offensive choric spot
Where we, who shrank from being shot,
    Had long since ceased to be;
And even Asiatic Anne*
Disgorged a bolt of monstrous plan,
    Which fell into the sea.

And our report, in pleasing wise,
Spoke of 'A novel enterprise
Against the enemy supplies'.
    'The General will note,
The casualties of the force
Were sixty men extremely hoarse
    And one severe sore throat.'

        Punch – December 1, 1915

THE CURE;

For a nation of shop-talkers

The fourteenth man said fiercely, 'At the third
I muffed my mashie – thing I never do;

---

* Asiatic Annie, a famous gun on the Troy side of the Straits.

I won the fourth, approaching like a bird,
    And at the fifth my iron came in two;
The sixth I did in just about fifteen,
    But won the seventh with a lovely three;
At number eight my drive was on the green;
    At number nine my drive was in the sea;
And then I put my second in the hay,
But at the –' Here I must have swooned away.

For far, far off there murmured in my head
    The talk of madmen – 'Seven on the green;
The King was guarded, but I laid it dead!
    And all the time I knew he had the Queen;
At the eleventh we were twelve above;
    Then Simpson missed a sitter at the net;
I took my baffie (it was forty-love);
    We never had a trump the second set;
But at the turn –' I don't know what occurred,
For I woke up and said a humble word.

I said, 'I took a ticket out to Kew
    And got into an Inner Circle train;
At High Street I was told it wouldn't do,
    So I went back to Gloucester Road again.
At Baron's Court they trampled on my feet,
    At Hammersmith I leaned against a door;
At Stamford Brook I sank into a seat;
    At Turnham Green I fell upon the floor;
But I arrived; I was not playing well,
But I arrived –' A perfect silence fell.

Punch – September 17, 1919

ON THE MARCH

(1)

LOST LEADER

The men are marching like the best;
　　The waggons wind across the lea;
At ten to two we have a rest,
　　We have a rest at ten to three;
　　I ride ahead upon my gee
　　　　And try to look serene and gay;
　　The whole battalion follows me,
　　　　And I believe I've lost the way.

Full many a high-class thoroughfare
　　My erring map does not disclose,
While roads that are not really there
　　The same elaborately shows;
　　And whether this is one of those
　　　　It needs a clever man to say;
　　I am not clever, I suppose,
　　　　And I believe I've lost the way.

The soldiers sing about their beer;
　　The wretched road goes on and on;
There ought to be a turning here,
　　But if there was the thing has gone;
　　Like some depressed automaton
　　　　I ask at each *estaminet*;
　　They say, *'Tout droit'*, and I say *'Bon'*,
　　　　But I believe I've lost the way.

I dare not tell the trustful men;
　　They think me wonderful and wise;
But where will be the legend when

They get a shock of such a size?
And what about our brave Allies?
    They wanted us to fight today;
We were to be a big surprise –
    And I believe I've lost the way.
            Punch – July 18, 1917 – *The Bomber Gipsy*

(2)

THE ROAD TO OONOESWARE

(*With apologies to the author of 'Mandalay'*)

There's a village in the distance, we'll be getting there tonight,
And per'aps we'll 'ave an easy or per'aps we'll 'ave a fight;
We don't know what we're doing and we ain't supposed to care,
We only know we're always on the road to Oonoesware –
    On the road to Oonoesware, and there *may* be billets there,
    Or there mayn't, and if there isn't there'll be 'eaps of open
        air,
                'Eaps of jolly open air;
                We can bivvy in the Square,
But our Cooker's ditched be'ind us and it's very 'ard to bear.

We walks along and wonders what on earth it's all about;
We 'ope that *someone* savvies, but at times we 'as our doubt,
When the Adjutant looks worried and the Colonel seems in
    pain,
And we whispers in our sorrow, 'Ah, 'e's lost 'isself again';
    Oh, 'e's lost us all again; can't we take the blooming train?
    The estaminays is shutting and it's coming on to rain –
                On the road to Oonoesware,
                'Course it isn't *our* affair,
But I wish some gent would tell 'em 'ow to get to Oonoesware.

We 'alts at level-crossings and 'as a lovely view
Of 'igh-class trains a-shunting, but they ain't for me and you;
We only go on railways when there's dirty work ahead,
And when we ride in motors, well, it means we're nearly dead –
    Yes, it means you're nearly dead, with your body full of lead,
    And a ticket on your tummy says, 'This man must not be
        fed' –
                But the Colonel sits 'is mare,
                And it don't seem 'ardly fair,
That we 'aven't all got 'orses on the road to Oonoesware.

And when our backs is breaking and death seems very near
We marches at attention and inspects the Brigadier;
'E sees our tin 'ats polished and our 'ipes got up to please,
But if 'e saw our blisters we should all be OBEs,
    Bloomin' blistered OBEs, all a-wobbling at the knees,
    And first we sweat like rivers and then we sit and freeze,
                On the road to Oonoesware,
                Ah, *ker voolay, c'est la gair,*
Only this 'ere step they're setting is enough to make you swear.

But the old sun comes out sometimes and the poplars climb the
    'ill
Like a lot of silly soldiers at extended order drill;
And there's bits of woods and scen'ry, and the 'Uns don't seem
    so near
When the band plays through the village and the kids come out
    to cheer –
    All the kids come out to cheer, and a man feels kind of queer,
    And the girls they blow you kisses and the mothers bring you
        beer,
                On the road to Oonoesware,
                Ah, it ain't all skittles there,
But I'm some'ow glad I'm always on the road to Oonoesware.

                        Punch – March 6, 1918

THE COMING OF PEACE

How will it be in Flanders when Peace comes
　　like a blow –
　Comes on a weary daybreak along the
　　startled wires
To where the grimy regiments sit on in slime
　　and snow,
　And the rich fumes of bacon hang round
　　the hissing fires?

How will it seem when sudden there are no
　　noises there,
　Save when from backward cities are heard
　　the tumbling bells,
Or some reluctant sniper forsakes his matted
　　lair
　To fire across the open incredulous
　　farewells?

But the loud guns are silent, and up the
　　Sunken Way
　The jingling teams come gaily to limber
　　up their lords,
With new-born dreams of Dorset and light
　　work in the hay,
　When foolish men for ever have sheathed
　　their foolish swords.

And in the fetid alleys men buckle on their
　　loads,
　And wind away to Westward along the
　　wooden track,
Wind singing round the shell-holes and up
　　the pitted roads,

And turn upon the hill-top to take a long
    look back –

Look back beyond the crosses star-spread
    about the lines,
    And looking, feel beside them their dead
        at last released
To see with them the sun rise above the
    broken shrines,
    And hear the German waggons roll back
        into the East.

But lonesome in the trenches the grey rat
    walks and grieves,
    Nor ever an English ration rewards his
        night-patrols,
And the shy birds come slowly to nest in the
    dug-out eaves,
    And crowding round the sand-bags red
        poppies hide the holes.

And stooping, from the cities, come soon the
    peasant crones
    To hunt for vanished homesteads across
        the withered plain;
Pale children play at battle about the
    hamlets' bones,
    And old men come with ploughshares to
        turn the fields again.

Punch – March 6, 1918, *The Bomber Gipsy*

SPRING CLEANING

The hailstorm stopped; a watery sun came out,
   And late that night I clearly saw the moon;
The lilac did not actually sprout,
   But looked as if it ought to do in June.
I did not say, 'My love, it is the Spring';
   I rubbed my chilblains in a cheerful way,
And asked if there was some warm woollen thing
   My wife had bought me for the first of May;
And, just to keep the ancient customs green,
We said we'd give the poor old house a clean.

Good Mr Ware came down with all his men,
   And filled the house with lovely oily pails,
And went away to lunch at half-past ten,
   And came again at tea-time with some nails,
And laid a ladder on the daffodil,
   And opened all the windows they could see,
And glowered fiercely from the window-sill
   On me and Mrs Tompkinson at tea,
And set large quantities of booby-traps,
And then went home – a little tired, perhaps.

They left their paint-pots strewn about the stair,
   And switched the lights off– but I knew the game;
They took the geyser – none could tell me where;
   It was impossible to wash my frame.
The painted windows would not shut again,
   But gaped for ever at the Eastern skies;
The house was full of icicles and rain;
   The bedrooms smelled of turpentine and size;
And if there be a more unpleasant smell
I have no doubt that that was there as well.

My wife went out and left me all alone,
    While more men came and clamoured at the door
To strip the house of everything I own,
    The curtains and the carpets from the floor,
The kitchen range, the cushions and the stove,
    And ask me things that husbands never know,
'Is this 'ere paint the proper shade of mauve?'
    Or 'Where is it this lino has to go?'
I slunk into the cellar with the cat,
This being where the men had put my hat.

I cowered in the smoking-room, unmanned;
    The days dragged by and still the men were here.
And then I said, 'I too will take a hand,'
    And borrowed lots of decorating gear.
I painted the conservatory blue;
    I painted all the rabbit-hutches red;
I painted chairs in every kind of hue,
    A summer-house, a table and a shed;
And all of it was very much more fair
Than any of the work of Mr Ware.

But all his men were stung with sudden pique
    And worked as never a worker worked before;
They decorated madly for a week
    And then the last one tottered from the door,
And I was left, still working day and night,
    For I have found a way of keeping warm,
And putting paint on everything in sight
    Is surely Art's most satisfying form;
I know no joy so simple and so true
As painting the conservatory blue.

Punch – May 14, 1919

THE TWENTIES

A CRIMINAL TYPE

Today I am MAKing aN inno6fvation. as
you mayalready have gessed, I am typlng this
article myself Zz½lnstead of writing it, The
idea is to save time and exvBKpense, also to
demonstyap demonBTrike= =damn, to demonstrat0
that I can type /ust as well as any
blessedgirl if I give my mInd to iT""
Typlng while you compose is realy
extraoraordinarrily easy, though composing
whilr you typE is more difficult. I rather
think my typing style is going to be
different froM my u6sual style, but Idaresay
noone will mind that much. looking back i
see that we made rather a hash of that
awfuul wurd extraorordinnaryk? in the middle
of a woRd like thaton N-e gets quite lost?
2hy do I keep putting questionmarks instead
of fulstopSI wonder. Now you see i have put
a fulllstop instead Of a question mark it
nevvvver reins but it pours.

    the typewriter to me has always been a
mustery£? and even now that I have gained a

perfect mastery over the machine in gront of
me i have npt th3 faintest idea hoW it
workss% &or instance why does the
thingonthetop the klnd of lverhead Wailway
arrange-ment move along one pace afterr every
word; I haVe exam aaa ined the mechanism
from all points of view but there seeems to
be noreason atall whyit shouould do t£is
damn that £, it keeps butting in: it is Just
lik real life. then there are all kinds oF
attractive devisesand levers andbuttons of
which is amanvel in itself, and does
somethI5g useful without lettin on how it
does iT.

     Forinstance on this machinE which is
Ami/et a mijge7 imean a mi/dgt,made of
alumium,, and very light sothat you caN
CARRY it about on your folidays (there is
that £ again) and typeout your poems onthe
Moon immmmediately, and there is onely one
lot of keys for capITals and ordinary
latters; when you want todoa Capital you
press down a special key marked cap i mean
CAP with the lefft hand and yo7 press down
the letter withthe other, like that abcd,
no, AECDEFG . how jolly that looks as a
mattr of fact th is takes a little
gettingintoas all the letters on the keys
are printed incapitals so now and then one
forgets topress downthe SPecial capit al key.
not often, though. on the other hand
onceone £as got it down and has written
anice man e in capitals like LLOYdgeORGE IT
IS VERY DIFFICULT TO REmemBER TO PUT IT DOWN

AGAIN ANDTHE N YOU GET THIS SORT OF THING
WHICH SPOILS THE LOOK OF THE HOLE PAGE . or
els insted of preSSing down the key m arked
CAP onepresses down the key m arked FIG and
then instead of LLOYDGEORGE you find that
you have written ½½96%: 394:3. this is
very dissheartening and ft is no wonder that
typists are sooften sououred in ther youth.

Apart fromthat though the key marked FIG
is rather fun , since you can rite such
amusing things withit, things like % and @
and dear old & not to mention = and ¼ and ¾
and ! ! ! i find that inones ordinarry (i
never get that word right) cor orrespon-
denfc one doesnt use expressions like @ @
and %%% nearly enough. typewriting gives
you a new ideaof possibilities o fthe
englifh language; thE more i look at % the
more beautiful it seems to Be: and like the
simple flowers of england itis perfaps most
beautiful when seen in the masss,   Look atit

```
% % % % % % % % % % % %
% % % % % % % % % % % %
% % % £ % % % % % % % %
% % % % % % % % % % % %
% % % % % % % % % % £ %
```

how would thatdo for a BAThrooM wallpaper?
it could be produced verery cheaply and
itcould be calld the CHERRYdesigN damn,
imeant to put all that in capitals. iam
afraid this articleis spoilt now but butt bUt
curse. But perhaps the most excitingthing

afout this macfine is that you can by
presssing alittle switch suddenly writein
redor green instead of in black; I donvt
understanh how ft is done butit is very
jollY? busisisness men us e the device a
great deal wen writing to their membersof
PARLIAment, in order to emphasasise the
pointin wich thefr infustice is worSe than
anyone elses infustice. wen they come to WE
ARE RUINED they burst out into red and wen
they come to WE w WOULD remIND YOU tHAT
ATtHE LAST EfECTION yoU UNDERTOOk they burst
into GReeN. thei r typists must enjoy doing
those letters. with this arrang ment of
corse one coul d do allkinds of capital
wallpapers. for lnstance wat about a scheme
of red £'s and black %'s and gReen &'s? this
sort of thing

```
£ % £ % £ % £ % £ %
& £ & £ & £ & £ & £
£ % £ % £ % £ % £ %
& £ & £ & £ & £ & £
```

Manya poor man would be glad to fave
that in his parLour ratherthan wat he has
got now. of corse, you wont be ab?e to
apreciate the fulll bauty of the design
since i underst and that the retched paper
which is going to print this has no redink
and no green inq either; so you must fust
immagine that the £'s are red and the &'s
are green . it is extroarordinarry (wat a t
erribleword!!!) how backward in MAny waYs
these uptodate papers are wwww $1/41/41/41/4$ $1/41/41/2=3/4$

now how did that happen i wond er; i was
experimenting with the BACK SPACE key; if
that is wat it is for i dont thinq i shall
use it again. iI wonder if i am impriving
at this½ sometimes i thinq i am and so
metimes i thinq iam not. we have not had so
many £'s lately but i notice that theere
have been one or two misplaced q's & icannot
remember to write i in capital s there is
goes again.

Of curse the typewriter itself is not
wolly giltless ½ike all mac&ines it has
amind of it sown and is of like passsions
with ourselves. i could put that into greek
if only the machine was not so hopelessly
MOdern. it's chief failing is that it
cannot write m'sdecently and instead of h it
will keep putting that confounded £. as
amatter of fact ithas been doing m's rather
better today butthat is only its
cusssedusssedness and because i have been
opening my shoul ders wenever we have come
to an m; or should it be A m? who can
tell; little peculiuliarities like making
indifferent m's are very important & w£en
one is bying a typewriter one sfould make
careful enquiries about themc; because it is
things of that sort wich so often give
criminals away. there is notHing a detective
likes so much as a type riter with an
idiosxz an idioynq damit an idiotyncrasy. for
instance if i commit a murder i sfould not
thinq of writing a litter about it with this
of all typewriters becusa because that fool

ofa £ would give me away at once I daresay
scotland Yard have got specimens of my
trypewriting locked up in some pigeonhole
allready. if they favent they ought to; it
ought to be part of my dosossier.

    i thinq the place of the hypewriter in
ART is inshufficiently apreciated. Modern
art i understand is chiefly sumbolical
expression and straigt lines. a typwritr
can do strait lines with the under lining
mark) and there are few more atractive
symbols thaN the symbols i have used in this
articel; i merely thro out the sugestion

    I dont tink i shal do many more articles
like this it is tooo much like work? but I
am glad I have got out of that £ habit;
    A.P.£.

Punch – July 20, 1920 – *Light Articles Only*

GIN AND MIXED

(WAITER *on his knee making notes on large writing-pad.*)

WITHERS (*with fitting Shakespearean gestures L.C.*)

Pluck me ten berries from the juniper
And in a beaker of strong barley spirit
The kindly juices of the fruit compress.
This is our Alpha. Next clap on your wings,
Fly south for Italy, nor come you back
Till in the cup you have made prisoner
Two little thimblefuls of that sweet syrup
The Romans call Martini. Pause o'er Paris

24

And fill two eggshells with the French vermouth.
Then home incontinent, and in one vessel
Cage your three captives, but in nice proportions,
So that no one is master, and the whole
Sweeter than France, but not so sweet as Italy.
Wring from an orange two bright tears, and shake,
Shake a long time the harmonious trinity.
Then in two cups like angels' ears present them,
And see there swims an olive in the bowl,
Which when the draught is finished shall remain
Like some sad emblem of a perished love.
This is our Omega. Go, fellow!
    WAITER (*rises from knee*) Sir,
It is too late. I cannot serve you.
    PLUM. Damn!

Two Gentlemen of Soho –
Lyric Theatre, Hammersmith, 1927

THE NOBLE ANIMAL

Well Trix dear I do think the *horse* is the *most* unbalanced and fraudulent object don't you, and that reminds me, *masses* of thanks for your *celestial* letter and it's *quite* angelic that you may be coming to London, but *no* darling I do *not* think that Mr Haddock would suit you, well of course it's *too* prohibitive to express in *words* but what I mean is well for *one* thing I *should* hate you to have the *weeest* whiff of unhappiness and really he *is* the most equibiguous man, well for instance, but *don't* think I'm *warning* you off or anything *female* because really my dear I'm *wildly* lukewarm and honestly my dear he spends the *whole* time introducing me to *nice friends* of his whom he'd like me to marry, my dear *too* Christian, and sometimes it *really* looks as if he *really* liked a girl and other times it *merely* looks as if he was merely *evading* her, so that what with one thing and another

25

one *simply* never knows *where* you are, but what I meant about *you* darling, well with *all* his faults he *does* strike a rather *spiritual* note, and my dear *don't* think I'm being the least bit *uncongenial* darling but my dear there *are* people who are obviously *incompatible* aren't there?

Well for instance I was going to tell you, you see after my scene with Uncle Arthur about the stags' heads and shooting and everything, well whether it was something *I* said or what but this time they asked *Mr Haddock* down here, because really my dear he's the *only* man I know who can look at a cock-pheasant without *wishing* he had a *gun*, and well Uncle Arthur said that since we were both so keen on dumb animals we'd better go *horse-riding* together, which was *rather* unworthy perhaps because as a *matter* of fact I'm not *Nature's* horse-woman, and I doubt if Mr Haddock was exactly *born* in the saddle, however they chartered two *anaemic* creatures from Wratchet-in-the-Hole and this afternoon off we went *hacking* or *hocking* or whatever it is.

Well my dear Mr Haddock had a sort of black creature and I had a blonde, my dear the *complete* image of Catherine Tarver with the same ten-and-sixpenny auburn and the same sloppy eye, but my dear they both looked *Nature's* lambs only as Mr Haddock said for *sheer* hippocrisy there's *nothing* like a horse and he said that lambs or not he has the most *corrupting* influence on them and *nearly* always they do something *perfectly* malignant and unexpected, well my dear of *course* he wore the *most* irrelevant clothes, my dear *grey* flannel trousers and *black* shoes and a pair of Uncle Arthur's gaiters and my dear I do think that horses feel it if you don't dress up for them perhaps, well as long as we were in the grounds they behaved like *nuns*, but my dear the *moment* we were on the road they developed the *most* congenital habits, well my creature had that *adolescent* trick of *tossing* its head back and flattening a girl's nose if you're not very careful and my dear the *whole* time it was wanting to *eat*, and Mr Haddock's horse was *quite* incapable of *trotting* or *walking* it *merely* ambled and my dear *whenever* he said 'Gee-up' or made those plebeian tongue-sounds which my dear *every* horse is supposed to understand it *simply* stood on its *hind-legs* and walked round in circles *waving* its fore-paws and my dear looking *too* self-satisfied, well Mr Haddock retained contact all right and really my dear he looked *rather* County but all the same we decided to cut out encouraging noises with the *result* my dear that we *simply* crawled and the *more* we crawled my dear the more my *sensual* horse was determined to *eat*.

Well Uncle Arthur had warned us not to go through Wratchet-in-the-Hole because it was market-day or something frantic, however Mr Haddock seemed to have a *particular* craving to go through Wratchet-in-the-Hole and call on some friends of his so we went through Wratchet-in-the-H, and my dear the *moment* we were in the main street of W-in-the-H my blonde beast *went mad*, and my dear it *gravitated* to the nearest shop and put its *head* in at the *window*, because my dear there was *no glass* and my dear if it had been a *greengrocer's* one could have *understood* it but what was so perfectly uncanny and *humbling*, my dear it was a *fish-shop* and what *do* you think it *merely* removed the *hugest* tin label with FINE FRESH HADDOCK on it and *lolloped* down the street with this *redundant* object in its teeth, well of course the *entire* population of W. followed us, my dear I blushed *all* down my *back* but worse *far* worse was to come, my dear you won't believe me but it went *straight* up to a policeman on point duty outside the Town Hall and *knelt down* on its *fore-knees* and dropped the FINE FRESH HADDOCK at his feet!!! And *then* my dear it *got* up and *walked on* in the *most* fraternal manner as if *nothing* had happened, well of course the policeman stopped us and he took the names and addresses of *everybody* present, and my dear *when* it came out that Mr Haddock's name was *Haddock* it *all* looked too *utterly* felonious and improper, well when at last we got away Mr Haddock said *I* know what, *these* horses have been in a *Circus*, and it turned out afterwards that's just what they were, my dear *my* creature had been one of those morbid *mathematical* horses which pick out the letters of the alphabet and everything, and they say whenever it sees *large print* it *loses control*, and Mr Haddock's horse used to do that *superfluous* hindleg waltzing act when the band keeps time with them, my dear *too* wearing, well they'd told us that the creatures had absolutely *no vice* which was *perfectly* true but my dear I do think that a horse's *parlour tricks* can be just as *anti-social* as its vices don't you?

Well after this we *ambled* along the road some way without a crisis and talked and Mr Haddock as usual said I ought to get married and I said why and he said because I was *Nature's* ray of sunshine and he knew herds of *distracting* bachelors who would *simply* tumble for me, so I said come to that why don't you get married yourself well, my dear he shook his head and looked *too* significant, my dear the *complete* secret-sorrow expression and I was just going to *press* him because I was sure he *wanted* to be pressed when as luck would have it he *sighed* loudly and his horse stood on its hind-legs again, my dear this is *gospel*, so after that we kept off *all* delicate subjects, well when we got to the Greens' place at that moment Mrs Green herself rode out of the gate on the most *expensive*-looking horse and my dear she's the *loveliest* girl, I loathed her at sight, and my dear she looked at me like something under a stone, and suddenly it *flashed* across me that perhaps Mr Haddock had a *hopeless passion* for her, well of course my dear I did the *Christian* thing, I took my horse along the hedge and let it *eat* while they talked, well my dear they *murmured* and all went well but when my *meretricious* horse had eaten *half* the hedge it cocked up its head and saw a large NO TRESPASSERS board stuck in the hedge and my dear without a moment's hesitation it merely *plucked* it out of the hedge and cantered back and *knelt* down and deposited it in front of *Mrs Green* (!), my dear *too* pointed, I was *wrapped* in shame, well of course after that I declined to have any more *truck* with the animal so we left the horses there and came home in the charmer's car, well my dear *all* the way Mr Haddock was perfectly lethargic and broody, so my dear you do see what I mean about your *happiness* darling because if it's a question of a girl's happiness I do *not* think that he's a *fraction* more reliable than that *ruddimentary* horse, and my dear in this life it isn't *enough* to be a *noble* animal and have no *vices*, so you see what I mean your *true* friend Topsy.

The Trials of Topsy, 1928

EQUALITY, ETC.: OR, CLAUSE FOUR

Song for a Socialist Sunday School

All are born equal. Counter this who can.
    Place in his cot some scion of the rich,
Lay at his side an infant artisan,
    And who shall say for certain which is which?

> *By reason, not ruction,*
>   *We soar to the skies;*
> *The means of production*
>   *We nationalize;*
> *While rapture surprising*
>   *We bring within range*
> *By nationalizing*
>   *The means of exchange.*

How comes it then that as the seasons pass
    These equal babes enjoy a different lot?
One steers the ship, one polishes the brass,
    While one is beautiful, the other not?

By reason, etc.

And who can doubt that in an ordered State
    No harsh distinctions should divide the twain?
Both, hand in hand, would rule the vessel's fate,
    And both be beautiful (or both be plain).

> *By reason, not ruction,*
>   *We soar to the skies;*
> *The means of production*
>   *We nationalize;*
> *While rapture surprising*
>   *We bring within range*
> *By nationalizing*
>   *The means of exchange.*

Laughing Ann – 1925

REDUCING

Trix darling, have you *ever* been to a Turkish Bath well *don't*, of course if you're *reducing*, but not unless you're *simply* mountainous, and even then, but don't go for voluptious pleasure that's all because my dear it's rather an *erroneous* entertainment, well recently darling I've had the *fraction* of a worry about my little figure, my dear *nothing* spectacular I'm still the *world's* sylph really, but there's just the *teeniest* ripple when I *bend*, and nowadays if a girl can't jump through her garter she's *gross*, well of course I did all those *unnatural* exercises and breathing through the hips and everything, but really my dear what with the hair and the face-cream and the care of the hands it's as much as a girl can do to get to bed as it *is* and if she's going to spend half the night expanding the *lungs* as well, well when *is* a girl to put in a spot of beauty-sleep, so the exercises *dwindled* somewhat.

Well then there's this *affected* fruit business, my dear Hermione eats *nothing* but radishes and she's *quite* invisible but looks like a ghost and my dear I do think breakfast is one of the *few* things worth clinging to in this life, don't you, however I kept on *noticing* this ripple in the bath, and that gave me the idea of this Turkish performance because somebody once told me that's the quickest thing ever and they say one of the Duchesses looked almost human after two.

Well I *crawled* in, all by myself, wasn't it heroic, but my dear *quite* petrified and feeling *just* like a human sacrifice approaching the altar, well my dear they take all your clothes away and give you the *most* mortifying garment in *thick* white linen my dear like an abbreviated *shroud* or the *Fat Boy's* nightgown, and wide enough for the *widest* Duchesses, so my dear you can *imagine* what your Topsy looked like, well the first place you go into is called the *teppidairium* or something, not very hot but quite hot enough, a sort of purgatory my dear, where you prepare for the bath to come so to speak, well I *crept* in my dear feeling like a dog that's done the wrong thing, and of course the *sole* soul in the place was the *most* redundant woman I know, the widow Wockley, my dear you know I can't *bear* to say an unkind thing but really my dear she *is* quite definitely *unmagnetic*, and my dear she looked like Mrs Caliban in the shroud and her hair like sea-weed and she has the *most* unseductive skin, well she was reading *Beauty While You Wait* and from what I can make out she takes a TB once a week, well she was all over me at once, you'd have thought we were *sisters* though really I've scarcely *met* the woman and never in shrouds, but my dear the *confidences*, well I gather she wants to get married again or something, though of course my dear she'll *simply* never be forty again, anyhow she plunged into the *most* embarrassing wail about 'Men' and all her *fatiguing* affairs and things, my dear she might have been HELEN OF TROY dictating her diary, Trix darling you *know* I'm not prudish *don't* you but I do think there ought to be some sort of *reticence* in the teppidairium don't you, and all in the *most* baneful we-girls-know-a-thing-or-two-don't-we style, my dear positively *leersome*, and as if she wasn't a *second* older than me, well after a bit something told me I should be *quite* ill *very* soon so I got up in the middle of a sentence and merely *fled* into one of the hot rooms.

Well, you go through a heavy curtain and the *most* awful *blast* of heat *strikes* you in the face, my dear *too* detonating, I just crumpled up and sat down and my dear the seat was *red-hot*, if you could have *seen* me leap up to the roof, well really I thought I should *burst* into *flames*, but rather than go back to the Wockley woman I thought I'd cheerfully be *insinerated*, so I tottered about like a cat on hot bricks, and my dear have you ever been to the *Aquarium* because if you have you know if you look closely into one of those tanks you generally see something perfectly *repugnant* lurking in a corner or sticking to a rock and you can't think *what* it is, it's just a *Thing*, and personally I move on to the next exhibit, well suddenly I realized that this room was full of *Bodies*, and my dear the most *undecorative* bodies, all *pink* and *shiny* with their eyes closed, and not a sound my dear, well if you can imagine a lot of *enormous* dead lobsters with white nighties on and very fat arms and my dear *one* of them was Lettice Loot, you know I do think there's a *lot* of nonsense talked about the beauty of the human form and everything, because really I do think that women are *about* the most hideous things there are don't you darling and that's why we have to be so careful about *clothes*, of course I think these artists are a lot to blame because my dear *look* at the lying pictures of women they do and really if anyone did a picture of a single corner in a Ladies' Turkish Bath well really I think that would be the finish of *matrimony*.

However, well then I took a peep into the *second* hot-room where there were only two dead lobsters, but my dear *too* squalid and the heat was *blistering* so I went back into the first room and my dear *imagine* my horror there was the Wockley body laid out with the others, I recognized it at once, well she opened one eye at me and I was *terrified* she'd *plunge* into her romances again so I escaped back into the teppidairium and read the Directions, well it said you pour teppid water over the *head* and await the *free* outburst of perspiration, and my dear you should have *seen* your poor Topsy sitting all by herself in a fat child's nightie *dripping* teppid water and waiting and waiting for the free outburst and everything, but my dear simply *nothing* took place, and I was petrified because I thought perhaps I was abnormal or coldblooded or something degrading, well at last the Wockley came out looking *yards* thinner already, my dear she'd practically *disappeared*, but not quite, unfortunately, well she said Have you sweated dear, and that will show you what I mean about a Turkish Bath, because my dear Trix *any* place where a woman like the Wockley can come up to a girl and ask her in cold blood if she's sweated well there *must* be a defect in the *whole* institution. Well I said No I hadn't sweated but I was doing what a girl could, and she said You're in the wrong room, if you don't sweat you'll have *pneumonia*, so I said I'd rather have *peritonitis* than go back into that *insanitary* oven with the bodies in it, and she said Come and try the Russian Steam Bath then, well my dear by this time I'd have tried the Russian Steam Roller to get out of the place, so she took me into the *most* antagonising cell and let off *masses* of Russian steam, my dear *too* alarming, but there was a capital free outburst and everything and I *rushed* out just before I was asphyxiated, well after that she began on her *odorous* adventures again and my dear you know I don't blush *gratuitously* but I got hotter and hotter and very soon, I said Thank-you Mrs Wockley, your conversation's done the trick, and I walked off, my dear *too* crude, I know, but *really*!

Well before I could get to my clothes I was caught by an *Amazon* of a woman and laid flat on a marble slab, my dear like a *salmon* or a side of ham, and my dear she scrubbed me and scraped me and prodded me and slapped me, my dear *too* humbling, and then she knocked the liver about and stood me up and turned the *hugest* hose on me, my dear I might have been a *conflagration*, well of course you know I'm not *built* for rough stuff and your *ill-treated* Topsy fell flat on her face, well then as if that wasn't enough she led me to the *most* barbarous *cold plunge* and said jump in Madam, well my dear only one thing *created* could have made me jump into *cold water* after all I'd been through and at that moment I heard behind me the *leprous* voice of the Wockley woman and rather than share the same *element* with the creature I *dove* into the frozen depths and stayed under water till she'd gone away, well after all this I lost four pounds but my dear I've had *such* an appetite *ever* since that I've put on six, so it's *rather* fallacious in the reducing line and perhaps it will have to be the *radishes* after all, O *dear*, farewell, your *unfortunate* Topsy.

The Trials of Topsy – 1928

'TWAS AT THE PICTURES, CHILD, WE MET

> 'Twas at the pictures, child, we met,
>   Your father and your mother;
> The drama's name I now forget,
>   But it was like another.
>
> The Viscount had too much to drink,
>   And so his plot miscarried,
> And at the end I rather think
>   Two citizens were married.
>
> But at the opening of the play
>   By Fortune's wise design –

Look Back and Laugh

It was an accident, I say –
    A little hand met mine.

My fingers round that little hand
    Unconsciously were twisted;
I do not say that it was planned,
    But it was not resisted.

I held the hand. The hand was hot.
    I could not see her face;
But in the dark I gazed at what
    I took to be the place.

From shock to shock, from sin to sin,
    The fatal film proceeded;
I cannot say I drank it in,
    I rather doubt if she did.

In vain did pure domestics flout
    The base but high-born brute;
Their honour might be up the spout,
    We did not care a hoot.

For, while those clammy palms we clutched,
    By stealthy slow degrees
We moved an inch or two and touched
    Each other with our knees.

No poet makes a special point
    Of any human knee,
But in that plain prosaic joint
    Was high romance for me.

Thus, hand in hand and toe to toe,
    Reel after reel we sat;

You are not old enough to know
   The ecstasy of that.

A touch of cramp about the shins
   Was all that troubled me;
Your mother tells me she had pins
   And needles in the knee.

But our twin spirits rose above
   Mere bodily distress;
And if you ask me 'Is this Love?'
   The answer, child, is 'Yes'.

And when the film was finished quite
   It made my bosom swell
To find that by electric light
   I loved her just as well.

For women, son, are seldom quite
   As worthy of remark
Beneath a strong electric light
   As they are in the dark.

But this was not the present case,
   And it was joy to see
A form as fetching and a face
   Magnetic as her knee.

And still twice weekly we enjoy
   The pictures, grave and gross;
We don't hold hands so much, my boy,
   Our knees are not so close;

But now and then, for Auld Lang Sync,
   Or frenzied by the play,

Your mother slips her hand in mine,
    To my intense dismay;

And then, though at my time of life
    It seems a trifle odd,
I move my knee and give my wife
    A sentimental prod.

Well such is Love and such is Fate,
    And such is Marriage too;
And such will happen, soon or late,
    Unhappy youth, to you.

And, though most learned men have strained
    To work the matter out,
No mortal man has yet explained
    What it is all about.

And I don't know why mortals try.
    But if with vulgar chaff
You hear some Philistine decry
    The cinematograph,

Think then, my son, of your papa,
    And take the kindly view,
For had there been no cinema
    There might have been no you.

Book of Ballads – 1926

TOPSY AND THE FRESH MIND

Trix darling I've made the *most* voluminous error I've *alienated* the Editor of *Undies* and now I don't believe I'll *ever* be a dramatic critic, well my dear you shall hear what happened and judge for yourself, well I told you he's been giving me *little* commissions to test a girl's mettle didn't I, and the other night he rang up in a *great* state my dear *two* minutes to cocktail-time and said *could* I fly *straight* off to Hammersmith (*Hammersmith!* darling) and go to the first night of a play called Othello, well my dear I'd *just* dressed as it happened but not for Hammersmith which it seems is half-way to *Bath* darling and *quite* insanitary, however that's the sort of horror an economic girl has got to face, well when I tell you that I had *no* dinner and the taxi took me *right* across England, my dear at Hammersmith they talk *pure* Somerset, well of course I was *madly* late and I merely *wriggled* over *nine* pairs of the largest knees, all in the dark, my dear *too* unpopular, and I had no programme and no dinner and no cigarettes so I merely *swooned* into my seat and prepared to enjoy the new play.

Well after all this *agony* what was my horror, well when I tell you that it was the most *old-fashioned* melodrama and *rather* poor taste I thought, my dear all about a *black* man who marries a white girl, my dear *too* American, and what was so *perfectly* pusillanimous so as to make the thing a *little* less incompatible the man who acted the black man was only *brown*, the merest *beige* darling, pale sheik-colour, but the *whole* time they were talking about how *black* he was, my dear *too* English. Well of course the *plot* was *quite* defective and really my dear if they put it on in the West End not a *soul* would go to it except the police possibly because my dear there were the *rudest* remarks, well this *inane* black man gets *inanely* jealous about his *anaemic* wife the *moment* they're married, and my dear she's a *complete* cow of a woman, my dear *too* clinging, only there's an *obstruse* villain called Yahgo or something who *never* stops lying and my dear for *no* reason at all that I could discover, my dear it was *so* unreasonable that every now and then he had to have the *hugest* soliloquies, is that right, to explain what he's going to do next, well he keeps telling the old black man that the white girl has a fancy-friend, well my dear they've only been *married* about ten days but the black man merely *laps* it up, one moment he's *Nature's* honeymooner and the next he's knocking her down, and what I thought was so *perfectly* heterodox he was supposed to be the *world's* successful *general* but my dear I've always understood the *sole* point of a real he-soldier is that they're the *most* elaborate judges of *character* and *always* know when you're *lying*, and if this black man couldn't see through Yahgo it's *too* unsatisfying to think of him winning a *single* battle against the *Turks*. Well for that matter this Yahgo was the *sole* person in the play who had the *embryo* of a brain and *whatever* he said they *all* swallowed it, but my dear I *do* think that a really professional liar like that must have had *years* of practice and you'd think anyhow Yahgo's *wife* would have known something about it, but *oh* no my dear she went on like the others as if Yahgo was *George* Washington, well so it went on and at last the black man smothers the girl, my dear *too* physical, but of course if *any* of them had had the *sense* of a Socialist it would *never* have happened, because my dear simply *all* the black man had to do was to say to the subaltern Look here they say you've been taking my wife out, is there anything in it, and be would have said Not likely General, I've a girl of my own, which be had though my dear the young man was *Nature's* fish and only a half-wit would have suspected him of an anti-conjugal *thought*, well then the black man would have said Well Yahgo says you have, and then there would have been explanations and everything, but of course it never *occurs* to the black man to talk to the subaltern, he *merely* goes and bullies his wife, who *merely* crumples up, poor cattle, but if only she'd said Look here less of it what's your evidence, oh yes and I forgot there's the *most* adolescent business with an *embroidered* handkerchief, my dear the wife drops her *favourite* handkerchief which the black man gave her and Yahgo's wife who adores her and looks after her clothes *picks* it up, but my dear *instead* of giving it back to the wife she gives it to Yahgo who puts it in the young man's room, and my dear the young man *must* have known it was the wife's because she *always* wore it, but *instead* of taking steps he *merely* gives it to his own girl and asks her to *take out* the embroidery, my dear *too* likely, well she gives it back to him in the *public* street while the black man is watching, and when the black man sees *another* girl giving the young man his wife's handkerchief *instead* of saying Hi that's my wife's property how did you get it he *merely* goes off and murders his wife, my dear *too* uncalled-for.

Well my dear when a play is *perfectly* hypothetical from beginning to end I do think a play is a little *redundant* don't you, even if it's very well written, but my dear *this* was written in the *most* amateur style, my dear never using one word if it was possible to use three, and my dear the *oldest* quotations and the *floppiest* puns, my dear *cashier* and *Cassio*, *too* infantile, and my dear the *crudest* pantomime couplets at the end of the scene, and immense *floods* of the *longest* words which *sounded* rather marvellous I must admit but my dear meant *simply* nothing, but everyone else seemed to think it was *too* ecstatic so perhaps they'd had dinner, well at the end there was the *most* unnecessary slaughter and the *entire* stage was *sanded* with bodies, because the black man having killed his wife Yahgo killed *his* too because she argued, my dear *too* Harrovian, and really my dear I thought the whole thing was a fraction unhealthy and *saditious*, don't you?

Well at the end there were the *most* reluctant speeches and dahlias and everything, and I stayed for a bit in case the author appeared, because I thought it might be one of those *primitive* women, and then I *rushed* home and wrote down *just* what I thought about it and really I was *rather* proud of it, but my dear this morning the Editor of *Undies* rang up, my dear it's *too* wounding it seems the *whole* thing was written by *Shakespeare* and it's *quite* well-known, well of course my dear I've scarcely *looked* at the man, so I said to the Editor Well you said you wanted a *fresh mind* didn't you, and he said Yes of course but you mustn't have a fresh mind about *Shakespeare*, because it isn't done and so there we are, well I rang up Mr Haddock and asked him to buy me a Shakespeare because I want to see if it's true, well he's been in and he gave me *rather* a lecture because he said it's a bad sign if a girl can't appreciate great tragedy because he said Aristotel or some *sedimentary* Greek said that tragedy was better than comedy because tragedy was about fine people and comedy was about mean people, well I said tragedy must have changed since Aristotel then because this play was about one absolute cad and one absolute half-wit and one absolute *cow*, and then suddenly my dear I had emotional trouble and merely *burst* into tears, my dear what *is* the matter with me I'm *always* liquidating these days, however Mr Haddock comforted me, my dear *too* understanding, and after a bit he sat down and read some Shakespeare to me, which was *rather* flower-like I thought, and really my dear on a comfy sofa in front of a good fire with Mr Haddock and some hot-buttered toast a great deal of Shakespeare sounds *quite* meritricious, so try it Trix, your *cultured* little Topsy.

The Trials of Topsy – 1928

'IT MAY BE LIFE…'

I wish I hadn't broke that cup.
I wish I was a movie star.
I wish there weren't no washing-up*
And life was like the movies are.
I wish I wore a wicked hat;
I got the face for it, I know.
I'm tired of scrubbing floors, and that.
It may be life, but ain't it slow?

---

* There are some, I know, who think that 'The Kitchen-sink' was discovered by daring young people in Sloane Square and the late Fifties: but honestly some of us had heard about it in 1926.

41

For I don't have no adventures in the street;
Men don't register emotion when we meet.
Jack don't register Love's Sweet Bliss;
Jack just registers an ordinary kiss.
           An' I says 'Evenin'',
            An' Jack says 'Evenin'',
An' we both stand there at the corner of the square,
Me like a statue and 'im like a bear.
He don't make faces like the movie men;
He just holds tight till the clock strikes ten.
Then I says 'Friday', and Jack says 'Right'.
Jack says 'The same time?' and I says 'Right'.
Jack just whispers, and I can hardly speak,
An' that's the most exciting thing that
    happens in the week.

Jack loves me well enough, I know,
But does he ever bite his lip?
And does he chew his cheek to show
That passion's got him in a grip?
And does his gun go pop, pop, pop,
When fellers gets familiar? – No?
He just says ' 'Op it', and they 'op –
It may be life, but ain't it slow?

           For I don't have no adventures in the street;
           Men don't register emotion when we meet.
           Jack don't register jealousy and such –
           Jack don't register nothin' very much.
                      But Jack says 'Evenin'',
                       And I says 'Evenin'',
           And we both stand there at the corner of the square,
           Me like a statue and 'im like a bear.
           He don't look lovin' like the movie men,

He just holds tight till the clock strikes ten.
Jack says 'Kiss me', and I says 'Right'.
Jack says 'Happy?' and I says 'Quite'.
Jack just whispers, and I can hardly speak,
An' that's the most exciting thing that
    happens in the week.

Sung by Dorice Fordred in *Riverside Nights* – 1926

MR MAFFERTY HAS A HAIR-CUT

'The hair's a little thin, is it?' said Mr Mafferty, taking his head out of the basin. 'Well, maybe it is thin, Mr Barber. An' what way would it not be thin, an' you diggin' in the roots of it with your sharp fingers, an' tearin' it out with your fierce machines, an' frettin' it with your rough towels, an' washin' it away with your cascades of water, like a Chinaman tormentin' the sands of the river for a few grains of gold? It's the wonder of the world, I'm thinkin', if there's one hair clingin' to the poor crown of me head, an' it swollen and sore with the great buffetin' it's had this day. It's not thin the hair is at all, Mr Barber, but sensitive itself. It isn't a doormat you have in front of you, or a frayed rug, or a piece of a carpet is hung in the backyard on a Saturday mornin' to be beaten by an old woman, an' she chokin' with the dust. It's a human head, an' it tender as a little child. But maybe it's in the stable you worked as a boy, Mr Barber, an' you mistakin' the top of me skull for the back of a horse, the way you'd be scrapin' an' scrubbin' it with your steel brushes to make a shinin' surface a girl could see her face in, an' she lost in the wood on a dark night. There'll be a grand shine on me head, surely, after this mornin's work, but it'll be the shine of nakedness and the glory of a bald crown. Will you wait now while I chase the soap out of me eyes, for there's a longin' in me heart to be lookin' in the glass an' takin' a peep at what's left of me.

'That's better now. I can see with one eye. Let's be viewin' the remains.

'So that's it, is it? The Holy Popes! did you ever see the like of that? Let you cast your mind back now, Mr Barber, to a piece of a talk an' conversation we had a great while ago, an' I throwin' out a small kind of a hint I'd have a little off the top an' divil a hair off the sides. You mind that, is it? Then it could be that you might have a note made in your capacious memory of the great oaths you let that time to be watchin' me wishes as careful as a young bride, an' she not wedded a week of days. An' if it's the truth I'm tellin', will you throw your tired eyes in the glass, Mr Barber, an' see the wreck an' havoc you've made of me noble head, an' it clipped an' shaven from ear to ear like a parson's lawn or a bagatelle-board itself? *Thin*, is it? If it's thin that it is, what word would you use for a man had no hair at all? There'll be no welcome any place for me from this out, I'm thinkin', unless it would be Portland prison or the county jail. An' it's a hard thing, Mr Barber, to take an' honest man an' turn him into a burglar with a pair of scissors an' an electric brush between the sittin' down of him an' the risin' up.

'But it's me own blame, surely, for it's meself was engrossed in the flow of your conversation, the way I'd not be noticin' what you were at, an' you charmin' the ear with the fine tales of your family, an' your prognostications of rain, an' your brother that keeps the chickens, an' your wife's sister has the asthma an' went to America itself. It's lost I was in the story, Mr Barber, an' half in love with your wife's sister already, an' she rangin' the ocean an' the countries of the West to be makin' her fortune in the movin' pictures. Half-way to Hollywood I was meself, an' it's a fierce thing for a man to be brought back from America in the flick of an eye to find his own head is like a football made out of the skin of a wet seal, an' it piebald. But it's not meself would be blamin' you, Mr Barber, for we've great trouble in this world, everyone of us, an' when a man has his wife's sister in his mind, an' she coughin' on the high seas, he'd have a right not to be frettin' himself will he be cuttm' a hair here or a hair there or maybe an ear itself. But it's not meself will be takin' a shave of the face this day, an' you distracted thinkin' of your brother's hens an' the fall of the rain.

'Is it a small bottle of lotion I'll be buyin' now, Mr Barber? It is not. It's a quare, fine, gratifyin' liquid, that one, I'm not denyin'. There's some kind of a magical oil in it isn't oily at all, the way the hair will never be greasy. An' there's some kind of a powerful astringent in it isn't astringent at all, the way the hair will never be dry. An' there's some kind of a supernatural glue in it, the way the hair will never fall out. An' there's some kind of an exceptional fertiliser in it, the way ten hairs will be growin' where one grew before. An' there's some kind of a miraculous polish in it, the way the hair will glow like the skin of a tiger, an' he preenin' an' prowlin' at the time of matin'. An' there's some kind of a juice of the hyacinth in it, the way the hair will curl like the fingers of a flower, an' it rollin' across the brow like the billows of the sea. It's a tonic it is, an' a stimulant, an' a brain-food, an' if you gave half a drop to a man with one lock it's two he'd have at the dawn of day. It's like the wine of Juppiter himself, it's what they drink in the Moon, it has the rose beat for scent, there's never a flower could stand up to it at all, an' if you take one smell of it you'll not be lookin' at a lily again on this side of the grave. There's all the perfumes of Arabia an' India an' the United States in one small teaspoonful.

'But no, Mr Barber, it's not meself will be buyin' a bottle. An' I'll tell you for why. I had a bottle the last time, an' by a quare sort of an accident I spilled a little drop of the liquid on me old Persian prayer-mat lies before the fire. Believe me or believe me not, Mr Barber – for it's all one at the end of Time – but in the half of a day, Mr Barber, that same small prayer-mat had grown so large it was fillin' the whole room, the creature, the way I'd not be openin' the drawin'-room door at all for fear it would be spreadin' over the hall-place an' maybe creepin' up the stairway itself. An' after that, for the sake of Science, I let fall a drop or two on the bit of a croquet-lawn I have, an' it as bare as the south face of a billiard-ball. Well, if it's a lie I'm tellin' you, Mr Barber, let you poke me with a razor between the stomach an' the midriff, but that same lawn grew up so thick with weeds an' the like it broke down me neighbour's wall, crash, in the midnight, the way a man would swear it was an explosion did it, and he comin' fresh an' ignorant from the Isles of Bute or a far place entirely. So it's in dread I was to be puttin' it on me head, Mr Barber, an' I thinkin' I'd be flowerin' cabbages or burstin' out with a great mop of black hair like the natives of Australia, to be trippin' the feet of me an' I walkin' the wood. It's not meself, Mr Barber, would take much pleasure goin' about the city with a long trail of hair behind me hangin' from the head, an' maybe furred like a rabbit from me top to me toes. Let you keep silence then, Mr Barber, for it's never a word I'm sayin' against the agricultural properties of your rare lotion, but the contrary altogether.

'An' now, Mr Barber, if you'll find me bowler-hat it's away I am out of this place for ever. What's that? Is it a bill itself? Is it money you have in your gross mind? Away now, Mr Barber, I'd be ashamed breathin' the same air with you! Is it payin' I'd be to have me grand head destroyed, an' I the mock of the city from this out? I wouldn't pay a tailor to cut great holes in me trousers, an' I wouldn't pay a doctor to cut off me right hand, an' I askin' for a soothin' medicine. An' why would I pay you for an Eton crop, when all I looked for was a little kindness an' to be tidied round the ears? It's yourself will be payin' at the latter end, I'm thinkin'. I'll not ask you for a contribution an' damages this moment, Mr Barber, but it's me own solicitor will be rampagin' at your doors before the moon rises on the city this night, an' he makin' the heart of you a jelly with writs and the like. Goodmornin', Mr Barber, an' misfortune follow you from this day to your life's end!'

Punch – March 28, 1928

WHY DOESN'T SHE COME?

Why doesn't she come?
   I know we said eight.
Or was it half-past?
That clock must be fast.
Why doesn't she come?
   She's ten minutes late.
I'll sit by the door
   And see her come in.
I've bought her a rose,
   I've borrowed a pin.
I'll be very severe,
I'll tell her, 'My dear,
You mustn't be late'.
It's a quarter-past eight.
   Why doesn't she come?

Why doesn't she come?
   This must be the place.
She couldn't forget,
Or is she upset?
Why doesn't she come?
   Am I in disgrace?
Oh, well, if it's that,
We were both in the wrong –
I'll give her the rose
And say I was wrong.

I'll give her a kiss
And tell her I'm sorry –
'I'm *terribly* sorry… '
Why doesn't she come?
   Perhaps she is ill –
I fancied last night
Her eyes were too bright –
   A feverish chill?
She's lying in bed –
She's light in the head!
She's dying – she's dead!
   Why doesn't she come?

Why doesn't she come?
   She's tired of me – eh?
I've noticed a change,
Last night she looked strange.
So this is the end?
   Why couldn't she *say*?
Well, never again!
She needn't explain.
I know who it is!
I know who it is!
I've done with her now.
   Why doesn't she come?

Why doesn't she come?
It's nearly half-past.
Well, never again!
I'll send her the rose,
I won't say a word,
Just send her the rose –
She'd *laugh*, I suppose!
A flirt and a fraud!
I'll travel abroad;

I'll go to the East;
I'll shoot a wild beast.
And now for a drink,
I'll have a stiff drink –
A brandy, I think –
    And drown myself in it.
I'll shoot myself… Oh,
How I loved her! –
                    Hul*lo!*
    What? Late? Not a minute!

A Book of Ballads – 1928

THE WASH: OR, DAWN IN HOSPITAL

I woke like a log, one eye at a time. Dimly I perceived beside my bed the night-nurse, basin of water in one hand, a thermometer in the other.

'Do you feel like a little wash now?' she said brightly.

'No, Nurse, I do not,' I said, and I went to sleep again.

When I re-woke (as the films say) there was a thermometer in my mouth, and the night-nurse had 'captured' (as the poets say) one of my hands.

'You know very well,' I said, taking out the thermometer, 'that my pulse and my temperature are always the same. I am very well. All that I need is sleep, and this is the hour of all hours in the day when I sleep the best. And if I am not to sleep I will not be washed.'

'You must be washed,' she said, 'before the doctor comes.'

'I am quite clean enough for a doctor,' I said. 'I will be washed at noon, when I stop sleeping.'

'You will be washed now,' she said, and, untucking all my snug bed-clothes, she piled them in a disorderly and draughty heap on my legs.

'This is barbarous,' I said.

'Shut the eyes,' said the night-nurse, and scrubbed my face with a hard rubber sponge.

'It is extraordinary.' I said. 'Whenever the doctor comes he inquires if I have slept well; when Sister comes in she asks anxiously how I slept; last night you gave me, yourself, *two* different preparations or drugs to make me sleep. One would think that the whole establishment had no other aim than to make me sleep; all the resources of medicine have been mobilized to make me sleep. Yet when I do sleep, or rather when at last I drop into a fitful doze, I am immediately woken up. And for what purpose? To be washed!'

'Quite a martyr, aren't you?' she said. 'Now the hands.'

'The hands do not want washing,' I said. 'Wash the hands if you must; but you will have no assistance from me.'

She dropped the hands into a basin of boiling water.

'I should have thought that you, at least, Nurse, would have seen the futility of these proceedings,' I said. 'That sleeping draught you gave me was wholly ineffective. All night I tossed upon my sleepless couch, counting the hours, and every quarter reviling the punctual clanging of your local clock. Before five, I know, I did not sleep a wink. About six I may have dropped off. And no sooner do I drop off than you wake me with thermometers and soap'.

'You have been sleeping like a log since ten o'clock', she said. 'Now the legs'.

'I deny it,' I said. 'What time is it now?'

'It's half-past-seven,' she said, 'and I'm late'.

'Do you realize,' I said, 'that when I am in full health I do not begin to *think* of washing till about nine, and even then it does not always happen? Yet now, when I am extraordinarily ill and cruelly deprived of my appendix, I am expected to endure this distasteful ordeal at day-break.'

'You're lucky,' she said; 'at some places they wash the bodies at six.'

'No one shall wash *this* body at six,' I said.

'Can you lift that leg?'

'I can not,' I said; 'I am very ill'.

She went out of the room, and I went to sleep again.

She came back with Nurse Andrews. They woke me up again and seized the right leg. They soaped the right leg and sponged it with a cruel sponge. They put the right foot in a basin, poured methylated spirit over the heel and sprinkled powder over the whole. They rubbed the right leg with a towel and hid it under a blanket Then they unveiled the left leg and started on that. Meanwhile the maid came in and did the grate, leaving the door open.

'Do you have many deaths in this hospital?' I said.

'Not so many,' said the night-nurse.

'Well, one of these days you will have an Abdominal dying of ablutions. Just because I have no appendix,' I said, 'you think you can humiliate and torment me how you like. And there's another extraordinary thing I've discovered. I have been lying in this bed for a fortnight, Nurse, with no tobacco, no alcohol, no late nights, no night-clubs nor dances, nor the pernicious society of your sex, Nurse. I have not so much as eaten a sweet. I have lived, in fact, a life of abstinence and virtue, gazing at flowers, reading good books and eating little but vitamins. And if there is anything in what the reformers of this world tell us, I should wake each morning as fresh as a lark, Nurse. As soon as my eyes are open, I should have all my faculties alert and buoyant, ready for anything. Well, they are not, Nurse. I am not fresh. I wake each morning feeling like an old piece of blotting-paper, as other men do. I wake fuddled and suicidal and quarrelsome and hog-like, as usual. I wake like chewed string. I wake as I might wake after a week's debauch.'

'If you will turn him over, Nurse Andrews,' she said, 'I will do the back.'

'You will kindly leave the back alone,' I said. 'And I will not be talked about as if I were something in a butcher's shop. I am a living soul, with aspirations and a future life, and you are not to keep speaking of *the back* and *the leg* – as if I were so many joints of beef.'

Neither of the ministering angels took any notice of this protest, so I resumed the main argument.

'There is this further consideration,' I said. 'So far (touching wood) I have made a most rapid recovery from the mutilations of the doctors. The wound is not septic, the tongue is clean, and, if all goes well, as you have told me, I shall escape from your clutches in record time. In fact, Nurse (making every allowance for the skill and attention of the medical and nursing professions), the conclusion is that, in order to be healthy and especially before an operation, a man should constantly absorb in enormous quantities all those poisons which modem civilization has made available, for this it is my habit to do, and you see the result; but you will find that long after I leave you the teetotallers and vegetarians and non-smokers will be stretched upon their beds about this hospital, feebly complaining and constantly ringing the bell. Which is the worst case here, Nurse?'

'The Abdominal in Number 9,' she said.

'An archdeacon, I believe. A non-smoker?'

'Yes.'

'And a teetotaller?'

'Yes.'

'Well, there you are,' I said.

'Now the teeth,' she answered.

I washed the teeth under protest, for this is a thing I hate to do before ladies. I then shaved by numbers and lay back exhausted. They then began the painful and fatiguing process which is known as making the patient comfortable. This took a quarter-of-an-hour. I am condemned for some reason to sit upon an aircushion, and while one is being washed one slides to the bottom of the bed. The two good women with heroic efforts hauled me up into a sitting position, but left the air-cushion behind. While the air-cushion was being placed in position, I slid down the bed again; it seemed to be a downhill bed. They heaved me on to the air-cushion, reviling me alternately for exerting myself too much and for making myself too heavy. When I was enthroned on the air-cushion at the right elevation the air-cushion was not central, and while the air-cushion was being centralized I slid down the bed again. When both the body and the air-cushion were right the pillows were wrong, and while the pillows were being put right, I did an avalanche, air-cushion and all. And all the time, with little anecdotes about abdominal cases they had known, the thoughtless women made me laugh, which hurts more than anything.

'Are you comfortable *now?*' said the night-nurse at last.

'I am not,' I said. 'But I would rather live on in discomfort than perish of exhaustion in a position of ease. I do not feel nearly so well. For a whole hour, Nurse, I have had worry and hard work, and all this before breakfast. When a man is in health, Nurse, a man takes great care of himself before breakfast, husbands his strength, nurses his soul and does as little as possible. But here upon a bed of sickness he does the equivalent of about two hours' hard labour before breakfast. It's extraordinary. And speaking of breakfast, Nurse – well, what about breakfast?'

The night-nurse arranged upon the table a number of nasty-looking steel instruments.

'The doctor is coming before breakfast,' she said, 'to take your stitches out. And,' she added wickedly, 'I hope it hurts.'

Honeybubbbe & Co – 1928

MR MAFFERTY TAKES A LADY OUT

'I know now why men stay at home,' said Mr Mafferty, 'for last night I took a lady out to dinner. I did it to oblige a friend, Mr Heather, an' he in love with her, so there's no call for your insinuatin' glances. It's a fine young lady she is surely, but hungry itself, though she lives in a rich house, with dogs an' footmen an' the like. I wonder now the like of her would not be takin' a little nourishment at home in the daytime, the way a gintleman could entertain her in the evenin' without sellin' his securities or borrowin' from the bank. An' I wonder there's no two people can meet together in this town without one of them gives food an' drink to the other. Is it unlawful talkin' between meals or what?

'Well, me friend is called away suddenly to the country, an' he asks me to console the lady with me genial society. I drive up punctual to the house in a motoromnibus, an' in less than half-an-hour she's dressed an' ready, like a flower out of the East in pink satin. "An'," says I, "what place would you like to take your food? I know a fine small place in Bloomsbury."

' "Bloomsbury's a fine place," says she, "but I know a fine small place behind Piccadilly itself."

' "Well, that's fine," says I; "we can go by the Underground train." For it's not meself was in love with the girl, an' the station two small steps from her house, no more.

' "D'you think I'd travel under the ground in me new pink?" says she.

' "I do so," says I. "It's clean an' dry below. An' you can read the evenin' paper."

' "Jumpin' James!" says she, "it's a quare strange man you are."

' "I am so," says I, an' I hired a motor-cab for the creature.

'Well, Mister Marini's little place was as large as a church, an' full of lords. I never saw so many rich folk before, an' I afeared me black tie would be slidin' up me collar behind, an' me fine gilt studs escapin' in front. Mister Marini an' me young lady is old friends, an' he sends six waiters to us. I picked up the programme of eatin' an' the blood ran cold in me bones, for it's a poor man I am. Bedad, there was nothin' to eat below five shillin's, an' it was three shillin's to sit down only. "I wonder now," says I, "there's no charge made for breathin'. What will you take, young lady? I see they have a nice grilled chop ready."

' "It's a small little cocktail I'll be takin'," she says.

' "Is it so?" says I in wonder, for it's a small slip of a thing she is, maybe nineteen or twenty years grown.

' "It is that," says she. "An *Uncle's Dream* itself."

' "The Saints preserve us!" says I. "Would that be an expensive beverage, Mister Marini?"

' " 'Tis three shillin's only," says the foreign gintleman.

' "Well, let you choose first what food you'll take," says I to the lady, "for it could be I'd not be able to pay for the two."

' "It's little food I'll be eatin' this night," says she, "an' I destroyed with the great fat I have on me."

' "Go fetch the lady a cocktail," says I, relieved in me mind. "An' then will you take some oysters or not?"

' "What's oysters?" says the innocent child.

' "It's a kind of edible bivalve they are," says I; "an' terrible fattenin' in the fall of the year."

' "I'll eat no oysters then," says she.

' "Maybe the lady has a hankerin' for lobster?" says the headwaiter; an' he reels off six or seven lobsters in the French language.

'Well, I cast an eye at the price of lobsters an' I made faces at the waiter the way he'd not be putting expensive notions in the lady's head. But the mean feller avoids the glance of me eye, an' she orders a Lobster du Maurier or the like of that.

' "It's fillin' food, lobster," says I. "You wouldn't want much after your lobster, I'm thinkin'."

' "I would not," says she, "I've a quare small appetite."

' "Would the lady be takin' a pheasant?" says the waiter.

' "I might," says she.

' "You would not," says I, "an' you in dread of the fat. I tell you now what you'd like, surely, an' that's a little chopped ham on a piece of toast. That's a darlin' little dish now, an' not fattenin', for you'd have the lean of the ham only. There's times I've gone for a week of days eatin' nothin' at all but chopped ham on toast."

' "We've no chopped ham on toast," says the waiter.

' "Then, may your bones rattle in your bed this night!" says I. "Haven't you all the birds an' the beasts an' the fishes of the sea in this place? An' is it hard set you'd be to find a small morsel of bread an' a few shavin's from the leg of a pig?"

' "There's no word said about chopped ham on the card," says he.

' "Well, it's the wonder of the world," says I, speechless.

'An' then the young lady says, "I'll have no more at all, waiter, only a small bowl of soup before the lobster an' maybe the half of a partridge after, with fried potaters an' a few small sprouts; an' after that nothin' at all unless it would be a small piece of an ice-puddin', an' maybe a dainty little savoury to finish, an' coffee an' liqueurs only, an' never a mouthful more, if you please."

' "Have nothin' you don't want, me darlin'," says I tenderly. 'Well, by the end of it, between the two of them, they'd ordered two meals would keep the Brigade of Guards from starvation, with fowls an' fishes an' angels on horseback an' the divil knows what besides. An' I took up the wine-list, an', begob, it opened itself at the champagne page! An' I turned over quickly to the still wines an' burgundies, an' says I, "What wine will you take, young lady? There's a grand Australian Burgundy they have here."

' "It's the strong joy I have to see the bubbles risin' in me glass," says she, "like the stars of heaven clmbin' the sky."

' "Is that a fact?" says I, "Well, I wonder now you wouldn't have more joy seein' the red wine of the Empire in your glass, like the red blood of the Australians – an' they shearin' the sheep."

' "I would not," says she.

' "I've seen the great trees of Australia," says I, "as high as the British Museum, an' they bearin' red grapes the size of cannonballs. An' Number 67 is a nice wine, I'm thinkin'."

' "It's not meself," says she, "would be drinkin' red wine in a pink dress."

' "Is it not?" says I. "Well, if it's white you have your heart fixed on there's a grand little white hock would warm the soul of a snake itself. It's Number 30 is in me mind."

' "I've no fancy for the German wines," says she, "since me aunt was drowned in the Great War."

' "It's noble principles you have, surely," says I. "An' there's no nobler wine than a cheap Sauterne, 'tis white as charity an' bottled by the French. Will you take a small sip of Number 17?"

' "It's quare an' heavy I am this night," says she, "after the long day, an' it rainin'. It's no more than a thimbleful I'd be takin', but there's a hunger in me heart for bubbles."

' "God help me!" says I, an' I ordered the champagne, for there's no goin' against a woman at the latter end.

' "The quare extravagant fellow you are!" says the young lady, reproachful. "It's soda-water was in me mind, no more."

' "Soda-water, is it?" says I. "It's a pity now you'd not remember the word before. Maybe it's not lobster you'd be wantin' truly, nor the half of a partridge, but one sardine an' the end of a cold sausage?"

' "It is so," says she. "Why would I be needin' grand food an' drink, an' I a simple girl with the stars in me soul an' a strong love for the wild places? I wonder now you'd bring me to a grand place the like of this one, an' I after tellin' you I'd be as happy standin' at the coffee-stall or takin' a poor crust in Bloomsbury."

' "Is it yourself," says I, the blood rushin' to me head – "is it yourself would be as happy eatin' at Bloomsbury as this place?"

' "I would so, surely," says she. "Why would I tell you a lie?"

' "Well," says I, "Mister Marini, is there a public omnibus goes from this place to Bloomsbury?"

' "There is that," says he.

' "Then let you stop it at the door," says I, "an' reserve two places. For it's to Bloomsbury we'll be goin' this livin' instant." An', begob, Mr Heather, it's to Bloomsbury we went.

'If it wasn't for the passion of love, Mr Heather, there'd be never a rich restaurant doin' business at all.'

Punch – November 6, 1929

LOVE IN THE NATIONAL GALLERY

Most lovers in London have found
   There is nowhere for lovers to go;
One look, and a crowd gathers round,
   And tomorrow the papers will know;
But still, if they want to embrace,
   For persons of tact and good sense
There is many a suitable place
   Maintained at the public expense.

And that's how I loved Mr Mallory;
We met in the National Gallery,
But I did not think much of his salary,
   And so I dismissed the poor man.
But now, when I see an Old Master,
My heart beats a little bit faster,
   For it may have been WATTEAU
   Or jolly old GIOTTO,
But that's where our passion began.

My mother's the difficult sort,
   And he'd a mamma of his own,
And so we were able to court
   At the Public Collections alone.
Ah! many the vows that we swore
   And many the kisses he took
As we sat with one eye on the door
   And the other on 'Crossing the Brook'!

> *And oh, how I miss Mr Mallory!*
> *We kissed in the National Gallery,*
> *And but for my sad shilly-shallery*
>   *I ought to have married the man.*
> *I tell you, I shake like a jelly*
> *When I look at a good Botticelli,*
>   *For we met as a rule*
>   *In the Florentine School,*
> *And that's where our passion began.*

Then I found, with my friend Mr Watts,
   The British Museum delicious,
As we studied Phoenician pots
   Till people became quite suspicious.
We went to South Kensington too,
   And oft we have told the fond tale
Behind a stuffed shark that he knew,
   Or safe in the shade of the whale.

> *And then there was dear Mr Rose,*
> *Who kissed me at Madame TUSSAUD'S.*
> *He was constantly blowing his nose,*
>   *And so I dismissed the poor man.*
> *But often my little heart throbs*
> *When I think of Lord NELSON or HOBBS*

It was just between those
That I kissed Mr Rose,
And that's where our passion began.

But now that I'm married to Watts,
    Museums don't play the same part;
I'm tired of Phoenician pots,
    But I still have a passion for Art.
Mr Watts is quite jealous, I find,
    But he can't have the smallest objection
To a person improving her mind
    At the TATE or the WALLACE Collection.

For oh, how I miss Mr Mallory!
We meet at the National Gallery;
I don't like to think of his salary,
    For now he is earning such lots.
I'm tired of Phoenician pots,
For that's where I met Mr Watts;
    But oh! how I thrill
    To a Gainsborough still,
For that's where I meet Mr Mallory.

A Book of Ballads – 1926

I TOLD YOU SO

The Smellies

(Written in 1929)

...Technically, the screen strode ever forward. When all the demands of hearing and sight had been perfectly satisfied, the best minds of the film-world were turned upon the other senses. A brilliant young American named Schwab invented an apparatus by which smells could be photographed and mechanically reproduced in conjunction with a noise-drama (a thing, of course, which the theatre has never done).

These early 'smellies' made a huge sensation, particularly *Fish*, a strong story written 'around' the life of a San Francisco fishwife with homicidal tendencies. The synchronization was exact: the moment Slooky Sal appeared on the screen with her fish basket a strong smell of lobster and dried haddock pervaded the auditorium. The lobsters were alive, and not only their smell but the petulant crunching of their claws was clearly apprehended by the audience, many of whom had never seen a live lobster before.

The next, and as it turned out, the fatal, step was the 'Feelies', in which not only the faces, voices and smells of the actors, but their *sensations*, were photographed, and by a delicate mechanical device conveyed to the public. That is to say, if a 'feelie' actor kissed a 'feelie' actress on the screen, every woman in the audience had the impression that she had received an embrace, passionate or paternal as the case might be; and, if the hero was knocked on the head by objectionable men, the whole house felt stunned for a moment or two.

And so the march of civilization proceeded.

Punch – May 8, 1929

MR MAFFERTY CONSIDERS THE OPPRESSED SUBJECT RACES

'I'm wonderin',' said Mr Mafferty, 'will I take a ship to Jamaica an' settle down easy in the sun. There's too much talk about work in this island. I never speak to a man or woman without they'll be tellin' me what work they're at or what work they're seekin'. I'm sick of the word employment. A million citizens lookin' for *work*! There's somethin' wrong with the country surely.

'An' them politicians! When they're not complainin' there's too little work for the poor unfortunit Englishman it's tragical tears they're weepin' because there's too much work for the poor unfortunit black man. I've heard a ton of talk latterly about the oppressed subject races of the British Empire, an' they trampled under the brutal heel of the white gentlemen that do be lyin' in the shade with a lemon-drink while the poor unfortunit black feller is perspirin' in the open. I've seen men standin' on tubs in the West of London with the hot tears scourin' their cheeks on account of the miserable negroes three continents away. I've seen men rantin' an' ragin' concernin' the British Empire the way you'd think it was an instrument of torture, though they've seen no more of the British Empire than you can see from the Isle of Wight on a fine day.

'Well, I've seen parts of it only meself, but I've seen the oppressed subject races in Jamaica, an' a fine an' peaceful kind of an oppression it is. Them negroes – I beg your pardon, there's no negroes in Jamaica, nor black men nor white; them words is forbidden, for it's grand an' democratic the little Colony is – there's Jamaicans only an' British citizens, though, if you want the truth, by reason of long residence in a hot sun it's kind of sunburnt some of them are, you understand. An' there's reason in it; for no man thinks shame of a freckle or two, an' what's a negro but a man with one large freckle? Well, them Jamaicans, I'm tellin' you, is fine friendly, freckled fellers; they have the teeth of tigers an' the grace of gods, an' they walkin' the road with a wide smile, singin'. They're fond of laughin' an' lovin' an' wearin' pink, an' talkin' nonsense at the market, an' singin' hymns, an' seein' the pictures in the moonlight. For they have no roofs to the cinemas there, Mr Heather, an' that's one more piece of cruelty an' oppression. An' they have their own Parliament, an' that's another.

'Well, you'll be thinkin' there's points of likeness between them Jamaicans an' me own poor countrymen, an' you'll be thinkin' the truth. An' there's one grand quality we have in

62

common. They've no nonsense in their heads about the joy of work nor the dignity of labour, nor none of that Saxon tomfoolery at all. There's reason in work in a cold climate where a man has to keep warm, and there's reason in work in a hot climate if a man wants something to eat. But there's no sense in makin' a virtue of it the way you do in this place. Wasn't it designed as a curse an' punishment from the very beginnin' by reason of the Fall of Man? I never heard of ADAM and EVE searchin' for employment in the Garden of Eden, an' they not stirrin' themselves unless it would be for a change of scenery or to take the peel off a pomegranate. But what was the first thing came to them when they misbehaved? Work, Mr Heather! There was no talk then of the joy of toil or the dignity of labour. Work? It's not a natural occupation at all.

'An' them Jamaican peasants have the true philosophy in these matters. Indeed, why would they not, and they residin' in a little Eden of their own, where you've only to look hard at a piece of land an' wish, an' up comes twenty-five banana-trees, or a shipload of sugar. An' every man has his own small little patch, with his palm-tree an' his mango-tree, an' his yams an' bread-fruit an' maybe an outlandish vegetable or two. It's fine an' happy he could pass his days, from the first of the year till the latter end an' he layin' quiet in the shade of his own trees, or maybe, another's, waitin' for the fruit to fall. But by reason of the great number of children he has, an' the great joy he has of wearin' fine coloured clothes an' dressin' his girls in pink cotton frocks, an' by reason of education an' the divil knows what misfortunes besides, he has to go against his nature an' his principles an' work. An' I'll tell you what kind of a week's work the poor unfortunit oppressed feller has to do under the cruel heel of the British Empire.

'Well, the week begins on Monday, the same as elsewhere. I tell you that because it's a quare strange little island, that one, an' things happen you'd not be expectin'. Ash Wednesday, now, is the first day of a time of fastin' an' self-denial, is it not, Mr

Heather, an' the whole civilized world, you'd say, thinkin' a sober thought or two, and tightenin' the belt? Well, you'd be wrong; for in Jamaica Ash Wednesday's a public holiday. The shops shut an' the Public Offices, there's horse fairs an' cricket matches an' eatin' an' drinkin' an' the girls walkin' abroad in their pink frocks an' powder. An' that's a lesson for us all, Mr Heather, the way we'd not be takin' annythin' for granted.

'But the Jamaica Monday begins the same as others, though it's quare an' different it continues. You'd say that Monday was the worst day in the English week, wouldn't you now, an' the whole nation crawlin' back to work reluctant, like sheep to the slaughter? Well, in Jamaica it's a day of quiet an' meditation for the down-trodden countryman. He begins the day talkin' about work, the same as yourselves, but that's as far as he goes. There's a great bargainin' an' argufyin' with the boss every Monday mornin' about the work he'll do in the week an' the wages he'll take; an' away he goes complainin' to his place of labour. An' he'll cut a couple of sugar-canes, or maybe one, or he'll make a small little hole with the harrow by the side of a banana-tree, so as to mark the job for his own, the way no man can come there on Tuesday mornin' an' take it from him. An' then he'll sit down a short space in the shade an' consider an' meditate upon the week to come, an' the great quantity of work he'll be doin' in that time. A kind of heaviness takes hold of him then, an' he mutterin' to his own self, "Can't cut cane at a shillin' a ton, Massa, can't cut cane at a shillin' a ton," or the like of that; an' then maybe he'll have a burnin' sense of injustice an' wrong, an' away he goes to his own home. Nor no man says a word to the contrary, for it's the custom of the country. An' a fine custom it is itself.

'Well, that's Monday in Jamaica, a day of injustice an' oppression an' peaceful meditation. But on the Tuesday mornin' you'll see him at work, as cheerful as a cockroach, an' it flyin' the fields on a hot night in the month of June. All Tuesday he works an' all Wednesday he works an' all Thursday he works as well. But about noon on Thursday he'll be overcome by a burnin' sense of injustice an' wrong, to think of the great space of time he's been at work for a poor small pittance unworthy of his exertions. An' this same sensation grows worse instead of better, till about noon on Friday he can bear it no longer, an' he takes his wages an' goes to his own place; nor no man hinders him, for it's the custom of the country. But when he comes to his own place there's a grand new energy an' determination in his movements, an' he makin' ready his yams an' mangoes an' bits of vegetables for the market on Saturday. On Saturday mornin' you'll see him marchin' into market with a great load balanced on his head, as straight an' easy as a tree walkin'. An' all Saturday he'll be talkin' nonsense at the market, an' laughin' an' arguin' an' sellin' his yams. An' on Sunday he'll be goin' to church an' meditatin' in the shade an' maybe singin' a song. But on Monday it's time to be thinkin' about work again, an' he spends Monday thinkin' about work, as I told you before.

'Friday noon till Tuesday mornin' – it's the longest weekend in the world, Mr Heather. An' it's meself could suffer gladly a little oppression an' tyranny of the same kind.'

Punch – June 5, 1929

THE DAILY SEVENTEEN

(Pardon. This was written in 1929, but it is still pretty topical, I feel)

To the Editor of *Punch*

Sir, – A rather serious word in your ear.

On the morning of Monday, November 11, Armistice Day, I found in small type in *The Times* the usual Monday bag of motor-murders, euphemistically described as 'Road Accidents'.

Twelve citizens were murdered (not counting those mutilated or maimed) in or by motor-cars in or about London during the three preceding days.

Perhaps, Sir, you will think some of the details worthy of larger type

EIGHT OF THE TWELVE WERE PEDESTRIANS.
FOUR OF THESE WERE CHILDREN UNDER TEN.
THREE OF THE TWELVE WERE PASSENGERS.
TWO ONLY WERE DRIVERS.
NO ONE WAS ARRESTED OR EVEN CENSURED.

The speed of the guilty motor-car is only given in one instance, and in that case (the common story, slippery surface – sudden emergency – brake – skid – crash) the Coroner said:

'There was no question of criminal negligence on the part of the driver. HE WAS GOING TOO FAST, but no motorist thought anything of thirty miles an hour these days.'

The jury returned a verdict of 'Death by Misadventure'.

At the other inquests the verdict was 'Accidental Death'.

In the same issue of *The Times* I read a very serious leading article on 'Measles', the tone of which contrasted strangely with an almost light-hearted leading article on road accidents which appeared a few days earlier. The article on 'Measles' concluded:

'Public money could not be devoted to a better object, for *this disease is the greatest of all the dangers to child life in this country*'.

I am sorry to have to say it, but this statement is fantastically erroneous. The greatest of all the dangers to child life in this country is the motor-car and nothing else. Ask any village mother which she fears most – measles or motors. Listen to them crying down the road as their children go off to school, '*Mind the motors, Maggie!*' It is the ruling terror in their minds, the first word on their lips. And, supposing they knew anything of statistics, they would have statistics to back them, for the measles mortality is negligible beside the motor mortality. Our charity and the doctors are bringing down the infantile death-rate by leaps and bounds, but the motor-cars are sending it up much quicker than that. You may say 'Nonsense!' I answer sadly, 'It is a fact'.

I do not venture to blame *The Times* either for its optimism or its error, for we are all in the same boat, the boat of complacency and resignation; and only you, Sir, perhaps can get us out of it. If as many people were dying of measles or machine-guns or railway accidents as are dying by motor-cars – what is it? – six thousand a year, or SEVENTEEN A DAY in England and Wales – there would be a national panic; we should stop going to the theatres. But somehow we have got it into our heads that highway massacre is natural and inevitable. I venture the wild suggestion that it is not.

'*He was going too fast*, BUT…'

That short sentence must somehow be torn out of our minds, coroners, juries and all. If I ran at my full speed along a crowded pavement and knocked down and killed an old woman or child there would be no 'buts' – slippery surface, child playing with hoop, slip, stumble, error of judgment, bad lighting or anything else. It would not be 'Accidental Death', it would be 'Manslaughter', and rightly.

Excellent gentlemen like Mr MERVYN O'GORMAN write expert, charming and learned letters to *The Times* enumerating the various 'buts' – the bad surface, the bumpy road, the jay-walker, the child at play, etc. They suggest that there should be wider roads, more foot-paths, more intelligent children, more agile and clever pedestrians. Certainly. But they never add that *until we have these things* the motorist must adapt himself to the present imperfect conditions. For all the experts have the fixed idea that the one thing that really matters is, not human life, but speed. The speed of motorcars has increased, is increasing, and ought to be diminished. Mr MERVYN O'GORMAN tells us complacently that 'safety in traffic can only be reached by study of its multifarious conditions'. Excellent! Keep an expert watch on the doomed seventeen every day and see how they die. And meanwhile, says the expert, *remove the speed limit altogether!*

I advance the perhaps daring thesis that motor accidents are caused in the main by motor-cars, and by motor-cars going too fast to brake without skidding, too fast to stop in time, too fast to avoid the jay-walker (if any). *Seventeen citizens died today on the high roads. Eighteen citizens will die tomorrow.* Four-hundred-and-fifty will be injured. Very few of them would be saved by better 'surfaces' or more foot-paths; a few might be saved by driving tests for drivers; *none* would be saved by removing the speed limit; many might be saved by enforcing it. I hope, Sir, that you will resist the total abolition of the speed limit tooth and claw. We do not say to the drunkard, 'You have had one bottle and got drunk – here is the key of the cellar'. Whatever speed limit is fixed for the public road should be enforced as strictly as the drinking limit of the public house. Indeed our roads have many drunkards on them – drunk with speed, impatience and power. For the present generation of drivers and walkers I should fix the limit without hesitation at thirty. It does not move me that '*no motorist thinks anything of thirty miles an hour these days*'. They must be *made* to think something of it. I would have pasted on every windscreen –

SEVENTEEN CITIZENS ARE DYING ON THE ROADS TODAY.

EIGHTEEN CITIZENS WILL DIE TOMORROW.

BY SUNDAY IT MAY BE TWENTY–

IS IT WORTH IT?

The deaths have doubled in four years, and the rate of advance is rising. No lecturing of the pedestrian can really check it, though that may help; none of the 'expert' proposals can really check it, though there may be something in some of them. Others of them will help it upwards. The suggestion, for example, that the monster motor-coach on the narrow country road should have a legal limit of thirty-five m.p.h. is sheer invitation to murder. No expert is any good unless he is prepared to say, 'By this or that means *I will bring the death-rate tumbling down, and bring it down at once* – narrow roads, jay-walkers, slippery surfaces or no'.

I, Sir, am modestly prepared to say that. It can only be done by stabbing the imagination of every driver on the road; and that can only be done by measures drastic, dictatorial and mad. I would proclaim a Reign of Terror on the roads – a six-weeks' campaign for the saving of life. During that six weeks whenever two cars crashed I would send the surviving driver or drivers to jail, innocent or guilty. Whenever a pedestrian was injured he would go to prison for three months, but the driver would get six. Very few pedestrians would die an 'Accidental Death' by motor-car; in most cases it would be either manslaughter or murder. For 'if a man do a thing deliberately which is calculated to endanger the life of another, and it causes his death, he will be guilty of homicide' – and that is the law. In a county which had more than a certain percentage of accidents all motor-traffic would for six weeks be prohibited. To travel over thirty miles an hour in any circumstances would be 'dangerous driving' – as it generally is – and punishable with imprisonment. To enforce these measures I would employ the British Army and give them useful occupation. During this mad six weeks there would be many hard cases, *but the death-rate would come down*. And I do not think we should find that the national life suffered in any way whatever. Not even the traffic would be dislocated. The reckless weekender might have less time at Brighton, *but the death-rate would come down*. At the end of it we might hope to have implanted a new psychology of the roads; the motorist would have ceased to 'think nothing of thirty m.p.h.'; and on that basis we could return to normal laws and some of the experts' pretty ideas. But at the first sign of a relapse – the moment the death-rate rose – my Minister of Transport would have power to declare martial law on the roads again. The expert may smile at this and the motorist may spit, *but the death-rate would come down.* And so long as they have nothing better to suggest than the abolition of the speed limit I shall continue to shout at them –

'SEVENTEEN CITIZENS WERE KILLED TODAY.
EIGHTEEN CITIZENS WILL BE KILLED TOMORROW –
IS IT WORTH IT?'

I know that we are all motorists now, and that is why we are so difficult to rouse from our complacent calm. In any other context those figures would make us hysterical; and perhaps we *ought* to be hysterical.

It is evening. Most of the seventeen will be dead by now. Two women have been burned to death in a ditch; another was thrown through a wind-screen and cut to pieces; an old man was killed as he was leaving a tram; a young girl was flung through a shop window; two children were crushed by a lorry at the door of their home; a motor-cyclist has been beheaded; three 'jay-walkers' were killed on the pavement. 'Accidental deaths!'

Worse things have happened on the British roads today than happened many a day in the whole British front line. More deaths too. And the expert says, 'More speed'. And Mr O'Gorman says, 'Abolish the speed limit'.

Ten o'clock. The seventeenth citizen is dead.

Punch – November 20, 1929

TOPSY GOES HUNTING

Well Trix my crystallized cherry I'm completing the cure down here at the Dilvers' my dear I'm having rather an *orgy* of air and exercise, disgusting for the brain darling, I can scarcely *think*, however I do feel less like a dried prune, anyhow we've had the *longest* paper-chase over absolute *hill* and bog and my dear whether it was the prunes or what to my *frank* surprise I discovered that *running* was *rather* congenial, because I have rather an antelope action and breathe *plausibly* through the nose, and my dear there's an *angelical* man here called *Colonel* Candy, my dear *too* boyish and beamy for a Colonel and he commands the *Guards* Cavalry or something, well he was a hound too and we *practically* caught the hares together only not quite because at the crisis I bounded gracefully into the *profoundest* brook, anyhow he said I was *Nature's* gazelle in the running department and I *rather* thought he was *rather* attracted so the next day I challenged him to a *handicap* Marathon round the private lake, which my dear is *quite* miles so of course he gave me the *most* benevolent handicap, I was half out of *sight* because of the shrubberies, but you know there's *no* doubt that girls were *not* designed for mobility in skirts, so my dear after about *half* a mile what with *agony* in the chest and the little breath *oozing* in *pitiful* sobs I paused at a convenient bush, discarded the lower garment, and darted on in my Parisian bloomers, *chaste* darling but of a *tangerine* hue, however *such* was the relief and I got my second wind, but my dear *what* was my horror when *thus* arrayed I crashed round a corner and met *one* Duchess and a Lady-in-Waiting taking a walk, my dear my *blushes*, and of course *what* they thought because by this time the Colonel had nearly caught me and my dear being *Nature's* knight he'd picked up the skirt and it seems was cantering behind me with the garment on his *arm*, however I waved *cheerily* to the ladies and panted on, my dear *too* insouciant but far from convincing.

However darling as if *that* wasn't enough *yesterday* I took the Colonel to an absolute *fox-meet* in the car, because it seems he's a *casual* hunter but had brought no spurs or anything, so he said we might follow on *foot* perhaps, well darling you know my views but I thought it was rather my duty to litterally *see* what happens, and of course the *magnetic* smile of the man, however Catherine Dilver said I wasn't to go unless I swore to be *too* restrained and not *head* the foxes or shoot them or anything, because she didn't want to lose caste with the Master and everybody, so I utterly swore because when you're a guest one must *rather* behave, whatever one's principles well don't you agree, darling?

Well my dear it was the *rudest* day and raining *too* cruelly however I must say the meet was *quite* pictorial, Only of course it was *rather* difficult to see the horses for the *cars*, and my dear the Colonel says there are *some* Hunts now where they don't allow horses at the meet at *all*, however the red-coats and everything and those *divine* dogs, which my dear I *patted* tenderly to placate the Master, but my dear *too* unresponsive I thought, the Master I mean, and of course I do *not* think that the British girl looks best in a *bowler*, not to mention a *veil*, my dear Margaret Dilver looked *quite* another person and *as* I told her I preferred the original, of course *quite* piquant and so forth but my dear as I said *why* must the fox-field be the *sole* place where the *men* dress gaudy and the girls go *plain*?

And my dear the whole thing was *rather* alarming because nearly *every* horse had a *red* ribbon on the tail to show that it kicked and scratched and was generally malignant, though of course if a horse had *blue* ribbons *all over* I wouldn't trust it *very* fanatically, and my dear as all horses do nothing but go round and round in the *most* suggestive circles one gets quite giddy with edging away from the scarlet sterns, however at last the dogs departed and we *spludged* after them along an *obscenely* muddy lane and I lost the Colonel almost at once in the crowd, and they all disappeared, so my dear forlorn and lonely I merely *waded* along till I saw a *distant* red coat beside a wood or spinney, which of course taking it to be the Master or something I *plunged* across the filthy fields through *streets* of barbed wire and two *definite* morasses, and when I tell you that it turned out to be a woman in a *red* mackintosh, my dear *too* galling, well after that I sort of *swam* back to the road where far away on the other side I saw *one* man with a *reluctant* horse constantly trying to jump the *same* fence, so then I crawled back to the car and merely flopped on the cushions to wait for the Colonel, my dear *quite* moribund, and now comes the drama, because my dear the whole time one could hear the dogs *vaguely* barking afar off because it seems it was one of these *circular* hunts, anyhow as I lay gasping with the door open what *do* you think the *largest* fox jumped into the car, my dear *quite* out of breath and *smelling* horribly but with the *most* appealing eyes, well my dear the little brain worked swiftly and I thought Catherine or no Catherine I *can't* have all those *dogs* in the car, so my dear I *closed* the door and I said to the faithful Parker *rather* casually Drive on.

Well darling we drove on slowly about *two* miles up the longest hill, me patting the fox and everything which apart from the smell gave *no* trouble at all, and of course it was rather a dilema because after what Catherine said I didn't think it fair to utterly terminate the hunt, so my dear the fox having rather a *moulting* tendency I plucked a fluffy bit from the back now and then and merely threw it out of the window, with the *result* my dear that *when* we stopped at the top of the hill I looked back and saw the whole *herd* of dogs quite pouring up the road and *one* man in red absolute *miles* behind and *rather* wildly playing the cornet.

Well *then* my dear foreseeing trouble and stress I told Parker to have no mercy on the accelerator and we departed at about sixty into the *heart* and bowels of the *next* county but *one*, where my dear at a *convenient* copse I opened the door and gently tried to *disembark* the fox, my dear *too* fruitless because the *wistful* creature declined to budge, so I thought perhaps in its *home-county* it would be more amenable, and of course I had to retrieve the Colonel, so my dear we slunk back by circumsical routes but my dear *what* was my horror when suddenly round a corner we ran into the *entire* hunt drawing a spinney or something however no dogs in sight, so I threw a rug over Reynard and drove past warily, well I picked up the Colonel who my dear had had *quite* enough of hunting on foot, and we'd just started again when out of the spinney came the principal dog, and my dear it gave the *loudest* sniff and bounded after us with alarming noises *followed* rapidly by *all* its colleagues, because it seems a bit of the fox-fluff had stuck to the *back* of the car, so I said Faster Parker, well my dear what *was* I to do because at *that* point *could* I eject the creature, well of course the Colonel was *too* mystified so I said quietly I can't explain but as a *matter* of fact there's a fox in the car and at that moment he put his foot on the fox and it nipped him *rather* familiarly in the calf, but my dear he *is a complete* lamb because he laughed and laughed only he said the whole proceeding was *utter* blasphemy and I ought to stop the car and explain to the Master, so I said that would be *too* fatal because of Catherine Dilver and everything, because probably I shouldn't tune in with the Master and anyhow it was MY car and for that matter it was MY fox, but if we could shake off the dogs then nobody would *ever* know, so my dear we drove like tigers along the *tiniest* lanes and at last escaped, only so hot was the hunt that we couldn't stop to evacuate the fox till a *secret* shrubbery on the Dilvers' own drive, and *now* my dear I hear that seven of the *prize* pullets disappeared last *night*, my dear *too* wearing, because I *did* mean to behave so *utterly* well, Oh dear, farewell your *misfortunate* TOPSY.

Punch – January 29, 1929 – *Trials of Topsy*

THE THIRTIES

HELEN

PARIS (*is heard singing below*).

HELEN. He loves me... It is Fate –

No, it is Folly. O Venus, could you not promise the shepherd some less embarrassing reward? (*Sitting down, she looks up at Leda and the Swan.*) I have always loved this family group. There they are, father and mother together. O Father Jove, assist me now. O mother, why must the gods select our family for all their experiments?

(*Invocation to Venus*)

    Ah, Venus, nobody could wonder
      If now and then a woman fell;
    Man is enough to make us blunder,
      And we must fight the gods as well;
    A man goes wrong of his own choosing,
      We only do as you dictate:
    Men sin because it is amusing –
      When woman falls it is her fate,
      When woman falls it is her fate...
        Ah, what a life
        For a virtuous wife!
    With men we struggle and struggle and struggle again;
      But if the gods
      Go and double the odds

A P Herbert

No wonder some of us struggle and struggle and
    struggle in vain!

For instance, there was my poor mother
    Who met a most attractive swan;
They fell in love with one another
    (Though I don't know quite what went on);
It seemed in need of some protection,
    For trembling to her breast it came,
And if she showed it some affection
    I think I might have done the same –
    I'm sure I should have done the same.
        Poor little waif!
        Do you wonder she erred?
    With men we struggle and struggle and struggle again;
        If it's not safe
        To be nice to a bird,
No wonder some of us struggle and struggle in vain!

Our virtue is a precious jewel,
    Our beauty is a thing accurst,
And while they last it's one long duel –
    The question is, which will go first?
But life's too good to be quite true in,
    And there's no argument with Fate,
So if the gods decree our ruin
    We must obey, and not debate –
    We know our doom – though not the date…
        What can I do?
        How I try to be true!
    Venus, I struggle again and again and again!
        If Heaven's plans
        Are the same as the man's,
Then I may struggle and struggle and struggle in vain.

        Sung by Evelyn Laye in *Helen* – 1932

FARDELL v. POTTS

The Reasonable Man

The Court of Appeal today delivered judgment in this important case.

THE MASTER OF THE ROLLS: In this case the appellant was a Mrs Fardell, a woman, who, while navigating a motor-launch on the River Thames, collided with the respondent, who was navigating a punt, as a result of which the respondent was immersed and caught cold. The respondent brought an action for damages, in which it was alleged that the collision and subsequent immersion were caused by the negligent navigation of the appellant. In the Court below the learned judge decided that there was evidence on which the jury might find that the defendant had not taken reasonable care, and, being of that opinion, very properly left to the jury the question whether in fact she had failed to use reasonable care or not. The jury found for the plaintiff and awarded him two hundred and fifty pounds damages. This verdict we are asked to set aside on the ground of misdirection by the learned judge, the contention being that the case should never have been allowed to go to the jury; and this contention is supported by a somewhat novel proposition, which has been ably, though tediously, argued by Sir Ethelred Rutt.

The Common Law of England has been laboriously built about a mythical figure – the figure of 'The Reasonable Man'. In the field of jurisprudence this legendary individual occupies the place which in another science is held by the Economic Man, and in social and political discussions by the Average or Plain Man. He is an ideal, a standard, the embodiment of all those qualities which we demand of the good citizen. No matter what may be the particular department of human life which falls to be considered in these Courts, sooner or later we have to face the question: Was this or was it not the conduct of a reasonable man? Did the defendant take such care to avoid shooting the plaintiff in the stomach as might reasonably be expected of a reasonable man? (*Moocat* v. *Radley* (1883) 2 QB) Did the plaintiff take such precautions to inform himself of the circumstances as any reasonable man would expect of an ordinary person having the ordinary knowledge of an ordinary person of the habits of wild bulls when goaded with garden-forks and the persistent agitation of red flags? (*Williams* v. *Dogbody* (1841) 2 AC.)

I need not multiply examples. It is impossible to travel anywhere or to travel for long in that confusing forest of learned judgments which constitutes the Common Law of England without encountering the Reasonable Man. He is at every turn, an ever-present help in time of trouble, and his apparitions mark the road to equity and right. There has never been a problem, however difficult, which His Majesty's judges have not in the end been able to resolve by asking themselves this simple question, 'Was this or was it not the conduct of a reasonable man?' and leaving that question to be answered by the jury.

This noble creature stands in singular contrast to his kinsman the Economic Man, whose every action is prompted by the single spur of selfish advantage and directed to the single end of monetary gain. The Reasonable Man is always thinking of others; prudence is his guide, and 'Safety First', if I may borrow a contemporary catchword, is his rule of life. All solid virtues are his, save only that peculiar quality by which the affection of other men is won. For it will not be pretended that socially he is much less objectionable than the Economic Man. Though any given example of his behaviour must command our admiration, when taken in the mass his acts create a very different set of impressions. He is one who invariably looks where he is going, and is careful to examine the immediate foreground before he executes a leap or bound; who neither star-gazes nor is lost in meditation when approaching trap-doors or the margin of a dock; who records in every case upon the counterfoils of cheques such ample details as are desirable, scrupulously substitutes the word 'Order' for the word 'Bearer', crosses the instrument 'a/c Payee only', and registers the package in which it is despatched; who never mounts a moving omnibus, and does not alight from any car while the train is in motion; who investigates exhaustively the *bona fides* of every mendicant before distributing alms, and will inform himself of the history and habits of a dog before administering a caress; who believes no gossip, nor repeats it, without firm basis for believing it to be true; who never drives his ball till those in front of him have definitely vacated the putting-green which is his own objective; who never from one year's end to another makes an excessive demand upon his wife, his neighbours, his servants, his ox, or his ass; who in the way of business looks only for that narrow margin of profit which twelve men such as himself would reckon to be 'fair', and contemplates his fellow-merchants, their agents, and their goods, with that degree of suspicion and distrust which the law deems admirable; who never swears, gambles, or loses his temper; who uses nothing except in moderation, and even while he flogs his child is meditating only on the golden mean. Devoid, in short, of any human weakness, with not one single saving vice, *sans* prejudice, procrastination, ill-nature, avarice, and absence of mind, as careful for his own safety as he is for that of others, this excellent but odious character stands like a monument in our Courts of Justice, vainly appealing to his fellow-citizens to order their lives after his own example.

I have called him a myth; and, in so far as there are few, if any, of his mind and temperament to be found in the ranks of living men, the title is well chosen. But it is a myth which rests upon solid and even, it may be, upon permanent foundations.

The Reasonable Man is fed and kept alive by the most valued and enduring of our juridical institutions – the common jury. Hateful as he must necessarily be to any ordinary citizen who privately considers him, it is a curious paradox that where two or three are gathered together in one place they will with one accord pretend an admiration for him; and, when they are gathered together in the formidable surroundings of a British jury, they are easily persuaded that they themselves are, each and generally, reasonable men. Without stopping to consider how strange a chance it must have been that has picked fortuitously from a whole people no fewer than twelve examples of a species so rare, they immediately invest themselves with the attributes of the Reasonable Man, and are therefore at one with the Courts in their anxiety to support the tradition that such a being in fact exists. Thus it is that while the Economic Man has under the stress of modern conditions almost wholly disappeared from view his Reasonable cousin has gained in power with every case in which he has figured.

To return, however, as every judge must ultimately return, to the case which is before us – it has been urged for the appellant, and my own researches incline me to agree, that in all that mass of authorities which bears upon this branch of the law *there is no single mention of a reasonable woman.* It was ably insisted before us that such an omission, extending over a century and more of judicial pronouncements, must be something more than a coincidence; that among the innumerable tributes to the reasonable man there might be expected at least some passing reference to a reasonable person of the opposite sex; that no such reference is found, for the simple reason that no such being is contemplated by the law; that legally at least there *is* no reasonable woman, and that therefore in this case the learned judge should have directed the jury that, while there was evidence on which they might find that the defendant had not come up to the standard required of a reasonable man, her conduct was only what was to be expected of a woman, as such.

It must be conceded at once that there is merit in this contention, however unpalatable it may at first appear. The appellant relies largely on *Baxter's Case*, 1639 (2 Bole, at page 100), in which it was held that for the purposes of *estover* the wife of a tenant by the mesne was at law in the same position as an ox or other *cattle demenant* (to which a modern parallel may perhaps be found in the statutory regulations of many railway companies, whereby, for the purposes of freight, a typewriter is counted as a musical instrument). It is probably no mere chance that in our legal textbooks the problems relating to married women are usually considered immediately after the pages devoted to idiots and lunatics. Indeed, there is respectable authority for saying that at Common Law this was the status of a woman. Recent legislation has whittled away a great part of this venerable conception, but so far as concerns the law of negligence, which is our present consideration, I am persuaded that it remains intact. It is no bad thing that the law of the land should here and there conform with the known facts of everyday experience. The view that there exists a class of beings, illogical, impulsive, careless, irresponsible, extravagant, prejudiced, and vain, free for the most part from those worthy and repellent excellences which distinguish the Reasonable Man, and devoted to the irrational arts of pleasure and attraction, is one which should be as welcome and as well accepted in our Courts as it is in our drawing-rooms – and even in Parliament. The odd stipulation is often heard there that some new Committee or Council shall consist of so many persons 'one of which must be a woman': the assumption being that upon scientific principles of selection no woman would be added to a body having serious deliberative functions. That assumption, which is at once accepted and resented by those who maintain the complete equality of the sexes, is not founded, as they suppose, in some prejudice of Man but in the considered judgments of Nature. I find that at Common Law a reasonable woman does not exist. The contention of the respondent fails and the appeal must be allowed. Costs to be costs in the action, above and below, but not costs in the case.

Bungay, L J, and Blow, L J, concurred.

Misleading Cases – 1935

'MR SPEAKER, SIR…'

MAIDEN SPEECH

'I have in my hand a Bill which I am ready to introduce next Friday, or on the Friday after, or on all the Fridays, until it is passed into law; and I swear that it shall be passed before this Parliament is over.* (*Laughter*) Hon. Members laugh. But I must remind them that all the serious politicians laughed when I disclosed my obscene designs upon my almost virgin University. They said that with my extraordinary opinions I ought to go to Hoxton, to the taverns, to the racecourses of our land, and hope perhaps to scramble together a discreditable vote or two, but that to go to Oxford, the citadel of Christian enlightenment and the stronghold of orthodoxy, a constituency with more parsons to the square vote than any other constituency besides – this was lunacy. However, I went on, and the walls of Jericho fell down. Therefore, I would ask hon. Members in the north-east corner of the House to consider again before they laugh at my intentions…

'So many years go by, so many Sessions, so many Parliaments, and nothing is done about these things. If we mention them at General Election time, we are told that we must not trespass upon what are called the major issues. If we mention them after

---

* This impious vow, which makes me blush when I read it now, was fulfilled in one year and nine months.

the election, we are told that since they were not mentioned at the election, the Government have no mandate for them. At the beginning of a Parliament the Government have no time to do anything; at the end of a Parliament they have no courage to do anything; and in the middle of a Parliament there is a change of Ministries. We are told that a party Government cannot do this thing, and it seems that a National Government cannot do it, though it would seem to me that if any Government could be fitted for such a task, it would be a National Government which claims to represent all sections of society...

'Sir, I have not come here to make jokes; nor yet to collect an agreeable background for a work of fiction, nor with any personal political ambitions. I have come here to raise my small voice for a large number of small people who think, rightly or wrongly, that a number of small but important things like this are, in the midst of our mighty cares, being thrust aside or wrongfully neglected. If I cannot make that voice effective I will go back to my books and plays. It was never my intention to start my Parliamentary career by dividing the House against His Majesty's Government, with which, on the whole, I am in sympathy. I am prepared to do it upon this point of principle, but apart from that, whatever may be said on the matter, and whatever may happen, I should like to say that I am proud indeed to be standing in this place among the faithful Commons of His Majesty the King.'

Independent Member
Hansard, Vol. 307, col. 134, 4 December, 1935

NOTHING'S BEEN THE SAME

Thank you, Mrs Thomas, and I don't mind if I do;
My dear, it seems an age since I was sitting here with you.
I only hope you're better, dear, than what I am, because –
Oh, well, we musn't grumble, but I'm not the girl I was.

Nothing's been the same since I took up with orange-juice,
  One always pays for foolishness, my dear –
    Pains in the back and side,
    My little bird has died,
  And bilious – well, I couldn't tell you here!
Then we had the Frost, my dear, and then we had the Flood,
And Bert's been quite a martyr to suppression of the blood.
Oranges? I tell you, dear, with me their name is mud –
  So what about a little drop of beer?

A tumbler night and morning! Well, I'd just as soon have ink;
It's what you're bred and born to is the safest, don't you think?
And don't you let 'em talk you round with this reducing stuff –
There used to be too much of me, and now there's not enough.

Nothing's been the same since I took up with orange-juice;
  It never does to shock the system, dear.
    My temper's kind of terse,
    The weather's worse and worse,
  And the Government is acting very queer.
Well, that's what comes of tampering with Providence, you see;
It's oranges for animals, but hops for you and me.
I wouldn't touch another if I had my private tree –
  But what about a nice drop of beer?

I've lost my loving-kindness, dear, I've lost my self-control,
And Mabel thinks that what I've got is jaundice on the soul;
You'd be surprised – this morning I had words with Mrs Drew,
And many of them words, my dear, I didn't know I *knew*!

Nothing's been the same since I took up with orange-juice,
  The slightest thing excites me now, my dear;
    I used to live and let,
    But now I seem to get
  A nasty sort of itch to interfere.

I'm not the Christian woman what I used to be before;
Poor Bert's took up with betting, dear, and I've begun to snore;
Oranges? If it's for me, they needn't grow no more –
  But what about a healthy drop of beer?

Derby Day – Lyric Theatre, Hammersmith – 1930

ENGHEIM, MUCKOVITCH, KETTELBURG, WEINBAUM, AND OSKI v. THE KING

Free Speech – Why?

This was a petition to the Crown by certain British subjects, made under the Bill of Rights, and referred by the Crown to the Privy Council.

THE LORD CHANCELLOR: This is a petition to the Crown by certain members of a political party who were convicted of holding a public meeting in Trafalgar Square contrary to the orders of the Home Secretary and police. The petitioners are keenly interested in the 'Hands Off Russia' movement, and, although there is no evidence that any person in this country proposes to lay hands on Russia, they have been in the habit for some weeks past of gathering at Lord Nelson's monument on Sunday afternoons and imploring the few citizens present to keep their hands off that country. At these meetings banners are held aloft which invite compassion for persons in a state of bondage, and songs are sung expressive of a determination to improve the material condition of the human race. These at first sight unobjectionable aims have unfortunately inflamed the passions of another body of citizens, who interpret them as an unwarrantable interference with the affairs of their own country, and have therefore banded themselves into a rival movement whose battle-cry is 'Hands Off England'. This party, though their banners and their songs are different, express the same general ideals as the petitioners, namely, the maintenance of liberty and the material advancement of the poor and needy. Their principal song has a refrain to the effect that their countrymen will never consent to a condition of slavery; while the songs of the petitioners assert that many of their countrymen are in that condition already, and resent it. So that at first sight it might be thought that these two bodies, having so much in common, might appropriately and peacefully meet together under the effigy of that hero who did so much to ward off from these shores the hateful spectres of tyranny and oppression. When, however, it was announced that the two movements did in fact propose to hold meetings at the same time and place, the police were so apprehensive of a disturbance of the peace that both gatherings were by order prohibited. For it appears that the spectacle of the national flag of these islands is infuriating to the petitioners, while the simple scarlet banner of the petitioners is equally a cause of offence to the other movement, though that same colour is the distinctive ornament of many institutions which they revere, such as His Majesty's Post Office and His Majesty's Army.

These, however, are political matters which fortunately it is not necessary for this Court to attempt to understand, though we may observe that an age in which it is possible to fly across the Atlantic in thirty hours might be expected to hit upon some more scientific method of deciding by what persons a given country shall be governed. The 'Hands Off England' movement obeyed the order of the Home Secretary, but the petitioners did not; their meeting was begun, and was dispersed by the police. They were prosecuted and fined, and they now ask for a gracious declaration from the Throne that these proceedings were in violation of the liberties of the subject as secured by the Bill of Rights, and in particular of the rights, or alleged rights, of Public Meeting and Free Speech.

Now, I have had occasion to refer before to the curious delusion that the British subject has a number of rights and liberties which entitle him to behave as he likes so long as he does no specific injury or harm. There are few, if any, such rights, and in a public street there are none; for there is no conduct in a public thoroughfare which cannot easily be brought into some unlawful category, however vague. If the subject remains motionless he is loitering or causing an obstruction; if he moves rapidly he is doing something which is likely to cause a crowd or a breach of the peace; if his glance is affectionate he is annoying, if it is hard he may be threatening, and in both cases he is insulting; if he keeps himself to himself he is a suspicious character, and if he goes about with two others or more he may be part of (a) a conspiracy or (b) an obstruction or (c) an unlawful assembly; if he begs without singing he is a vagrant, and if he sings without begging he is a nuisance. But nothing is more obnoxious to the law of the street than a crowd, for whatever purpose collected, which is shown by the fact that a crowd in law consists of three persons or more; and if those three persons or more have an unlawful purpose, such as the discussion of untrue and defamatory gossip, they are an unlawful assembly; while if their proceedings are calculated to arouse fears or jealousies among the subjects of the realm they are a riot. It will easily be seen, therefore, that a political meeting in a public place must almost always be illegal, and there is certainly no right of public meeting such as is postulated by the petitioners. It was held so long ago as 1887 by Mr Justice Charles that the only right of the subject in a public street is to pass at an even pace from one end of it to another, breathing unobtrusively through the nose and attracting no attention.*

There are, in fact, few things, and those rapidly diminishing, which it is lawful to do in a public place, or anywhere else. But if he is not allowed to do what he likes, how much less likely is

* This was confirmed in a recent Court case, 1959.

it that the subject will be permitted to say what he likes! For it is generally agreed that speech is by many degrees inferior to action, and therefore, we should suppose, must be more rigidly discouraged. Our language is full of sayings to that effect. 'Speech is silver', we say, and 'Silence is golden'; 'Deeds – not words'; 'Least said – soonest mended'; 'Keep well thy tongue and keep thy friend' (Chaucer); 'For words divide and rend', said Swinburne, 'but silence is most noble till the end'; '"Say well" is good, but "Do well" is better'; and so on. The strong, silent man is the admiration of us all, and not because of his strength but because of his silence. The talker is universally despised, and even in Parliament, which was designed for talking, those men are commonly the most respected who talk the least. There never can have been a nation which had so wholesome a contempt for the arts of speech; and it is curious to find so deeply rooted in the same nation this theoretical ideal of free and unfettered utterance, coupled with a vague belief that this ideal is somewhere embodied in the laws of our country.

No charge was made in this case of seditious, blasphemous, or defamatory language, and in the absence of those the petitioners claim some divine inherent right to pour forth unchecked in speech the swollen contents of their minds. A Briton, they would say, is entitled to speak as freely as he breathes. I can find no authority or precedent for this opinion. There is no reference to Free Speech in Magna Carta or the Bill of Rights. Our ancestors knew better. As a juridical notion it has no more existence than Free Love, and, in my opinion, it is as undesirable. The less the subject loves the better; and the less everybody says the better. Nothing is more difficult to do than to make a verbal observation which will give no offence and bring about more good than harm; and many great men die in old age without ever having done it. The strange thing is that those who demand the freest exercise of this difficult art are those who have the smallest experience and qualifications for it.

It may be well argued that if all public men could be persuaded to remain silent for six months the nation would enter upon an era of prosperity such as it would be difficult even for their subsequent utterances to damage. Every public speaker is a public peril, no matter what his opinions. And so far from believing in an indiscriminate liberty of expression, I think myself that public speech should be classed among those dangerous instruments, such as motorcars and fire-arms, which no man may employ without a special licence from the State. These licences would be renewable at six-monthly periods, and would be endorsed with the particulars of indiscretions or excesses; while 'speaking to the public danger' would in time be regarded with as much disgust as inconsiderate or reckless driving.

What is in my mind is well illustrated by this case; for the evidence is that the one manifest result of the 'Hands Off Russia' movement has been to implant in many minds a new and unreasoning antipathy to Russia; while the cry of 'Hands Off England' has aroused in others a strong desire to do some injury to their native land. We find therefore that there is no right of Free Speech recognized by the Constitution; and a good thing too.

Uncommon Law – 1935

A NICE CUP OF TEA

Some folks put much reliance,
On politics and science:
 There's only one hero for me.
His praise we should be roaring,
The man who thought of pouring
 The first boiling water onto tea...

I like a nice cup of tea in the morning,
For to start the day, you see.
And at half past eleven
Well, my idea of heaven,
Is a nice cup of tea.
I like a nice cup of tea with my dinner,
And a nice cup of tea with my tea,
And when it's time for bed,
There's a lot to be said,
For a nice cup of tea.

They say it's not nutritious,
But darn it, it's delicious,
And that's all that matters to me.
'It turns your meat to leather',
Well, let's all die together,
The one drink in Paradise is tea.

I like a nice cup of tea in the morning,
For to start the day, you see.
And when I've sent the breakfast in,
Well, my idea of sin
Is a fourth (or fifth) cup of tea.
I like a nice cup of tea with my dinner,
And a nice cup of tea with my tea.
And when it's getting late,
Why, most anything can wait
For a nice cup of tea.

Sung by Binnie Hale in *Home and Beauty* – 1937

SCENE SEVENTEEN

(They tell me this piece is not so 'dated' as all that)

Sequence 49, Scene 17, did not, on paper, present many difficulties. Just a simple piece of dialogue:

MURIEL. Give me that letter!

GEORGE *(crunching the letter in his hand)*. Never!

MURIEL *(she hears a twig snap in the jungle and whispers)*. What is that?

GEORGE. Elephants.

That was all. But when I arrived on the 'location' they had been working at this scene for four hours.

The scene of the incident was a clearing in the jungle of Ceylon, near which it was known that a dangerous 'rogue' elephant was roaming, seeking somebody to trample on.

But the scene of the 'shooting' was a desolate area of stubblefields and barbed-wire fences in Herts. Two hundred yards away from the tropical grove was a British railway-station, which appeared to be the centre of the shunting operations of Great Britain. Through this station express trains ran frequently and noisily, careless of the trouble they gave to the producers of a sound-film operating in the open air. The studio unfortunately was built before the talkies were thought of.

It was a typical spring day in August – 'showers and bright periods', as the forecast describes it. A fitful breeze blew across the fields and made noises in the microphones; the sun appeared now and then between racing clouds, and rain fell every fifteen minutes.

The difficulties of reproducing the hot stillness of a tropical jungle in these conditions can scarcely be exaggerated. Nor was the tropical atmosphere heightened by the numerous arc-lamps, cameras, hanging microphones, bits of scaffolding, and labyrinthine wires that surrounded the tropical palms and banyan-tree, not to mention three or four directors, five or six sound experts, twenty-five camera-men, and a miscellaneous army of electricians, carpenters, and tropical scene-shifters.

There are three main troubles in the production of a talkie out-of-doors – the actors, the sound, and the light. The first thing is to decide what the actors are to say and to get them to say it correctly and audibly. When I arrived the actors were still being rehearsed; they seemed patient but mad. George had hissed 'Never!' for the forty-first time, and Muriel was about to hear the broken twig and whisper, 'What is that?' when an express train rushed roaring through the station. A man was sitting about a hundred yards away beside a telephone connected with the sound-cabinet far away in the studio; and this man shouted, 'Can't be heard!' Muriel with pardonable irritation shouted back, 'I'm WHISPERING! WHAT IS THAT?' And George yelled, 'ELEPHANTS! MY SACRED AUNT!'

But these were the only signs of strain I detected: the patience of every one was quite amazing. In Scene 17, Sequence 49, there are, as you will have noted, three separate sound-effects, all rather fine – the crunching of the letter, the snapping of the twig, and the whispering of Muriel. After long labours, rehearsals, and tests, the correct volume for all the sounds and speeches was ascertained and fixed. Muriel's whisper was no longer likely to break the ear-drums of the film-fan, and the snapping of the twig no longer sounded to the unseen fellows in the sound-cabinet like a twelve-inch log falling from a great height. All that remained was to turn on the four expensive lamps which were to bring the English sunshine up to tropical standard, start the sound-machine, set the cameras going and shoot the scene.

The sun was shining brightly. A red light shone. The tropical lamps shone. 'All quiet, please!' Perfect silence. A green light shone. A cold breeze blew across the fields. Muriel, wilting in the heat of Ceylon, said, 'Give me that letter!' The cameras madly photographed her. And then from nowhere a big black cloud rolled up and buried the sun; and the darkness of Britain descended on Ceylon.

For fifteen minutes the whole crowd patiently watched the cloud. Then it rained for ten minutes. Then the sun emerged. A red light shone. 'Quiet, everybody!' Deathly hush. Lamps, cameras, green light. Scene 17 was off again. Muriel wound up her weary emotions for the fifty-seventh time and said, 'Give me that letter'. George said –

But at that moment round the corner came the 'Flying Scotsman' or some such train. Muriel made a rather pathetic little whimper and I went off to tea.

When I returned it seemed that Scene 17, Sequence 49, was really about to be recorded. The tropical sun was visible, and though it was now low the arc-lamps supported it powerfully. The breeze had fallen with the sun, and there was a strange quiet, broken only by some desultory shunting. The red light shone. The green light shone. The cameras whirred. Away in the sound cabinet the sound-gentleman listened tensely. And then an awful thing happened. Muriel forgot her words.

Thrilled, no doubt, by the prospect of finishing with Scene 17 at last, Muriel stared blandly at George and said nothing at all for a full half-minute. And at last she murmured diffidently, 'Where is the letter?'

George stared at her and shook like a jelly, realizing that to this question it was impossible to reply 'Never!' and he said, 'I don't know'. But the quick-witted fellow then remembered that he had the letter in his grasp, so he added, 'Here it is,' and handed it to Muriel. They then turned off the expensive lamps and began again. No cross word passed. Everyone seemed to realize that this sort of thing was only to be expected. I was proud to be a Briton.

The sky was now clear, but the sun had nearly set. At the next attempt it was George who lost his nerve, and when Muriel said, 'Give me that letter', George replied, 'All right', and tore it up.

Perfect patience continued to reign. I thought as the night fell that Muriel perhaps had a suicidal impulse or two, but neither she nor the directors expressed their secret thoughts.

The biggest blow, perhaps, came about sunset. More lamps had been brought out, there was neither rain nor train, both Muriel and George remembered their words, said them perfectly and even acted a little (this was the hundred-and-first-time), and the whole scene was played through without interruption or fault of any kind. Smiles and sighs of relief all round. And then the camera-man revealed that the film had run out half-way through the scene.

Not a word was said. I went home and left them at it. But I believe that Scene 17 was successfully recorded about nine.

I know that, later, when the film was finished, the film was too long, and Scene 17 was cut out altogether.

And now you know:

(*a*) Why the 'pictures' have sometimes a certain spasmodic effect.

(*b*) Why the radiant heroine of one scene looks as if she had slept under a steam-roller in the next.

(*c*) Why film-actors are highly paid.

(*d*) Why the invention of the 'talkies', though a marvel of modern science, has not so far perhaps made many staggering contributions to Art.

And

(*e*) one or two other things.

Mild and Bitter – 1936

NINTH WICKET

The bowling looks exceptionally sound,
   The wicket seems unusually worn,
The balls fly up or run along the ground;
   I rather wish that I had not been born.

I have been sitting here since two o'clock;
   My pads are both inelegant and hot;
I do not want what people call my 'knock',
   And this pavilion is a sultry spot.
I shall not win one clap or word of praise,
   I know that I shall bat like a baboon;
And I can think of many better ways
   In which to spend a summer afternoon.
I might be swimming in a crystal pool;
   I might be wooing some delicious dame;
I might be drinking something long and cool –
   I can't imagine why I play this game.

Why is the wicket seven miles away,
   And why have I to walk to it alone?
I hope that Bottle's bat will drive today –
   I ought to buy a weapon of my own.
I wonder if this walk will ever cease;
   They should provide a motorcar or crane
To drop the batsman on the popping-crease
   And, when he's out, convey him back again.
Is it a dream? Can this be truly me,
   Alone and friendless in a waste of grass?
The fielding side are sniggering, I see,
   And long-leg sort of shudders as I pass.
How very small and funny I must look!
   I only hope that no one knows my name.
I might be in a hammock with a book –
   I can't imagine why I play this game.

Well, here we are. We feel a little ill.
   What is this pedant of an umpire at?
Middle and off, or centre – what you will;
   It cannot matter where I park the bat.

I look around me in a knowing way
　　To show that I am not to be cajoled;
I shall play forward gracefully and pray…
　　I have played forward and I am not bowled.
I do not like the wicket-keeper's face,
　　And why are all the fielders crowding round?
The bowler makes an imbecile grimace,
　　And mid-off makes a silly whistling sound.
These innuendoes I could do without;
　　They mean to say the ball defied the bat,
They indicate that I was nearly out;
　　Well, darn their impudence! I know all that.
Why am I standing in this comic pose,
　　Hemmed in by men that I should like to maim?
I might be lying in a punt with Rose –
　　I can't imagine why I play this game.

And there are people sitting over there
　　Who fondly hope that I shall make a run;
They cannot guess how blinding is the glare;
　　They do not know the ball is like a bun.
But, courage, heart! We have survived a ball;
　　I pat the pitch to show that it is bad;
We are not such a rabbit, after all;
　　Now we shall show them what is what, my lad!
The second ball is very, very swift;
　　It breaks and stands up steeply in the air;
It looks at me, and I could swear it sniffed;
　　I gesture at it, but it is not there.
Ah, what a ball! Mind you, I do not say
　　That Bradman, Hobbs, and Ranji in his prime,
Rolled into one, and that one on his day,
　　Might not have got a bat to it in time…
But long-stop's looking for my middle-stump,

And I am walking in a world of shame;
My captain has addressed me as a chump –
I can't imagine why I play this game.

Mild and Bitter – 1936

OTHER PEOPLE'S BABIES

A SONG OF KENSINGTON GARDENS

Babies? It's a gift, my dear; and I should say I know,
For I've been pushing prams about for forty years or so
Thirty-seven babies – or is it thirty-nine?
No, I'm wrong; it's thirty-six – but none of them was mine.

> *Other people's babies –*
>   *That's my life!*
> *Mother to dozens,*
>   *And nobody's wife.*
> *But then it isn't everyone can say*
> *They used to bath the Honourable Hay,*
> *Lord James Montague, Sir Richard Twistle-Thynnes,*
> *Captain Cartlet and the Ramrod twins.*
>   *Other people's babies,*
>   *Other people's prams,*
>   *Such little terrors,*
>   *Such little lambs!*
>   *Sixty-one today,*
>   *And nothing but a Nanny!*
>   *There, ducky, there,*
>   *Did the lady stare?*
>   *Don't cry! Oh, my!*
>   *Other people's babies!*

Isn't he a pet, my dear – the spit of Lady Stoop?
Looks a perfect picture, yes – I nursed him through the croup;
But I shall get my notice just as soon as he can crawl –
It's a funny thing to think he won't remember me at all.

> *Other people's babies,*
> *Nothing to show –*
> *Twelve months' trouble,*
> *And out I go.*
> *Of course, it isn't everyone can say*
> *They used to bath the Honourable Hay,*
> *Lady Susan Sparrow, what was dropped in the pond,*
> *And now, Cook tells me, she's a well-known blonde.*
> *But forty years of croup,*
> *Forty years of frights,*
> *Long, long days, dear,*
> *And short, short nights –*
> *Sixty-one today,*
> *And ought to be a granny,*
> *Pensions for the widows, eh?*
> *But what about the Nanny?*
> *There, ducky, there,*
> *Nannies don't care!*
> *Don't cry! Oh, my!*
> *Other people's babies!*

Sung by Norah Howard in *Streamline* – 1934

'NOT CATCHY'

or

A LACK OF FUN

When the critic says that the composer's music is pleasant, graceful or inoffensive, but not noticeably tuneful, I comfort the composer with the following story.

A friend of mine remembers his father coming home from the first performance of *The Gondoliers* (by Gilbert and Sullivan). When asked what the piece was like his father said: 'Not bad. But of course there's only one tune in it.'

Any composer or librettist who needs further comfort should turn back the pages of *Punch*, as I have been doing, and read the 'notices' of the other operas by the immortal pair.

I cannot find any contemporary criticism of the first five works – *Trial by Jury, Sorcerer, Pinafore, The Pirates of Penzance* or *Patience* – though that may be my fault.

But there is a long notice of *Iolanthe* on December 9, 1882. And very familiar stuff it is. The critic fills a column and a half with a teasing account of what is now called the advance 'ballyhoo' by Mr D'Oyly Carte, 'who can bang Barnum himself as a Showman and is up to every move on or off the theatrical boards...'

'After this came the Manager's final achievement of putting the right people in the right places for the first representation... The result was a large gathering of Enthusiastic Gushers with whom the success of the new piece was, as one discriminating critic wrote, "a foregone conclusion" ... It forcibly struck us that if such an audience as jeer'd and guy'd the first representation of the Laureate's *Promise of May* at the Globe had been assembled at the Savoy...the Second Act, after the first quarter of an hour, would have met with rather a warmer reception than the Authors had anticipated... '

(This note, not unknown, they tell me, today, is sounded in many of the critiques – the note of surprise and resentment that people should actually go to the theatre in a friendly mood, determined to enjoy themselves, and, having gone, insist on enjoying themselves.)

'*Iolanthe* begins brightly enough, though the fairy music *is from the first disappointing.*

'...having once laughed at the procession of Peers, at Mr Grossmith as *Lord Chancellor*...there is nothing else to laugh at, because the Author has himself destroyed the incongruity of his own creation...

'...but for Mr Sullivan's music (very far from his best, and not up to his *Patience* or *Pinafore*), *Iolanthe's* Fairies *with a less select audience*, would have only narrowly escaped the fate of *Foggarty's Fairy* at the Criterion.

'Mr Gilbert started with a funny idea, not perhaps quite pleasant when too broadly insisted upon...

'The idea seems to have been too much for him... "Said I to myself, said I" – not exactly a new and original refrain, by the way...

'...the patter-song seems to have been suggested by Planché's well-known "I'm in such a flutter."...

'...the rhymes clever, but not absolute marvels of rhythmical ingenuity...

'...the dialogue is not worthy of the author...

'As a musical or humorous work *Iolanthe* is not within a mile of *Pinafore* nor a patch on *Patience* – nor has it anything to equal the "When Constabulary Duty's To Be Done" which enlivened the Second Act of the not too lively *Pirates of Penzance* – and after the first burst of curiosity has been exhausted we do not fancy that the public will take to

Iolanthe as they have to Messrs G and S's previous productions.'

The notice of *Princess Ida* (in January, 1884) begins with the familiar complaint that there is not enough scope for the comedian (Mr George Grossmith).

'You will thoroughly sympathize with an audience who come "for the fun of the thing" and who don't get it at the Savoy in *Princess Ida*, because they see next to nothing of the only person on that stage capable of raising a laugh.

'Nobody else is funny *per se*.

'The best *jeu de mot* in the piece is where *Ida* tells the old woman who could not say *Amen* that "are men" stuck in her throat.

'The scenery is perfect.

'…a meaningless monotony about the actions of everyone in *Princess Ida* which is infinitely wearisome.

'…the song-words (excepting the one for GG, which is simply first-rate) are not a patch upon those in *Pinafore* or *Patience*.

'… For, honestly, though it is all pretty and nice and smooth, with quaint conceits and a fair amount of dry humour, yet there is a *lack of fun*.

'I am sure that the Public, after the first curiosity is satisfied, will grumble at not having enough of "Gee-Gee".'

Coming to *The Mikado* (March 28, 1885), I expected to find a more enthusiastic tone. But this is the most surprising and entertaining of all the notices. Here again our critic gave three quarters of a column to the same complaint – that the comedian was not (at first) "well served".

'The first performance, which would have been good enough anywhere else, was not quite up to Savoy mark…

'It broke upon many of us there as quite a revelation that our GG's real humour had hitherto been less in his face and voice than in his legs (!). Throughout the First Act his legs were invisible…and the audience (were horrified to find that) their favourite was not being funny!

'Suddenly, in the Second Act, he gave a kick-up, and showed a pair of white-stocking'd legs under the Japanese dress. *It was an inspiration*…a shout of long-pent-up laughter… George took the hint; he too had found out where the fault lay, and now he was so pleased at the discovery that he couldn't give them too much of a good thing… From that time till the end of the piece there wasn't a dull minute.'

(So that the success of the master's masterpiece at its first performance seems to have turned upon the accident that the comedian, more than half-way through the play, was "inspired" to kick up his legs.)

The character of *Pooh-Bah*, according to the critic, was anticipated years ago by Planché, in *The Sleeping Beauty*

'As Lord High Chancellor I slumber never;
As Lord High Steward in a stew I'm ever;
As Lord High Constable I watch all day;
As Lord High Treasurer I've the deuce to pay… ' etc.

'…some capitally written songs and telling lines, but…

'*I must see it again to be able to judge of Sir Arthur Sullivan's music*, which struck me as peculiarly graceful, *if not quite so immediately catching* as his *Pinafore* and *Patience*…. Of course, it is a success.'

Ruddigore (January 29, 1887) was treated very shortly and sharply. '…excellent scenery, exquisite costumes…a gushingly enthusiastic audience…and yet, somehow, *Ruddigore* wasn't happy.'

'At any other Theatre the same piece, with different names attached to its production, would have had a bad time of it…

'*Ruddigore* is not even (!) up to the mark of the *Princess* or *Iolanthe*, and not within measurable distance of *The Mikado*, which, by the way, might be successfully revived.'

(The critic, you will observe, is now almost 'gushing' about the former works.)

The notice of *The Yeomen of the Guard* (October 13, 1888) begins with some caustic remarks about the 'gush' of the Press generally. If it had been anybody else but G and S, our critic asks, 'wouldn't the virtuously indignant critics have been down on the librettist for not informing the public that the plot was founded on that of *Maritana*?'

He goes on to support this allegation in detail and concludes: 'But for Mr Gilbert the critics have nothing but obsequious compliment and good-natured excuses.'

As for the music, it is:

'...genuine Sullivan and charming throughout, *though not at first hearing very catching* – with the exception of the duet, repeated with chorus* as finale, "I have a song to sing-O", the first phrase of which I did manage to carry away with me, but while humming it on my road home I found myself imperceptibly wandering into the "Lullaby" in *Box and Cox*...

'Courtice Pounds sings prettily a ballad about "Moon" and "June"...

'In a week or two *Jester* George Grossmith will introduce some of his gaggery-waggery – (O dear, what did Mr Gilbert say?) – no doubt, when he has exaggerated his dances, developed his comic business, and made the part quite his own, it will go with roars.

'My summary is this: *Cut at least twenty minutes out of the First Act; take a quarter of an hour out of the Second Act...* Induce Mr Temple to abandon all attempt at playing his part seriously.'

---

* i.e. 'plugged'.

And of *The Gondoliers* (January 4, 1890):

'There is nothing in the music that catches the ear on a first hearing as did "The Three little Maids" (but it didn't! see above) or "I've got a song to sing-O"; but it is all charming.'

You will observe, then, all whom it may concern, that Sir Arthur Sullivan's music, all through this collaboration, was *never* 'very catchy at a first hearing'.

There is nothing surprising in this. The only surprising thing is that so many people who ought to know better should go on through the ages making these dangerous judgments. If you have one or two not very good tunes and play them over and over again it is fairly easy to make the audience – and even the critics – go away humming them. But if you have a number of tunes (good or bad) and do not 'plug' any, your music is bound to be 'not very catchy at a first hearing', because no human brain can catch so quickly, especially if the tunes are good – that is, not 'obvious'.

After my first hearing of *The Beggar's Opera* I could not hum a tune; but after a third I could hum a dozen. And, speaking roughly, the tune that you know the third time is generally better than the tune you know the first – and lives longer. But the critics, those over-worked men, can seldom go a third time. So life rolls on, the composer tears his hair, and people wonder why songs are 'plugged'.

Sip! Swallow! – 1937

THE COMMON COLD

The Common Cold! The Common Cold!
The doctors really must be told
It's really time that they controlled
The horrors of the common cold.

I love the doctors – they are dears;
But must they spend such years and years
Investigating such a lot
Of illnesses which no one's got,
When everybody, young and old,
Is frantic with the common cold?
And I will eat my only hat
If they know anything of that!

Mark with what long and patient care
The doctor studies what is rare.
He cannot do too much for you
If you have something strange and new,
Nor can he quite conceal his bliss
If it should chance to end in -is.
Moreover, if the thing's obscure
He may be slow but he is sure.

He knows the perfect pill or paint
For every tropical complaint,
Which is not likely to occur
In Battersea or Westminster.
But there are fortunately few
Who suffer from the strange or new;
I do not know a single case
Of Indian Itch or Persian Face,
Nor do I think that I have met
A man with sleeping-sickness yet.

But all of us have one disease –
We all sniff, snuffle, cough, and sneeze.
The common cold! The common cold!
If all the populace was polled,
A large majority, I'm told,
Would register a common cold.

This is the universal plague,
And here I find the doctor vague:
To poly- this and poly- that
He plays a straight and pretty bat,
But when it is the common cold
The man is absolutely bowled.

And you would think that Harley Street
Would be ashamed of this defeat;
You'd think, I say, that here and now
The Street would vow a holy vow –
'Whatever any doctor's at
We will desist from doing that,
No more inquire the cause of twins,
And stop inventing vitamins,
And drawing teeth and drawing fees
Till we have done for this disease;
We will not sleep, we will not eat,
Nor shave the face nor wash the feet,
Nor shall our boots be heeled and soled
Till we have killed the common cold.'

But if, in fact, you chance to meet
A specialist in Harley Street
And say to him, 'Look here! Behold!
I have – again – the common cold',
The gentleman will only stare;
He really does not seem to care.
He then remarks without remorse,
'Oh, well, the thing must take its course'.
But I reply with frank chagrin,
'Why must the blasted thing *begin*?'

Mild and Bitter – 1936

LOVE LIES BLEEDING

(This drama, 'written by a Russian during his residence in Hammersmith', is from the Revue *'Riverside Nights'*, which Sir Nigel Playfair and I put together at the Lyric Theatre, Hammersmith, in 1926. Mr Ridgeway had been running a season of Tchehov plays at the Barnes Theatre across the River. It is, I fear, a little like some of these modem plays.)

CHARACTERS

EBENEZER STEPHEN STEPHENSON, *a lunatic.*
THOMAS WILLIAM LOVE, *a footballer.*
HENRIETTA JOLLY, *an aunt.*
JONATHAN NATHANIEL JOLLY, *a gambler.*
ALICE MARGARET JOLLY (*his daughter*), *a bride.*
HENRY HIGGINBOTTOM, *a steeplechaser.*
HARRIET ELIZABETH HIGGINBOTTOM, *his mother.*
REGINALD ARTHUR FOSTER, *a best man.*
HEZEKIAH TOPLEY, *a newspaper seller.*

SCENE: *A room in the house of the* JOLLYS, *Blythe Road, Hammersmith.*

The furniture crowded against the walls. One table with white table-cloth, glasses, etc., being an attempt at a buffet.

At a small table (right) sits STEPHENSON, *who is very old and untidy. He wears a most ancient second-hand frock-coat which is too large for him, and a straw hat with a hat-guard. He has his back to the room, and seems to be writing, referring now and then to a pile of papers and a number of great books, some of which have overflowed from his table to the floor. He looks woebegone and works feverishly, muttering. Indeed, he seems a little mad, and sometimes chews a cucumber.*

On the other side of the room (left) sits LOVE, *who is young and sulky. He is dressed in a football jersey and shorts, for he is a footballer, and plays goal for Chelsea. His boots and shorts are muddy, and one would say that he had been playing for Chelsea quite recently.*

He is sitting in front of a wireless set, with loudspeaker, and is tinkering with the controls. He wears an expression of profound discontent.

STEPHENSON (*not looking up*). What is the time, Thomas William Love?

LOVE (*after a pause – and with a shrug of utter disillusionment*). What does it matter?

HENRIETTA *drifts, or rather staggers, into the room; she is extremely old, though not as old as* EBENEZER; *she looks as if at any moment she might die, not from ill-health or age, but from concentrated melancholy. She carries a plate with some cake on it.*

HENRIETTA. Here is the seed cake for the wedding breakfast. There is something peculiar about this house. The pork sandwiches have gone bad.

STEPHENSON *looks at her suspiciously and mutters;* LOVE *pays no attention to her; she puts the plate down and drifts out again.*

LOVE. I admire pork. (*Sighing*) It is a quarter past three, Ebenezer Stephen Stephenson.

STEPHENSON (*not looking up*). Morning – or afternoon?

LOVE *shrugs hopelessly.*

STEPHENSON (*turning round – darkly*). As a matter of fact, when you come to think of it, it matters to a quite extraordinary degree. At half-past three the 3.30 is run; and you know what that means to the head of this house. (*Confidential*) And then, you must be aware, Friday is the end of the financial year, and I am still at Schedule A (*Wildly*) A fortnight! Only a fortnight to fill up all my forms! The forms of a whole family! (*Fiercely*) Oh, my forms! My beautiful forms!

He buries his face in them, sobbing, as though they were roses.

LOVE (*is not much affected by this sad scene – but continues to tinker with the wireless*). As for me, I have never been able to share your enthusiasm for the Income Tax. But, then, there is absolutely no seriousness in me. All my life I have been a failure, and yet, as you see (*looking very lugubrious*), I am as gay as a spark. Even now, look at me (STEPHENSON *does not*), I sit here trying to extract music from the ether with this utterly ridiculous machine, and, do you know, I simply do not care whether I succeed or not?

HENRIETTA *drifts in again from the other side of the room with a plate of sandwiches and a small teapot.*

HENRIETTA. The gold-fish are swimming round in circles. Alice Margaret's canary is lying dead in its cage. It would not surprise me if something quite unusual took place in this strange house. (*Going over to* STEPHENSON, *in a humouring voice*) Dear Uncle Ebenezer Stephen Stephenson! It is good of you to calculate the assessments for us all. But this is a day of joy.... You should have put on your black clothes like the others and gone to the church.

She lays a hand on his shoulder.

STEPHENSON (*starting violently, covers his forms protectively with his hands*). Don't touch me! Keep away! (*Cunningly – looks at her searchingly, as if seeing her in a new light*). Are you a relative incapacitated by age or infirmity, Henrietta Jolly, or a daughter upon whose services the individual depends by reason of old age or infirmity, where the said relative, widowed mother, or daughter is maintained by the individual? (*Beating his forehead*) So much depends on that! (*Confidential*) But listen, Henrietta Jolly – if Love Lies Bleeding does not win the 3.30, then even I cannot save your brother. Oh, my forms! (*He returns to them.*)

HENRIETTA (*wringing her hands*). Oh, this house is dreadful – dreadful! My poor brother! Yesterday he was misinformed by a gypsy at Sandown, and today his daughter is married to a steeplechaser. Oh!

Suddenly, behind her, LOVE'S *labours are rewarded, and a gay dance-tune pours from the loudspeaker.* LOVE *sits listening to it with an expression of abject sorrow.*

HENRIETTA (*turning – horrified*). Stop it, Thomas William Love. (*He stops the music.*) And why are you in fancy dress?

LOVE (*rising, with more vigour*). Will you have the goodness to tell me, Henrietta Jolly, the name of the detestable individual who is at this moment marrying your brother's daughter, Alice Margaret?

HENRIETTA (*wearily*). I forget whether his name is Foster or Higginbottom. It is all the same.

STEPHENSON (*wildly – to himself – reading from his forms, and tearing his hair*). Wear and tear of machinery and plant!

HENRIETTA. But excuse me, why are you not playing in the cup-tie, Thomas William Love?

LOVE. To be perfectly accurate, I am. Or, rather, shall we say, I was. I will tell you what happened –

STEPHENSON (*vaguely – as he works*). Nine-tenths of the amount of such earned income (subject to a maximum additional allowance of £45) –

LOVE (*annoyed by the interruption, resumes*). I was standing in goal. The score, as we say, was five goals each (and half the game to go). Five times the ball had passed me and entered the net. (*Bitterly*) That is the sort of man I am. The centre-forward of the other side was running straight for me with the ball. He had passed the backs – there was nothing between him and me. Suddenly, at that moment, I realized the utter futility of my whole existence. What in the world, I reflected, does it matter whether a goal is scored or not, by one side or the other? Will anybody be wiser, more beautiful, have more elevated ideals? Besides, now that all things are held in common, is it right for one brother to have more goals than the rest? Some of the crowd, it is true, will cheer louder, and some will utter blasphemy and threats. But what, after all, is the crowd? What are they *for?*

STEPHENSON (*muttering*). Retirement, bankruptcy, death, etcetera.

LOVE. Well, you will understand, Henrietta Jolly, that, having reached that conclusion, there was only one thing for me to do. Without so much as another glance at the advancing centre-forward, I turned on my heel, walked away from the goal, and came to this house.

STEPHENSON (*who seems to have been listening all the time, looks up but not round*). Did he score a goal?

LOVE (*indifferently*). I did not notice.

HENRIETTA. This is a very peculiar house. (*With her woman's intuition*) It is evident from what you have said that you are in love with Alice Margaret.

LOVE (*shrugs, hopelessly*). Could anyone love a person so exceptionally second-rate as myself? (*He returns to the wireless.*)
    Clatter, conversation, and wedding-bells outside.

HENRIETTA. Here they come, and now I dare say the tea is cold. (*She pours out tea, etc.*)

    LOVE *turns on the wireless, and another dance-tune is heard as the wedding party enter.*

    The BRIDE (ALICE MARGARET JOLLY) *and the* BRIDEGROOM (HENRY HIGGINBOTTOM) *come in hand in hand. She is slight, pinched, and intense; she wears a very dingy wedding-dress, worn by her great-grandmother in the year ?? He is in a very horsy black-and-white check suit, with breeches, and has bow legs. The* BRIDE *looks as if she has been crying, or is just about to. The* BRIDEGROOM *looks like death.*

    The other three are dressed almost entirely in black. JONATHAN NATHANIEL JOLLY, *the father of the bride, is a robust, florid, hearty, and cheerful person in a long frock-coat and brown boots.*

HARRIET ELIZABETH HIGGINBOTTOM, *the mother of the bridegroom, is stout and short of breath. She wears a good deal of jet, sequins, and lace. She carries smelling-salts and a fan.*

REGINALD ARTHUR FOSTER, *the best man, is natty and perky and efficient – perhaps a clerk or young salesman. He is supporting* MRS HIGGINBOTTOM, *who seems much exhausted.*

LOVE *sits tinkering with the wireless, and* STEPHENSON *goes on with his work. Neither looks at the party.*

The BRIDE, *as soon as she sees* LOVE, *detaches her hand from* HIGGINBOTTOM'S *and goes quickly up to* LOVE, *who looks up and stops the wireless. The others make for the refreshment table.*

FOSTER. Perhaps a little tea, Mrs Higginbottom?

MRS HIGGINBOTTOM (*nigh spent*). Tea? I could drain a samovar! (*Sinks into a chair.*)

She and FOSTER *are at one side,* MR JOLLY *and* HIGGINBOTTOM *at the other.* HENRIETTA *carts refreshments about.*

ALICE MARGARET (*intensely*). Thomas William, I cannot endure my married life. My husband sings in church. We have never been to church together before. It is dreadful. I detest music. What am I to do?

LOVE *looks darkly over her shoulder and takes a revolver from the pocket of his shorts.*

LOVE (*laughing sardonic-like*). And now I suppose you expect me to gratify your absurd passion for me by killing your husband? But let me tell you, young lady, you have come to the wrong shop. For I shall certainly miss him.

ALICE MARGARET (*putting her arms round him*). Do not be morbid, Thomas William. I have always loved you, but I married him to please my father, because he said he could spot winners.

They embrace passionately, a little hampered by the revolver. None of the others seems to observe these goings-on.

JONATHAN (*comfortably – having had a little wine – looking at the clock*). They should be off by now, Henry Higginbottom. You still have faith in Love Lies Bleeding?

HIGGINBOTTOM (*pontifical*). Mr Jolly, the horse that beats Love Lies Bleeding will win.

STEPHENSON (*totters to his feet and feebly waves a form or two at them*). If Love Lies Bleeding does not win – (He sinks back into his seat).

JONATHAN.* Ha! I tell you what it is. I believe I am the most extraordinary character alive. I have absolutely no influence over a single human being. I say to one 'Come!' and he goes, 'Do this' and he does exactly the opposite. But when it comes to horses, I have the power of an archangel. Put me on the back of a horse and it becomes possessed of a devil, flies over mountains, jumps hedges, plunges into ponds. Put my money on a horse, and it stops dead. I do not believe that in all the world there is an animal so mild and swift that I cannot turn it into a wild beast by sitting on its back, or convert it into a lumbering cart-horse by putting half a crown on the creature. I have only to draw a horse in a sweepstake, and it bursts out coughing or swells at the knees. (*Drinking*). Ha! Truly a remarkable power! (*To* HIGGINBOTTOM). But now that *you* are a member of the family – we shall see a change, eh, Henry Higginbottom?

HIGGINBOTTOM *nods, and they drink together.*

STEPHENSON (*pricking up his ears, totters over to* HIGGIN-BOTTOM). A new member of the family? Then naturally you will want your forms filled up? (*Taking his arm, he leads the bridegroom over to the table, delighted, still croaking.*)

HIGGINBOTTOM, *humouring him, goes quietly.*

JONATHAN (*looking at his watch*). Go, Henrietta Susan Jolly, and buy an evening paper.

* Nigel Playfair.

HENRIETTA (*going out*). As you will, Jonathan Jolly, but I never yet knew any good to come out of an evening paper. There is something very queer about this party. (*She drifts out*).

Enter, right, along the street, an old NEWSPAPER SELLER, *drunk.*

NEWSPAPER SELLER.* Paper! Paper! All the losers! (*Highly amused.*) He! He! The trouble about me is that half the time I yearn after beauty and the other half I drink gin. Paper! He! He! I remember when there were larks singing in the Broadway. Did anyone want an evening paper then? Everyone was content with his own misfortunes – his own and his neighbour's. But nowadays a man bears on his back the calamities of the whole world. Earthquakes and murders with his breakfast; floods, strikes, and railway-smashes on his way to work. He! He! (*Waving his papers.*) And, not satisfied with so much misery in the morning, he must needs have another dose of disaster in the evening. He! He! (*To* HENRIETTA JOLLY, *who now approaches*). Paper, miss? I tell you what it is, miss, there's more joy in Fleet Street over one sinner that cuts his sweetheart's throat than over the ninety and nine just men who marry and live happily ever after. (*Going off*) I never sell one of these things without thinking I've made another fellow-creature miserable. But I keep on doing it! He! He! Paper! All the losers!

(EXIT)

MRS HIGGINBOTTOM (*panting and puffing*). It is difficult to see why people continue to get married in this country, Mr Foster, for sooner or later they go mad or have a baby, and then everything begins all over again.

> JONATHAN, *meanwhile, has closed his eyes, and is humming drunkenly to himself.*

* Miles Malleson

REGINALD FOSTER. At home, Mrs Higginbottom, I have a tame salamander, which continually stands on its hind legs. I have sometimes wondered why.

THE BRIDE (*who all this time has been locked in* LOVE'S *arms whispers tensely*). Let me go! Someone will see us!

> LOVE *releases her, and she sits down by the wireless. He stands fingering his revolver, and gazing darkly at the inoffensive* FOSTER.
>
> HENRIETTA *then bounces into the room with an evening paper – saying almost gaily*

HENRIETTA. Did I not tell you that some misfortune would befall us?

ALL. What is it?

> STEPHENSON *and* HIGGINBOTTOM *turn in their chairs* (*right*), JONATHAN *jumps up and looks over* HENRIETTA'S *shoulder at the paper.* FOSTER *pushes over and stands centre.* MRS HIGGINBOTTOM *waddles over to the paper group. The* BRIDE *and* LOVE *remain where they are* (*left*).

JONATHAN (*reading – in sepulchral* tones). 'Love Lies Bleeding fell dead at the starting-gate.'

THE BRIDE (*gives a little scream*). Oh! And he *promised* it should win!

Silence – broken at last by a rending sound. It is STEPHENSON, *tragically tearing up the forms on which he has laboured so long. All gaze straight in front of them.*

Perhaps by accident, the BRIDE *turns the appropriate lever, and dance-music again issues from the loudspeaker.*

Then LOVE *moves a step, and raising his revolver, shoots* FOSTER *through the head.* FOSTER *falls to the ground. No one at first appears to notice the incident.* LOVE *stands over the body and shoots it again. The* BRIDE *stops the wireless.* LOVE, *to make quite sure, fires another shot at the defunct* FOSTER.

THE BRIDE. What are you doing, Thomas William Love?

The others slowly begin to take things in.

LOVE (*with an eloquent gesture towards the body*). Well, at any rate you will admit that we can now be married, and live happily ever after.

THE BRIDE. But that is not my husband. That is the best man.

LOVE (*throwing down his revolver, with a shrug*). Now *that* is just the sort of thing that happens to me.

CURTAIN

Riverside Nights – 1926

MULLION

My ball is in a bunch of fern,
A jolly place to be;
An angry man is close astern –
He waves his club at me.
Well, let him wave – the sky is blue;
Go on, old ball, we are but two –
We may be down in three,
Or nine – or ten – or twenty-five –
It matters not; to be alive
Is good enough for me.

How like the happy sheep we pass
At random through the green,
For ever in the longest grass,
But never in between!
There is a madness in the air;
There is a damsel over there,
Her ball is in the brook.
Ah! what a shot – a dream, a dream!
You think it finished in the stream?
Well, well, we'll go and look.

Who is this hot and hasty man
That shouteth 'Fore!' and 'Fore!'?
We move as quickly as we can –
Can any one do more?
Cheer up, sweet sir, enjoy the view;
I'd take a seat if I were you,
And light your pipe again:
In quiet thought possess your soul,
For John is down a rabbit hole,
And I am down a drain.

The ocean is a lovely sight,
A brig is in the bay.
Was that a slice? You may be right –
But goodness, what a day!
Young men and maidens dot the down,
And they are beautiful and brown,
And just as mad as me.
Sing, men and maids, for I have done
The Tenth – the Tenth! – in twenty-one,
And John was twenty-three.

Now will I take my newest ball,
And build a mighty tee,
And waggle once, or not at all,
And bang it out to sea,
And hire a boat and bring it back,
And give it one terrific whack,
And hole it out in three,
Or nine – or ten – or twenty-five –
It matters not; to be alive
At Mullion in the summer time,
At Mullion in the silly time,
Is good enough for me.

Mild and Bitter – 1936

'MR SPEAKER, SIR...'

ROYAL COMMISSIONS

MR ALAN HERBERT: I am sure that the Financial Secretary will get this Vote without any difficulty, but I should like some assurance that this money is not going to be wasted. I am probably the only Member of this Committee who in his election address boldly asserted that when he became a Member of Parliament he would set his face against the habit of Government Departments asking Royal Commissions to find out things which they ought to know already themselves, and which almost everybody else knows. Therefore, I am bound to make my protest now. A Royal Commission is generally appointed, not so much for digging up the truth, as for digging it in: and a Government Department appointing a Royal Commission is like a dog burying a bone, except that the dog does eventually return to the bone.

In my short experience of Royal Commissions I find that they spend perhaps years going into a question, that public-spirited ladies and gentlemen give their services free in doing that work, that they produce portentous and expensively-printed reports and that nothing happens.

THE DEPUTY-CHAIRMAN (Colonel Clifton Brown): The hon. Member is now discussing Royal Commissions as a whole, but the Supplementary Estimate with which we are dealing refers only to certain Commissions.

MR HERBERT: With great respect, Colonel Clifton Brown, my argument was that I feared that this particular sum of money might be wasted. I was offering evidence to justify my fear, in obedience to the rule that one should not make general assertions and accusations without offering evidence of them. I was about to refer to what has happened in the past. Take the case of the Royal Commission on Canals and Waterways.

THE DEPUTY-CHAIRMAN: It would be quite out of order to go into that now. This discussion can only refer to those Commissions and Committees which are the subject of the Supplementary Estimate.

MR HERBERT: I apologise if I have erred, and in that case I can only express the hope that my fears will not be justified in the case of these Royal Commissions which, for all I know, are admirable and worthy bodies, although two of them look to me to be the kind of Royal Commissions which would probably be quoted on a Friday afternoon to stop the passage of a private Member's Bill... Do I understand, Colonel Clifton Brown, that under your Ruling I am not allowed to give examples?

THE DEPUTY-CHAIRMAN: The hon. Member must not go beyond the Commissions and Committees to which the Estimate refers.

MR HERBERT: It is constitutionally impossible, Colonel Clifton Brown, that you should be wrong, and it is Parliamentarily impossible for me to suggest that you are, but I feel that if I were in a higher sphere and looking down upon this little incident, I might consider that there was the possibility of the faintest scintilla of injustice attaching to the verdict which you have just pronounced... After all, it is impossible to consider any particular except as part of a whole. I think that is a Eucidean proposition with which everybody will agree; and I cannot entirely forget when I look at this list of Royal Commissions the fate of the others to which I was about to refer. I have often felt that it was a wondrous thing that His Majesty should still be able to get the devoted services of public-spirited men and women to act on these Royal Commissions, knowing very well that, in all probability, nothing whatever will be done as a result of their reports... I shall have to support this Vote very reluctantly, and with the feeling that I am helping to add just one more stone to the mountain of inertia, indecision and delay.

Hansard, Vol. 344, Cols. 649/651, February 23, 1939.

119

DO YOU SAY 'DORN'?

In our youth, when, trembling but hopeful, we sent humorous verse to the editor of *Punch*, the great Sir Owen Seaman used to write tartly in the margin of the said composition:

Do you say 'dorn'?

For we had committed the then unpardonable offence of rhyming 'dawn' with 'morn'.

The rebuke was just, the answer could only be 'No'; yet the question, we felt, was not quite fair.

For if the editor had said –

Do you say 'mawn'?

the answer would have been, 'Well, since you ask, we do. For we are miserable Cockneys and have no "r's". And the fact is that when we say "lawn" and "forlorn" the sound is very much the same – indeed, it is the same'.

But that would have been no excuse. For there are people, even in the Southern Counties, who do possess an 'r' or two; and even those who don't are rightly offended when they read:

Upon the lawn

A worm was born.

Why not? Ask a Scot.

Well, we have a good conscience. Mindful of our early mentors, we have all our lives resolutely refused, even on the stage, to rhyme 'Malta' with 'falter' or 'Britannia' with 'pannier'. And the temptations, believe us, in a lifetime of bardery, have been numerous and powerful. This single self-denying ordinance alone must have added several years to our hours of labour and by so much diminished our total output and earnings. The 'laughs' we lost in the theatre!

And who cares? Not many.

The admirers of the late Sir W S Gilbert care, we hope, for he played the game always. At least, on the very rare occasions when he transgressed the rule, he did it in such a way as to show that it was a conscious and exceptional piece of naughtiness.

But the authors (and audiences) of this generation do not seem to care two hoots. The great Mr Noël Coward gaily shatters the rules and would falter at Malta without any visible regret. Such famous pieces as 'Nina' are the successful result. You may say that to his London audiences the sound is the same; but then his lyrics are sung not by or to Southerners only. Besides, he afterwards publishes them in books.

You might think that the serious poet would be more severe in such a matter than the mere light-hearted singer for the stage. Not a bit of it! The serious modern poet is much more loose and undisciplined than the base and 'commercial' leg-show lyric-monger.

We pick up one of the works of Mr W H Auden, who, they tell us, is prince of the 'new poets'.* On the first page my finger touches I see:

> The shutting of a door,
> The tightening jaw.

Another poem begins:

> On Sunday walks
> Past the shut gates of works
> The conquerors come
> And are handsome,

and lower down I see:

> Pursued by eaters
> They clutch at gaiters.

Here is another poem of couplets, most of which rhyme in orthodox fashion: 'fires – wires', 'doors – floors', 'girl – whirl,' 'camp – damp', 'bad – cad,' also, by the way, 'canals' and 'rails.' And suddenly we are confronted with:

> afford
> abroad.

Do you say 'affoad'?

---

* Now Professor of Poetry at Oxford University

Do you say 'abrord'?

You and I may, for our diction is deplorable. But surely the sensitive and scholarly Mr Auden does not?

We seem to hear already the hum of the highbrows like hornets round our head. Rhyme, they buzz, is an out-worn convention, and the cultivated modern poet will not be the slave of it. He expresses deep psychological mysteries and discovers new aspects of beauty by the use of assonance and dissonance and crashonance and sprung rhythm and split heads and Heaven knows what. He has not much use for what we know as metre, and he frankly despises the pedantic rhyme.

All this would be more convincing if he did despise rhyme. But he doesn't. Whenever rhyme comes easily he employs it: whenever it doesn't he gives up. And that, Bobby, is the difference between his generation and ours.

If you really despise rhyme don't put 'eaters' next to 'gaiters', or 'walks' next to 'works', or 'door' next to 'jaw' in a poem the rest of which is composed of correct rhymes like 'night' and 'fright' and 'date' and 'gate'. If you don't want a rhyme you can put 'gate' instead of 'door' or 'leggings' instead of 'gaiters'. That will be more honest and give no offence.

Is this not the age of efficiency and thoroughness and precise attention to technique? What should we say of the boxer who, having engaged to fight with his fists, let out with his foot when that became too difficult; of the steeplechaser who ran round the most formidable obstacles and said that jumping was, after all, an outworn convention? We should say that they did not know their jobs, and we might say other things as well. And these, we maintain, should be said about the poet, serious or sprightly, who announces by his deeds that he is going to write a rhymed poem according to the ancient rules, and in the middle decides that they do not matter.

We may, upon this theme, be in a minority of one – or rather two. The other is that brilliant performer E V Knox, who followed Sir Owen Seaman into the editorial chair of Punch, and is faithful to his standards too. Never mind, we raise the standard of the Anti-Dorners, the League for the Prohibition of Faltering at Malta. And, whatever may be the cause of our ultimate demise, we trust that none will be permitted to grave upon our tomb:

Here lies Haddock,
He died of Medoc.

Yet a couplet like that would be enough to make the reputation of a really modern poet. Heigh-ho!

General Cargo – 1939

PS. (1960) In a Birthday Song for a Royal Child (music by the Master of the Queen's Music) Mr C Day Lewis wrote:

'*Touched with a primrose bloom of dawn*
For every child that's born'.

In a recent revue we heard, without surprise, 'chartreuse' coupled with 'furs'.

'MR SPEAKER, SIR...'

TUBERCULOUS BEVERAGES

'It would be refreshing if, for a change, we could refrain from giving this dog a bad name. It is very easy to throw a cloud of prejudice over things by using such pseudo-scientific terms as "alcohol", "liquor", "intoxicating liquors", "vested interests" and so forth. I shall not follow the hon. Member for West Bermondsey (Dr Salter) in his medical researches, but I would say this to him: "So far as I know, beer does not have to be boiled before it is fit to drink; and the Minister of Agriculture and Fisheries and the Minister of Health are not racking their brains in order to regulate, certify and pasteurize it in order to make it fit for human consumption." I might easily go around describing milk as a tuberculous beverage, or motor-cars as homicidal vehicles, but that would be nonsense. Therefore, I ask hon. Members not to use that kind of language. One more word to the hon. Member for West Bermondsey. I believe that certain temperance associations, and perhaps himself, are in the habit, for the purpose of conveying an awful warning against the use of beer, of exhibiting in bottles, for instance to the children in the schools, the livers of deceased club-men, for all I know, past Members of this House. In that case, I would gladly offer my liver to the nation. But I suggest in our great educational scheme, which I believe is to be extended, he should make a further exhibition to the unfortunate children of the lungs of somebody who has perished through tuberculosis contracted from milk...

'What is a pub? We can agree that the pub is, on the whole, a social centre and, I suggest, a very valuable social institution. It is a place to which people can go for political sanity and for temperance purposes, for it is an instrument of control. It is a place where people who do not own rich houses, who have no billiard rooms or gardens of their own, are able to go for social intercourse and the news of the day. I would ask hon. Members, in discussing this question, to remember that the public-house is not a sink of iniquity, and that the publican is not a man who is ruining his fellow countrymen. It is said in the Trade that it is more difficult to become a publican than a parson...

'My mind goes back to a year ago, when I was naughtily and boldly laying an information against the Kitchen Committee of this House. There was not then light-hearted talk about 'intoxicating liquor' and about 'liberty which nobody wanted'. There was indignation, and rightly. This House did not then say, 'Oh, well, these things do not really matter, let us have more control, let us obey the law which we have imposed on the people'. This House marched out to battle – horse, foot, and Attorney-General – to defend its rights and privileges, and I congratulate them. I am very glad that they succeeded. The High Court decided that continual access to refreshment of every kind was essential to the conduct of the business of this House, although the business of this House is the most important business of making laws. I do not say that people demand the same privileges as there are in this House – I think they are glad that this House has special privileges – but they would like to have the same spirit shown in this House when their simple human desires are being considered.'

Hansard, Vol. 309, Col. 1725 – March, 1936

SONG OF SPORT

THE EARL
 It's really remarkably pleasant
  To wander about in the wood
 And to kill an occasional pheasant,
  Provided the motive is good.
 And one of the jolliest features
  Of slaying superfluous game
 Is the thought that we're saving the creatures
  From a death of dishonour and shame –
   Every bird has to die
   By and by, by and by,
 And they're lucky to die as they do,
   For if they do not
   They're sure to be shot
 By someone who's not in 'Who's Who'.
   And I give you my word
   That a sensitive bird –
 A point for our foolish reproachers –
   Prefers its career
   To be stopped by a peer
 And not by unmannerly poachers.

Dumb creatures with me are a passion:
    I've a special regard for the fox:
And I try in my fatherly fashion
    To spare him excitement and shocks:
The farmer is anxious to fill him
    With pellets, as farmers are wont,
And it's really a kindness to kill him
    For he's certain to die if we don't.
        Every fox has to die
        By and by, by and by,
But what he abhors is a gun,
        So we hunt him with hounds
        Over other folk's grounds
For that is his notion of fun.
        And I vow and aver
        That foxes prefer
To be killed, as it were, in their armour
        By an aristocrat
        In a shiny top-hat
And not by an underbred farmer.

ALL *It's all for the sake of the fox, poor thing –*
    He likes to go down in his armour,
        And oft on his face
        At the end of the chase
        A smile of serene
        Satisfaction is seen –
    To think that it wasn't a farmer!

Tantivy Towers – 1931

BOARD OF INLAND REVENUE v. HADDOCK

Why is the House of Lords?

We are able today to give some account of a startling judgment in the Court of Appeal delivered a few days before the end of term and, for reasons unknown but suspected, not hitherto reported in the Press.

The Master of the Rolls, having expressed a desire to hear no more argument from the learned counsel for the Crown, said:

This is an appeal from a judgment of a Divisional Court reversing an order by Quarter Sessions, allowing an appeal on a case stated from a decision of the magistrates granting an order to eject against an official of the Board of Inland Revenue upon a summons to show cause why the respondent should not have vacant possession of his own premises under an instruction of the Commissioners for Income Tax, afterwards reversed by the Board.

The point at issue is whether the appellants are entitled under the Land Tax Clauses of the Finance Act, 1931, to enter upon the window-box of the respondent, Mr Albert Haddock, and there remain for the purposes of measurement and assessment on the neglect or default of the respondent to supply particulars of his window-box upon the Land (Expropriation) Tax Form Q1/73198.

The point appears to be short and simple, but this Court does not intend to consider it. It will be observed from the history of the case as already recounted that a number of intelligent dispensers of justice have already addressed their minds to it with varying results. We are asked to say that the learned High Court judges who last considered the case were in error, and that the lay magistrates whose order they reversed were right. Whatever our decision, it is certain that an indignant appeal against it will be directed to the supreme tribunal, the House of Lords, since the resources of the Crown are as

127

inexhaustible as its impudence, and the blood of Mr Haddock is evidently up.

In these circumstances, at the end of a long and fatiguing term of appeals, we do not feel called upon to consider this particular appeal with our customary care. But a few general observations upon our appellate system may not be out of place, and will at least satisfy the public that they are receiving full value from this distinguished Court.

The human mind is admittedly fallible, and in most professions the possibility of occasional error is admitted and even guarded against. But the legal profession is the only one in which the chances of error are admitted to be so high that an elaborate machinery has been provided for the correction of error – and not a single error, but a succession of errors. In other trades to be wrong is regarded as a matter for regret; in the law alone it is regarded as a matter of course. The House of Lords, as an appellate tribunal, is composed of eminent and experienced lawyers; but, if I may say so with respect, they are only by a small margin more eminent and experienced than the lawyers who compose this Court; indeed, it is frequently a matter of accident whether a judge selected for promotion is sent to this Court or reinforces the House of Lords. The difference in capacity is one of degree; indeed, the only real difference is that the House of Lords has the last word. But the difference in estimation is substantial, and in practice great issues and the destination of enormous sums of money are allowed to be determined by it.

Now, this is strange. The institution of one Court of Appeal may be considered a reasonable precaution; but two suggest panic. To take a fair parallel, our great doctors, I think, would not claim to be more respected or more advanced in their own science than our greatest jurists. But our surprise would be great if, after the removal of our appendix by a distinguished surgeon, we were taken before three other distinguished surgeons, who ordered our appendix to be replaced; and our surprise would give place to stupefaction if we were then referred to a tribunal of seven distinguished surgeons, who directed that our appendix should be extracted again. Yet such operations, or successions of operations, are an everyday experience in the practice of the law.

The moral, I think, is clear. A doctor may be wrong and he will admit it; but be does not assume that he will be wrong. In difficult or doubtful cases he will accept, and may even seek, the opinion of a colleague more experienced or expensive; but if he had to pronounce every opinion with the knowledge that in all probability it would be appealed against and publicly condemned as erroneous, there would be little confidence in the consulting room on one side or the other, and few medical men would consent to continue in practice. Indeed, it says much for the patience and public spirit of our inferior judges that they devote such thought and labour to their work in these discouraging conditions, and show no resentment towards junior counsel who, at the close of a ten days' inquiry and a protracted judgment, inform the learned judge responsible for both that they will appeal against his decision.

In short, the existence side by side of the Court of Appeal and the appellate House of Lords appears to me to be indefensible in logic and unnecessary and even vicious in practice. If it be assumed that the House of Lords is in fact possessed of exceptional acuteness and knowledge of the law, it may well be said that every case of exceptional difficulty should have the benefit of these exceptional powers. But it follows from this that every such case should be certified at an early stage as one that can be usefully considered only by the House of Lords, and to that House it should be at once referred; just as a general practitioner in medicine, confronted with an obscure disease or unusual conditions outside the range of his experience and knowledge, will at once refer the sufferer to a specialist. But the litigant whose case is exceptionally complex cannot now avail himself of the supreme wisdom of the House of Lords until he has trailed his coat through a number of inferior Courts, which are *ex hypothesi* incompetent to secure his rights or remove his doubts. Which is evidently a waste of time and money.

But it is perhaps a generous assumption that the litigant thinks of the House of Lords as the possessors of exceptional wisdom. The very similar composition and capacity of that House and this Court, to which a respectful allusion has already been made, are well known to him; and that similarity must suggest to him that when the House of Lords thinks differently from us it is not so much evidence of their superior wisdom as a matter of luck. At the end of certain hotly contested cases, decided only by a majority in both the Court of Appeal and the House of Lords, the weary and impoverished litigant, adding up the number of judges who have voted for and against him in the various Courts, has found that, *per capita*, His Majesty's judges were equally divided on the point in dispute. It is not surprising, then, if many appellants present themselves to that House in a reckless or at least a speculative mood, as a gambler who has backed a succession of losers still hopes to recover all by a wild wager on the final race. The Court of Appeal, to one in this mood, must represent a minor handicap taking place at 3.30. It is not desirable that our great tribunals be regarded in this light; but at present it is inevitable. The people may be taught to believe in one Court of Appeal; but where there are two they cannot be blamed if they believe in neither. When a man keeps two clocks which tell the time differently, his fellows will receive with suspicion his weightiest pronouncements upon the hour of the day, even if one of them happens to be right. Moreover, the expense of successive appeals must make the acquisition of justice difficult for the rich and impossible for the poor. The unsuccessful litigant who cannot afford to go beyond the Court of Appeal must always be haunted by the thought that in the House of Lords he might have won; while the Inland Revenue, relying on the public purse, can pursue their unjust claims to the end and, if they lose, can send the bill to the taxpayer.

For all these reasons we recommend that either this Court or the House of Lords (as a Court of Appeal) be abolished; or, in the alternative, that the House of Lords retain its appellate functions as a specialist body for the settlement of questions of exceptional difficulty, such cases to be referred to them upon the order of a High Court judge.* As for the present case, we decline to discuss it. It will go to the House of Lords in any event, so let it go at once. The appeal is formally allowed, and good luck to Mr Haddock!

Lord Justice Ratchet and Apple, L J concurred.

Uncommon Law – 1933

I TOLD YOU SO

A H
(An Epitaph)

Pause, pray, and pity, passer-by:
Here, as in life, I, Hitler, lie.
Forbear from mockery or mirth,
These are the saddest bones in earth:
For they reluctantly recall
The mightiest might-have-been of all.
    It is unusual to find
A perfect thing of any kind;
The *prima donna's* charms are small;
The beauty has no voice at all
(God has insisted, some believe,
On keeping something up His sleeve).

---

* Something like this was recommended by the recent Evershed Committee.

So I, who had so much of what
The other fellow hadn't got –
A new, unnatural cross between
A mystic, monster, and machine;
From every weakening force apart,
Untouched by alcohol – and heart;
Who shunned tobacco – and the truth;
Who dazzled, yet degraded, Youth;
Who drove my country to the top
And then insanely let her drop –
Half devil and half dynamo,
No man could tell how far I'd go;
And, but for one unhappy trait,
I might be going strong today.
I had momentum, I had weight,
But I could simply not go straight.
      Like others in the history book,
I lost a crown by turning crook.
I might have worn the Hero's robe,
A Washington to half the globe:
Instead of that I chose to be
The world's Horatio Bottomley.

Siren Song – October 25, 1939

THE FORTIES

'MR SPEAKER, SIR...'

BOOKS TAX

I hope that the relations of Oxford and the City of London will always continue to be friendly, but when I hear the representative of the City of London referring to a tax on books, the 'machine tools of education', as someone has said, of the great craft of literature, the great profession of learning, as a tax upon a mere 'hobby', to be compared with golf, then that is a mind with which I can make no contact, and I do not propose to try. I address myself with much more confidence, to the Chancellor of the Exchequer. Great qualities, such as geniality and tact, have carried the right hon. Gentleman from one office to another, with the goodwill of all and the hopes of many, as you may see some cheery reveller staggering from pub to pub, emerging from each with such a radiant smile that no one has the heart to stop his passage to the next. But, in this affair, without intention, I am sure, he has added insult to injury...

It is a sad and shocking thing that at this time in this titanic conflict, when we are saying, and saying truly, that there are arrayed, on one side, the spirit of force and, on the other, the forces of the Spirit, we should have sunk so low as to be seeking to put a tax upon, and to treat all learning and enlightened literature in the same way as we should treat brooms or

something which is kept under the bed.* The right hon.
Gentleman had a great opportunity. He might have said,
'However many Hitlers are at the door, however many dangers
and difficulties confront us, we are not so down and out and so
poor in resources that for the sake of £500,000, which is my
estimate of the yield of this miserable tax, we are going to do
this barbarous thing'. That appeal I should have addressed with
confidence to the right hon. Gentleman's predecessor,**
because, whatever his detractors may say, he had a real love and
understanding of the language and the fine things that make
literature. I say, with regret, that I believe I shall address this
appeal without avail to the right hon. Gentleman. In friendship
and courtesy I will not give reasons why I say that. But well may
the shades of Milton, of Caxton, of Sheridan, and of Charles
Dickens, and of those brave men, who in the last century fought
and won the principle of free enlightenment, groan in their
honoured graves today to think that that lamp which they hung
on the walls of Westminster has been clumsily torn down at last
by a Chancellor of the Exchequer, who, at this hour of
civilization, sees no important distinction between boots and
books.

Hansard, Vol. 363, Col. 1040 –July 25, 1940

The tax was withdrawn in August

---

* Books and 'domestic hollow-ware' were in the same list.
** Sir John Simon.

INVASION

Napoleon tried. The Dutch were on the way,
    A Norman did it – and a Dane or two.
Some sailor King may follow one fine day:
    But not, I think, a low land-rat like you.

September 15, 1940

(Three days later Hitler scrapped his plan. A constant reader?)

To WSC

(The Prime Minister is sixty-seven today)

Many happy returns of the day
    To the father of purpose and plan,
To the one who was first in the fray,
    Never doubted, or rested, or ran,
To the Voice of old Britain at bay,
    To the Voice of young men in the van,
To the Voice of new worlds on the way –
    To 'We must – and we will – and we can.'
May he live to hear History say,
    'This was their finest man'!

Bring Back the Bells – November 30, 1941

WE WERE THE FIRST…

Ah, yes, we are lazy, and foolish, and fat;
    And nothing we do is just what it should be;
And Russia does this, and America that –
    But we were the first to fight for the free.

For twenty-five years we've done everything wrong;
  And no wonder the clever ones giggle with glee;
For we tried to be kind, and we failed to be strong –
  Yet we were the first to fight for the free.

So let the bright fellows make hay with our fame!
  This is the truth the simple can see;
This is the claim that will cling to our name;
This is the boast that no beating can shame;
This is the picture our children will frame –
We did not wait till the enemy came:
  We were the first to fight for the free.

May 10, 1942

'LESS NONSENSE'

Let's have less nonsense from the friends of Joe;
We laud, we love him, but the nonsense – NO.
In 1940, when we bore the brunt,
We could have done, boys, with a 'second front'.
A continent went down a cataract,
But Russia did not think it right to act.
Not ready? No. And who shall call her wrong?
Far better not to strike till you are strong.
Better, perhaps (though this was not our fate),
To make new treaties with the man you hate.
Alas! These shy manoeuvres had to end
When Hitler leaped upon his largest friend
(And if he'd not, I wonder, by the way,
If Russia would be in the war today?).
But who rushed out to aid the giant then –
A giant rich in corn, and oil, and men,
Long, long prepared, and having, so they say,

The most enlightened leader of the day?
THIS tiny island, antiquated, tired,
Effete, capitalist, and uninspired!
THIS tiny island, wounded in the war
Through taking tyrants on two years before!
This tiny isle of muddles and mistakes –
Having a front on every wave that breaks.
We might have said, 'Our shipping's on the stretch –
You shall have all the tanks that you can fetch'.
But that is not the way we fight this war:
We give them tanks, *and* take them to the door.
And now we will not hear from anyone
That it's for us to show we hate the Hun.
It does not profit much to sing this tune,
But those who prod cannot be quite immune,
And those who itch to conquer and to kill
Should waste less breath on tubs on Tower Hill.
Honour the Kremlin, boys, but now and then
Admit some signs of grace at Number Ten.

Truth – October, 1942

BLOW THE BLUES!

I'm sick of the songs
About people with wrongs,
And lovers who love them no more,
Especially sung
By a girl with one lung,
Or a man with a voice like a snore.
I'm sure it's not true
That everyone's 'blue',
And human affection is vain:
And, if it were so,

The news is *de trop*,
And I don't want to hear it again.

Well, I can't pretend that I'm blue,
    For the girl that I love loves me:
She lives at Number Two,
    And I live at Number Three.
    We're as happy as happy can be,
There's nothing at all that's tough;
    For the girl that I love loves me,
And I see her quite often enough.

Then I weary of those
    Who must whine through the nose
With a bogus American twang,
    When it's perfectly clear
    To a sensitive ear
It was Hoxton from which they sprang;
    The singers who yearn
    For a rapid return
To places they never were at,
    And in no way suggest
    They were born in the West
Except that they sing rather flat.

I cannot *pretend that I'm blue,*
    For the girl that I love loves me:
We don't want to go to Peru,
    Or Texas or Tennessee.
    We're as happy as happy can be;
She comes from Potter's Bar;
    The girl that I love loves me,
And we like being where we are.

In these tricky times
The music and rhymes
Should surely be more up to date.
How seldom does Jazz
Reveal – if it has –
A constructive approach to the State!
Not a ghost of a plan
For the future of Man,
Not a message unless it's a moan.
There is song after song
Biologically wrong,
And some anti-social in tone.

But I can't pretend that I'm blue,
  For the girl that I love loves me:
I quite like her mother too;
  They call us the Harmony Three.
  I'm glad to record we agree
About Currency and the Beveridge Report;
  The girl that I love loves me,
And, as a matter of fact, she's a jolly good sort.
                    Full Enjoyment – April 14, 1943

MONTY THE 'MARTINET'

To complete the picture of the 'inhuman martinet', I must relate, I think, what had happened earlier. As I have said, a small battle had begun very early that morning – it had been postponed for a few days because of the weather – a battle, I gathered, to clear away the last pocket of Germans on our side of the Meuse. After breakfast, as the great Damon Runyon might have said (and it is a fairy story deserving special treatment, I think):

I am sitting in the ante-room, rather cold, reading the newspapers, when who comes in but the Field-Marshal, bearing a bottle of brandy across his breast, like a bride with lilies.

'A bottle of brandy' (he says) 'captured from the Germans. A present for Gwen (who is my ever-loving wife). Would you like it? Would you like it?'

Now, as a matter of fact, brandy is one of the very few drinks with an alcoholic foundation which I do not value very highly. I do not mean that I am unable to swallow it: but I do mean that if I am asked what drink I should choose to accompany me during a protracted visit to a desert island brandy would be quite a way from the top of the list. But my ever-loving wife has no objection to harbouring brandy in the home, and I am thinking it is a much more sensational present than the bottle of red wine I have bought for her in Brussels. In addition, it is not every morning that a guy is fitted up with a bottle of brandy by a teetotal Field-Marshal who has just begun a battle: and I am so moved by the scene and spectacle that I cannot think of any suitable response. I say weakly 'Thank you very much, Sir.' And then, because I think I have not played my full part in the conversation, I say: 'I wonder what the Customs will have to say about this, Sir?' But there is a little more in what I say than keeping the conversation alive, because I have just remembered that the little guy called Henderson who is one of the Field-Marshal's ADC's, has said to me in Brussels 'Do you like Bols?' and I have said 'Yes, I do like Bols' (which is a kind of Dutch gin, very good, they say, for the backache). So he says 'We have captured from the Germans huge quantities of Bols, to which, if the truth must be revealed, we are not extremely partial. We will give you a bottle.' So he gives me two great earthenware bottles of this Bols. And I am thinking that what with the two Bolses and the bottle of red wine and the Field-Marshal's bottle of brandy I am likely to be taxed like a wine-importer on my arrival in Old England, though it true that I have also acquired some toys for some of the seven grandchildren and these – who knows? – may soften the heart of the Customs. While I am reflecting after this manner the Field-Marshal says 'Oh, well, I will write you a letter' and scrams. I go up to my apartment and there is the nice little guy called Henderson, with the batman, which is a military man's man, and they are trying to thrust the two Bolses into my poor man's grip, which, what with the toys and the bottle of red wine, is not coming very easy. When I am sighted with the bottle of brandy they are discouraged somewhat, and it is decided after a few experiments that I will leave the bottle of red wine behind as a loving tribute to the Mess. At this moment who should sail in but the Field-Marshal himself with a letter he has just written in his own fair hand, and it goes like this: 'Mr A P Herbert MP has been staying with me as my guest. I have presented him with a bottle of brandy captured from the Germans. I hope the Customs will take a kindly view of this. I am sure they will. B L Montgomery, Field-Marshal'.

Now, once again, I am standing there like I have been hit by a hammer, because, believe me, by all the tales in town, this guy has as much loving-kindness as a goldfish and is by no means one of the Friends of Liquor. Moreover, this morning he is fighting a battle. I say 'Why, thank you, Sir'; but again I feel that I have not done justice to the situation. So I add, by way of a nervous crack, 'I suppose, Sir, you could not add a footnote about these two bottles of gin the boys have given me?', and I look down at the two guys still in a clinch with my small grip on the floor. The Field-Marshal takes one look at the scene, and he says 'What, gin? What, gin? Why, I'd better write you another letter.' And I am telling you, on oath, if you insist, that he goes out and writes the letter again, with a new piece about the Bolses. After that, I think I will not say any more, for fear he will give me a case of champagne and send a telegram to King George.

Well, I come down at the airport in an Anson machine that bounces so many times I think we are going to start again, and here I am, half-deaf, before the Customs. Two of the Customs guys know me because they have served on the River. The chief guy gives me a loud 'Hallo' and asks if I have anything to declare. I say, 'Why yes, I have something rather special to declare', and I show him the letter. He grins, and shows it to his colleagues, and they read it and grin and chuckle like mad. 'Well', says the chief guy at last, 'I guess that will be OK, Mr H, seeing it's all presents.' 'But,' he says, and I see very well where this cunning old guy is steering, 'I expect we'd better keep this document, hadn't we?' Now, if it is me, I would much rather keep the document and pay the duty, or abandon the cargo of liquor. But I think, if I do this, I am making a vain thing of the Field-Marshal's care and trouble. So I hand over the document, and I am telling you that there is some Customs guy who has the finest autograph of any Field-Marshal since Field-Marshals were invented.

Independent Member – 1944

MORNING PAPER

(*A Belated Bouquet*)

Morning paper Here you are!
   Morning papers everywhere –
Bed or Breakfast – tram or car.
   'Nothing in it.' But it's there.

Banging bombs and sweating men –
   Nights of terror in the Street:
But they cannot stop the pen,
   And the printer can't be beat.

There is havoc in the town,
    And the telephone is dumb,
Milkman's late – a bridge is down –
    But the morning paper's come.

Yes, they also serve the King,
    Though their medals may be rare.
'Nothing in it?' 'Not a thing.'
    Yet be thankful it is there.

Light the Lights – September 17, 1944

'THE CHANGE'

(*A Minister To His Successor*)

Here's the portfolio. In the cupboard there
'The sweets of office'. Yes, the cupboard's bare.
Here is the IN-tray – full of dynamite,
Your doom by daylight, and your dream by night.
Goodbye. Good luck. And do not pity me:
I am again respectable, and free.
But you, the Minister, become today
A public enemy, the public prey.
In opposition you were proud and pert,
Spoke when you willed, and cared not whom you hurt.
Now, to your Party and your desk a slave,
You must be silent, and you must behave.
And when at last you leave this stuffy place,
Worn out with service to the human race,
The office cat may thank you if it can.
Expect no gratitude from any man.

Full Enjoyment – August 5, 1945

THE LORDS

LORD LAVENDER. All I say, Madam, is that you'll never get
   your pestilent Bill through the House of *Lords!* (*cheers*)

LAVENDER
   There's a lot to be said for the House of Peers,
      Though it shouldn't be said by me.
   We've all the best Bishops, we make the best beers –
      We're top of the nation's tree.
   Field-Marshals and Admirals – Doctor and Judge,
      With the Chairmen of Banks and Boards –
   You have to take care what you bet about there!
      There's a lot to be said for the Lords.

   We don't represent anybody, it's true,
      But that's not a thing to regret:
   We can say what we think – and I know one or two
      Who've never said anything yet.
   While the Commons must bray like an ass every day
      To appease their electoral hordes,
   We don't say a thing till we've something to say –
      There's a lot to be said for the Lords.

   There are people who grouse at our excellent House
      Because the attendance is small;
   But a question that ought to have kindlier thought
      Is why we attend it at all.
   The Commons, perhaps, are superior chaps
      And richly deserve their rewards;
   But you don't pay a peer a thousand a year
      There's a lot to be said for the Lords.

   From father to son our high offices run:
      What a sensible way to proceed!

It's not any old horse you support on the course
    You go for a creature with breed.
I'd very much rather succeed a good father,
    Who wore a top hat and a sword,
Than be chosen by masses of ignorant asses –
    There's a lot to be said for a Lord.

They try to reform us; the plans are enormous:
    No wonder that nothing is done.
You might as well try to remodel the sky,
    Or construct a superior sun.
Why tinker at what is the best thing you've got,
    A House that is free from discords –
The one place in the land where women are banned?
    There's a lot to be said for the Lords – the Lords!

                Sung by Eric Fort in *Big Ben* – 1946

BIG BEN

(*Scene – The Chamber of The House of Commons*)

CLERK'S VOICE. Prohibition of Drink Bill – Second Reading.

MRS BUSY
    I move the Second Reading of this admirable Bill,
    To rectify our feeding and remove an ancient ill.
    I need not tell the House, I think, in all the sad details
    How dangerous it is to drink fermented wines and ales.
    A visit to a hospital, a prison, or a Court,
    Or lunatic asylum, will provide the right report.
    There is no character so strong, no intellect so sound,
    The ruthless Demon Alcohol will not at last confound.
    One drop of spirit such as men are fond of swilling down

Will kill a healthy rat or burn a hole in half-a-crown.
One bottleful of brandy is enough to drive a train;
Imagine the effect upon the kidneys and the brain!
First Memory departs: Imagination follows fast;
Then Moral Sense collapses quick, and Sanity goes last.
The liver, to a frightful size expanded, soon acquires
The consistency of granite and the shape of motor tyres.
The other organs follow suit and grow as tough as Turks
Till, in the normal cases, absolutely nothing works.
The sufferers, to ease the pangs incurred the day before,
Turn to the same old poison and, most rightly, suffer more.
Hangover follows hangover; they still increase the doses,
And day by day paralysis comes near – if not cirrhosis.
Meanwhile, the victim's morals very naturally fail,
And now the question is – will it be hospital or jail?
He falls to frightful passions, and his speech is rude and wild,
He throttles some young woman or assaults a baby child.
And happy are the tipplers who in agonies have died
Of cirrhosis or a stroke, but were not hanged for homicide.
Clause One of this fine Measure brings this traffic to a stop:
In Britain shall no alcohol be taken – not a drop.
All these bizarre particulars I am prepared to prove,
For I drank like a fish till I was thirty-six. I beg to move.

GEORGE. Mr Speaker, Sir.
    The painful narrative we have heard might have impressed
        us more,
    If we had not heard every word so many times before.
    The Honourable Member did her best our blood to curdle,
        Sir,
    But there are other kinds of pest to which I might refer.
    A man may fall beneath a bus or die of poisoned silk,
    Or find himself tuberculous from drinking dirty milk.

And many a corpse beneath the grass would still be living
    here,
If he had let French water pass and stuck to British beer.
Nor is it true that crime and vice are rigidly confined
To those who shun vanilla ice and orgies of that kind.
It is not in the village pub that slander flows most free,
But in the virtuous shop and club where women swill their
    tea.
Indeed the argument is hot against her every time:
It needs a sober man to plot and execute a crime.
But there is more. Though I am loth to mention cads and
    curs,
Hitler and Mussolini both were staunch teetotallers.
Did not the dictatorial itch to which I've just referred
Disfigure the oration which the House has lately heard?
What sort of prospect do we face, if we, the legislators,
Propose to make the British race a lot of damned dictators?
Just one more word – the Revenue is dear to every heart:
Whatever kind of tax is due we love to play our part.
But now observe how sharp the line between the taxes paid
By those who love cigars and wine – or sweets and lemonade.
The Fleet should give a daily cheer for those who swill or sip,
For every time we sink a beer we float a battleship.
On all these counts, and I expect that there are others still,
I hope this House will now reject this most un-British Bill.

MR JONES (*a feeble fellow*)
        This Bill, I think, goes far too far;
           And yet there is no doubt,
        For some restriction at the bar
           A case has been made out.
        May I suggest a compromise
           Before I cease to speak,
        Which is that this great country tries
           Prohibition half the week?

GRACE   I disagree; for Nature's laws
         Are generally sound.
    And everywhere for some good cause
         Some alcohol is found.
    There's alcohol in plant and tree:
         It must be Nature's plan,
    That there should be, in fair degree,
         Some alcohol in Man.

Big Ben – 1946

MY BIG MOMENT

If I'd only done the things I thought of doing,
    What a lot of splendid things I should have done!
Something big is always brewing –
    But it never sees the sun.
I long to hear the populace hallooing,
    But the populace are lamentably dumb:
For I never do the things I thought of doing –
    When will my Big Moment come?

Horse runs away. I think 'Now then!'
But while I think it's stopped by other men.
Girl is insulted. I go red:
While some pale nincompoop kills the man instead.
House is on fire. I run for the Brigade,
And some damn fool puts it out without their aid.
Join the Volunteers. We don't go to war:
And everybody asks what the devil we are for!
    All my swans as geese hatch out.
    Shall I ever hear men shout
    'Bravo, Thomas! Well done, Trout!'

If I'd only done the things I thought of doing, *etc.*
Sung by Brian Reece in *Bless the Bride* – 1947–9

FROM THE RUSSIAN

THE DAWN

Little Brother, why do you sigh?
Do you not see, across the fields,
   Beautiful against the sunset,
The Collective Sewage Farm,
   And the fine house
They are building for the Commissar?
   The peasants, too,
With merry songs
Are sowing the wheat
   For the cities,
For Stalin, the Good and Great,
   Our Father and Mother,
Who wrote Shakespeare
   And invented the camera;
Little Brother, why do you sigh?

Little Brother, why do I sigh?
   I wait for the Dawn.
For fifty years
   I have waited for the Dawn.
Under the cruel Tsars
   My father went to Siberia:
But he came back.
Under Stalin, the Good and Great,
   My brother and my brother's son
Have gone to the uranium mines:

149

But they have not come back.
Thirty years ago
When the cruel Tsar was liquidated
   I saw the Dawn:
   All would be different.

   Every year for thirty years
      I have said:
   'This year, truly,
Is no cause for fireworks
   Or festive drinking,
   But next year, surely'.
But *nothing*, Ivan Ivanovitch,
   Is different,
Except that there is less to eat,
The great Stalin
Has invented the submarine,
And I know more people in Siberia
   Than I did before.

Full Enjoyment – June 21, 1950

DOOMED – AN EPITAPH

Here, a dead horse, I lie in some dismay:
I should have won, at 8–1, they say.
My fate was sealed before I made the leap:
One A P Herbert drew me in a sweep.

March 29, 1949

'THE DEPOSIT'

And so you wish to serve your country, Sir,
In Britain's Parliament at Westminster?
You would give up your quiet and your job
To aid the State and represent the mob?
You are prepared, rash, patriotic soul,
To pay the large expenses of the poll;
And then to spend unnumbered years ahead
Listening to speeches when the world's in bed?
All this is very impudent and tough;
And if you do not satisfy enough
That for this act you have sufficient grounds
You will be fined £150

Full Enjoyment – January 25, 1948

IN A GARDEN

Greenfly, it's difficult to see
Why God, who made the rose, made thee.

ANYWHERE

God gave us eyelids: we can hide the eyes
From what is hideous or horrifies.
I wonder greatly that in recent years
We've not grown little flaps to close the ears.

A P Herbert

'MR SPEAKER, SIR...'

DOUBLE SUMMER TIME

I have other objections to the principle of summer time which may seem fanciful to some, but are very real to me, and to many thousands of my fellow citizens. First, we all hate public, national lying. I hate to have that great clock above our heads not telling the truth. Hon. Members may laugh, but I feel passionately about it. I hate to think that Big Ben, that great bell which has been such a voice in the councils of the world, will be heard booming, over the BBC, around the world, first Berlin time, and for the rest of the summer, Moscow time. I do not need to inform the Home Secretary that Berlin lies near Longitude 15 degrees East, and that Moscow is in Longitude 30* degrees East, and that if we advance the clock one hour, we shall use Berlin time, and if we advance it two hours, Moscow time...

My second objection has already been referred to by another hon. Member. I think that summer time, single or double, is the most frightful confession of weakness of which the human race has ever been guilty. By all means let us change our habits according to the seasons. Even the dumb animals do that. Even the uneducated cock does not crow at the same time all the year round. But let us change our habits without necessarily changing the clocks. I do not see why it is not possible for us to get up one hour earlier because it is good for us, because it is good for trade, or even because it is good for the country; but we seem able to do it only by means of a silly mechanical trick with the clock. That is an idea which must be repugnant surely to anybody who has the smallest respect for the human race. Surely, in the normal times to which the Home Secretary

* Inaccurate, I fear; it should be 37 degrees East.

152

referred – I do not say now – especially when the Government either run or control so many things, it should be the simplest thing in the world for the Government to say that, beyond a certain date, all Government offices would begin work one hour earlier and it was hoped that industry would follow suit? The only snag, I quite agree, would be the railway timetables: but in normal times, when there is more paper and less panic, that would be fairly easy to get over by having a second timetable.

Thirdly, what about the navigators, and the great position of this country in the world of navigation? An hon. Gentleman deprecated, with my hearty agreement, the possibility – and it is a possibility – that the Government may, under this Bill, at some time bring in permanent summer time. A great many people in this country want that, and I believe that Russia and possibly other countries have already done it. Suppose all the countries of Europe decided to do that, decided, in other words, to abandon Greenwich time. Let them do it: but surely this country should be the last to abandon Greenwich time? It is no small thing that the Prime Meridian runs through a small but historic suburb in the east of London. It is no small thing that you can steam seven miles down the river from this House and pass from west to east longitude. It gives me a thrill every time I do it, and I invariably draw the attention of my passengers to the experience which they are enjoying. It is no small thing that all the navigators and seamen of the world fix the position of their ships and aircraft by reference to Greenwich and Greenwich time. The stars themselves are fixed by reference to Greenwich time (*Laughter*). They are. In a humble way, I am a deep sea navigator, and I have travelled all over the world, and navigators at this moment are turning up their Tables and finding the Greenwich Hour Angle of the sun, the moon, the planets, and the stars. That is a terrific thing; it is not a thing to throw away lightly.

Suppose, as I say, that the whole of Europe decided that it will have permanent single summer time and we, because of our fuel crisis, decide to do the same thing. I am sure that, if Hitler had conquered the world, the first thing he would have done, having a certain imagination, would have been to say, 'The Prime Meridian shall run through Berlin and not through Greenwich.'* The same thing can be done in another way. Once we have permanent single summer time it is quite easy to do it without changing the clocks. It can be done by changing the maps and putting the Prime Meridian 15 degrees to the West, out in the Atlantic, and then we shall talk not of Greenwich time but of Iceland time or of Teneriffe time. I will not go on with this, but it is the kind of thing which ought to be gone into by some committee sometime before the end of next year.

Do not let us get it into our heads that Greenwich Mean Time is just some pedantic nonsense which does not really matter. It is one of the great glories of this country that all the nations have agreed that Greenwich and Greenwich time shall be the centre of all astronomy and navigation. It would be a terrible thing if we got into the habit of saying that it does not really matter, although I believe that not one among a million citizens really knows what Greenwich Mean Time really means. I shall invite the next speaker to explain it... I want this House, at the end of next year or the beginning of 1949, to challenge the whole principle. Let us believe that Greenwich Mean Time means something. That Greenwich is the centre of astronomy and navigation is a thing that we must not throw away. Let the Empire go if you must, but cling fast to the Prime Meridian.

Hansard, Vol. 434, Col. 267, March 1947 – Independent Member

* This was discussed, I learned later, in Germany.

FROM THE CHINESE

THE TRAVELLER

Life
Is a most extraordinary thing.
    I always think
As I travel through the country:
        Why
Are there so many other people,
    And what are they for?
In the little towns
    They crowd the streets and pavements,
        Busy with their baskets
        And hand-carts
    And ridiculous children.
They are a nuisance,
    They delay
        The passage of the carriage.
How do they exist
    In this small place
Where nothing important,
    It seems, is done?
Do they attend
    To each other's washing?
Do they receive lodgers?
    No – surely:
For who would live
In this place
    Unless he had to?
Intellectually,
    How barren are their lives,
Far from the delights
And diversions
    Of the capital.

What was the idea
    Of Providence?
What accident
    Of history –
What folly
    Of Man –
Caused this small town
To occupy the soil
        At all?
            Yet
In my mind
    There is a queer feeling
That all these people
    Think themselves just as important
As me,
    And would not live
In the capital
    For anything.

Full Enjoyment – August 6, 1947

SPELLING – AND MR SHAW

After the debate on Mr Follick's Reformed Spelling Bill
(defeated on Second Reading by three votes) 1949, Mr Shaw
wrote to *The Times*. We are used to the great man's superiority
to other men, especially the half-witted citizens who inhabit
the House of Commons. But he now spent a haughty paragraph
on me, and ended with a challenge which could hardly be
ignored. Mr Shaw wrote:

In the debate Sir Alan Herbert took the field as the
representative of Oxford University, the university of
Henry Sweet, greatest of British phoneticians. After
debating the stale tomfooleries customary when spelling

reform is discussed by novices and amateurs he finally extinguished himself by pointing out that a sample of Mr Follick's spelling saves only one letter from the conventional Johnsonese orthography. This was the champion howler of the debate. I invite Sir Alan to write down that one letter, and measure how long it takes him to get it on paper, and how much paper it covers: say a fraction of a second and of a square inch. 'Not worth saving' is his present *reductio ad absurdum*. But surely a University Member must be mathematician enough to go deeper. In the English-speaking world, on which the sun never sets, there are at every fraction of a moment millions of scribes, from book-keepers to poets, writing that letter or some other single letter. If it is superfluous, thousands of acres of paper, months of time, and the labour of armies of men and women are being wasted on it. Dare Sir Alan now repeat that a difference of one letter does not matter?

The rest is poppycock...

I replied:

To the Editor of The Times

Sir, – 'Dare', indeed? I eagerly accept Mr Bernard Shaw's challenge. I still think nothing of one letter (in 31 words) to be saved (perhaps) by the Follick plan, however many millions are now writing or printing it. Nor am I worried about the millions who are spending time or space this morning on shaving their chins or spelling God with a capital G.

I am sorry to say, by the way, that I may have been too generous about that one letter. I have again done the long title of the Bill into Follick English, as I understand it; and this time I make the scores equal (145 letters). I may be wrong: but look, Sir, at the following phrases, set down at random:

'The United Nations need a philosophy.' (31 letters.)
'Dhe Iunaited Neishuns niid ei filosofii.' (34 letters.)

'No sage is as wise as he looks.' (23)
'Nou seij iz az waiz as hi lwks.' (24)
'You are going round in a circle.' (25)
'Iu ar gouing raund in ei serkel.' (25)
'No elephant is a Socialist.' (22)
'Nou elefant iz ei Soushalist.' (24)

Here, if Ai hav dun it rait, Mr Follick is six letters down. It is easy to see why. He pulls out the 'ph' from 'elephant' and says 'What a good boy am I!' But what does it profit a space-saver if at the same time he spells 'go' 'gou' and 'a' 'ei'? Now for the time-saver. See what he has done (above) to such words as 'United', 'Nations', 'circle', and 'Socialist'. Such words, at present, are easily apprehended by millions of the Latin (and the English) speakers. Let Mr Shaw, the great mathematician, consider how many trillions of important seconds are going to be wasted by Frenchmen, Italians, Spaniards, and Americans wondering what on earth the English mean by 'serkel' or 'neishun', which are related to nothing they know, and do not even represent phonetically the way we say 'circle' and 'nation'. As for our children, Mr Shaw and his like are distressed by the time spent in teaching them that 'nation' and 'national' are not pronounced the same way. But how much time shall we have to spend on teaching them that 'neishun' and 'nashunal' are really the same word and spring from the same root?

Of course, as I said in the debate which Mr Shaw seems to have read, you can save paper space (though not, I think, much printer's or student's time) if you have a thoroughgoing phonetic system with an enormous alphabet and a lot of weird signs that make the printed page look like a bowl of tadpoles. Both Mr Shaw and Mr Follick, I gather, shrink from this. But Mr Shaw and others want to use several of our present letters upside down. Imagine the trouble of teaching a child to write 'c' or 'e' upside down! How many adults are likely to do it efficiently? And in print, as Sir Harry Johnston has remarked, how should we be sure that it was not a printer's error? The reformers, it seems to me, are in a dilemma which they will not face. Either they save no space worth mentioning, or they make the page repulsive and the sense obscure.

Going back to the challenge, even if I were persuaded that Mr Follick was going to save that one letter, I should not be impressed. What is the hurry? If we wish to communicate swiftly we have shorthand, morse, the telephone, and loudspeaker. The printed page is read at leisure: and other qualities get marks. We could save much time if we all wore beards and no collars. It would save time if Black Rod ran up the floor of the House without the stately gait and bows. We could save street-space if the Colonel marched in column of threes and there were no intervals between the companies. We could save paper if we cut out stops or ranthewordstogetherlikethis. All books, no doubt, could be printed in shorthand, and all citizens compelled to learn it. But in all these cases there would be a loss to elegance and understanding and the pleasures of the mind and eye which no mere saving of time, space, or trouble could justify. For example, it does not upset me to see Mr Shaw spell 'Labour', 'Labor'. Let him carry on. What a wonderful saving! But suppose the one letter were the 'y' in 'you' (Mr Follick wants to abolish 'y'). I do not find it any easier to write 'iu' (try it, Sir); it is not so legible in cursive script and might be taken for 'in'; it does not seem to me to be quite the same sound; and I, for one, should miss the word 'you'. So, with due apologies to the children and foreigners, I hope that letter will be spared, not 'saved'.

Mr Shaw should be almost old enough to know that you prove no case by shouting words like 'tomfoolery' and 'poppycock'. My own 'tomfooleries' I believe to be facts. From Mr Shaw we get nothing but dogmatic assertion and vague invective. But I hope that the writing of this long letter shows my proper respect for our oldest writer. Mr Follick wants to represent the 'aw' sound in 'paw' by the letters 'oo'; and I was tempted simply to say 'Pw! Mr Shoo!' It would have saved much time.

I am, Sir, your obedient servant,

A P HERBERT

Now, I thought, surely a thunderbolt will fall. But there was not a word.

Independent Member – March 1949

'MR SPEAKER, SIR…'

SWAN SONG –THE FESTIVAL OF BRITAIN

May I say how disappointed I am at some of the talk in some of the papers – this very gloomy talk, with petulant letters saying, 'What, after all, have we to celebrate?' Surely right hon. and hon. Members on this side of the House, at least, will agree that if, in 1951, we have survived five years of war, and five years of His Majesty's Government, then even they will have something they will like to celebrate, to dance and sing about. 'Faith,' I think Mr G K Chesterton said, 'is the capacity to believe in that which is demonstrably untrue.' If that is the only sort of confidence we have in our future, then let us have that.

I think there are other causes. I am no historian; but if the House will bear with me for one more minute, I will present another historical reason why we should celebrate, not only with the main Exhibition but with the arrangements set out in this Bill. After all, we are emerging from the murky forties into the fifties, and it has been pointed out to me by a better

160

historian than myself that the forties have always been a pretty wretched sort of decade. A hundred years ago there were the Hungry Forties, with the whole of Europe in chaos and revolution, with the Communist Manifesto, with crowned heads falling everywhere and rulers taking refuge in this island, and with the Chartists massing on Kennington Common. However, after that period we emerged into what was almost the most prosperous, happy period in this country's history.

In the seventeen-forties, I think, we were at war with France, Spain, and Scotland. A predecessor of mine in this House, Sir Charles Oman, records that when Charles Edward arrived at Derby 'Panic prevailed in London, the King's plate had been sent on shipboard, the Bank of England had paid away every guinea of its reserves, and the citizens of London were fully persuaded that they would be attacked next day by 10,000 wild Scottish clansmen'.

In the sixteen-forties there was civil war and King Charles I had his head cut off. In the fifteen-forties, I see, 'The time was a very evil one for England'. King Henry VIII was marrying too many women, executing too many men, and persecuting everybody else. I need hardly add that we were at war with Scotland, and France as well; but the historian adds, rather woundingly, that 'the French War was far more dangerous'. In the fourteen-forties we had a weak king, King Henry VI. We were at war with France, and we were gradually losing everything King Henry V had won. In 1431 we had burned Joan of Arc – and our publicity on the Continent was not good. In the thirteen-forties we were at war with France, and the Scots invaded the North of England. Also, a small detail, there was the Black Death. In the twelve-forties we invaded France. In the eleven-forties we were ruled by an unpleasant woman called Matilda and there was civil war all the time. In the ten-forties we were invaded by the Danes.

Now, whatever else may be laid at the door of His Majesty's Government, we are not now at war with France or Scotland or even Denmark, and I do not think that we shall be in 1951; and my hope is that in some way we shall emerge from the nineteen-forties into the fifties in such condition that we shall be justified in celebrating. But if not, even if we are going down, it is not the habit of the British Fleet to haul down the ensign when about to begin a doubtful engagement. On the contrary, each ship flies two or three to make sure that one shall be seen. It is in that spirit, I feel, that we ought to go forward with this bold, imaginative, attractive scheme, and show, whether we go up or down, that we can be gracious, gallant, and gay.

'Loud cheers', said *The Times*: and I was told by a friendly Minister that 'I had changed the whole course of the debate'. I can't say about that: but I know that Herbert Morrison made a very conciliatory and persuasive speech and the Conservatives did not vote against him after all. So I did feel that, at least, I had played the part of the child in the pictures who helps to bring Daddy and Mummy together – a fitting part for an Independent, singing his swan song, though he did not know it.

Hansard, Vol. 470, Col. 408, 23 November, 1949 –
Independent Member

THE FIFTIES

WHAT CAN YOU DO IF YOUR MUM'S NOT A PSYCHIATRIST?

I'm just a howling hepcat kid,
    But that's no fault of mi-i-ine:
It comes of what my Nanny did
    When I was eight or ni-i-ine.
She shut me up in a cupboard, she did,
    Under the kitchen stair;
You bet I yelled and blubbered, I did,
    An' pulled her silly hair.
But ever since then I've been shut in,
      I'm a moth on a pin,
      I'm an eel in a tin,
    An' I gotta get out,
    I must have a shout,
    That's what it's about,
      I must have a din.
I gotta express myself,
    They keep me mute,
An' so I dress myself
    In a screaming suit,
An' I jerk my knee
    An' I wag my fanny
So the world can see
    What I think of Nanny.

I gotta express myself some way,
I don't quite know what I want to say,
But I gotta get even with Nanny,
    An' all of the old queen bees,
With Teacher an' Preacher an' Granny –
    They all grow moss on their knees,
They haven't got rhythm, they're hardly alive,
There's no living with 'em – they jabber – I jive –
    For I gotta get even with Nanny.
Their world is a bore and a bungle,
I gotta get out in the jungle,
    I gotta get even with Nanny.
They don't like noise, an' they don't like boys,
    An' so when I go to the halls
I climb on the stage for to register rage,
    An' break up the seats in the stalls,
        An' I sway when I sit
        Like a frog in a fit,
    For I gotta get even with Nanny.
I gotta get out,
    They're shutting me in,
    I gotta get even with Nanny.
        They natter –
        I matter –
    I must have a din –
    I gotta get even with Nanny.
Look at me! I'm alive!
They can jaw – I can jive –
Look at me – I'm the loudest bee in the hive!
    I gotta get even with Nanny –
        Too many like her on the planet –
    An' so if a cop says 'Stop'
        I'll kick him an' say he began it –
    An' then I'll be even with Nanny.
                Punch – September 26, 1956

LONDON RIVER MEN

(From a speech proposing 'The Immortal Memory of Nelson' at Chatham Barracks, October 21, 1955)

I am proud indeed to be invited to the Ward Room of HMS *Pembroke II*, where I was rated a Petty Officer and 'kitted up' in 1940, and demobilized in 1945... Sir, they talk of Portsmouth and Plymouth, but without doubt Chatham, the Medway, and London River can strongly claim to be the true nursery of the Navy and the school of the greatest British seamen. Last year, in HMS *Drake* at Devonport, I had the honour to propose the Memory of Francis Drake. As I studied the history of that great mariner I found that in many ways it resembled my own. For one thing, as few know, he was, for several years, a Member of the House of Commons. I do not think he made many speeches, but he served diligently on the Committees. Then, as all know, he was fond of bowls and I am the President of the Black Lion Skittles Club. Also, in a sense, his base was Chatham. In spite of all the poetical talk about 'Drake, he was a Devon man' – and it is true that he was born there – he learned his seamanship like this humble sailor in the estuary of the Thames. At the age of 2, I believe, his father removed him to a hulk lying near Gillingham in the Medway. (Strange, by the way, how the parallels run on – Drake's father was a Bible–reader, Nelson's father was a rector, and my great-grandfather was a Bishop). And while Drake's father was away reading the Bible to the Fleet, young Francis, you may be sure, learned the secrets of the tides, and the mysteries of sand and shallows. He watched the hulk that was his home swing slowly to the flood tide, and the banks being covered by the rising river. Perhaps the Bible-reader knew his knots and taught him to make a bowline there. Perhaps in some old dinghy he learned to 'scull' with one oar over the stern, that useful and often necessary accomplishment. Drake's first sea-voyage, I seem to remember, was 'down Swin' and up the East Coast. On his first ocean voyage – and this is a thing for the young Paymaster to remember if ever he is put upon by executive officers – he signed on as Purser.

Nelson, too, began in the Medway and did much small-boat work in the lower reaches of London River. 'In this way' he wrote 'I became a good pilot for small vessels from Chatham to the Tower of London, down the Swin, and the North Foreland, and confident of myself among rocks and sands, which has many times since been a great comfort to me.' As the humble captain of a tiny vessel, which, proudly flying the White Ensign, plied up and down the Thames for five years of war, I know what he meant. Yachtsmen may yearn for the nearly tideless Mediterranean, with deep water always and everywhere, but there is no doubt that the ruthless, complicated tides of this island, with all their tricks and dangers, are a great school for seamen. Southey speaks of the 'intuitive genius' with which Nelson seized the situation at the Battle of the Nile. He saw at once that where there was room for an enemy ship to swing to an anchor, there was room for an English ship to enter. But he saw it with a mind and eye that had been trained in the tides and shallows of the Thames and Medway.

It has been well said: 'If Nelson had never existed in real life, no novelist would have dared to invent him.' For this hero, this leader of men, had no commanding presence or physique. He was 'a little man' with 'a feeble body', some 'oddity of appearance'; and he was 'always seasick'. What a comfort for any of us now who feel that the Creator dealt them a poor hand of cards! For in that slender shell there glowed a furnace – fired by religion, superstition, sense of destiny and prophetic power, and above all duty and devotion.

Apart from the courage of this frail fellow, consider the *endurance*. Not less remarkable than the Battle of Trafalgar was the long watch and chase that preceded it. For two whole years and a month he was at sea – with one arm, and 'always seasick'. There was one year and nine months turning and tossing in the

Gulf of Lyons, then the dash to the West Indies. Then at last Gibraltar. On July 20, 1805: '*I went ashore for the first time since June* 16, 1803'.

And here is a tale of comfort for our Frustrated Young. At the age of 16 or 17 he was sent home from the 'East Indies' sick and 'reduced almost to a skeleton'. On the voyage he was as unhappy as any teenager today. But 'After a long and gloomy reverie in which I almost wished myself overboard a sudden glow of patriotism was kindled in me and presented my king and country as my patron. "Well, then" I exclaimed, "I will be a hero, and, confiding in 'Providence,' I will brave every danger."' From that time, he often said, a radiant orb was suspended in his mind's eye, which urged him onward to renown.

The radiant orb not only led him on but seemed to disclose the future. For 'always on the eve of action he was in high spirits'. Before Copenhagen he said, 'I would not be elsewhere for thousands,' and before the Nile 'That we shall succeed is certain.' Before Trafalgar he said 'I shall not be satisfied with less than 20' enemy ships. And though he did not live to know it, 20 of the enemy 'struck'…

'Never was any commander more beloved,' says Southey. 'He governed men by their reason and their affections: they knew that he was incapable of caprice or tyranny; and they obeyed him with alacrity and joy, because he possessed their confidence as well as their love. "Our Nel," they used to say, "is as brave as a lion and as gentle as a lamb".'

This is the boy who felt like jumping overboard, this is the little and feeble sailor who was always sea-sick.

None of us, I fear, is likely to behold such a 'radiant orb' as led and illuminated the life of Nelson. But we may hope that some small orb of our own may serve us in the storm, so that, however the day has gone, we may whisper to ourselves the seaman's cry

'Lights burning brightly. All's well.'

VARIATIONS ON A THEME

VITAL STATISTICS

(1)

No more they laud the features of the fair,
The eyes, the nose, the grace of head and hair.
Instead, as if the lady were a ship,
They state her measurements at heart and hip:
And many a maid wins prominence and pence
Not for her charm but her circumference.
But Woman, shorn of voice and eyes and smile,
Is no more fetching than a measured mile.
Oh horrid Age, you make me rather sick
Who value Venus by arithmetic,
And think more saleable than sweetness is
The accidental adiposities.
And then – how strange! – they never give the fan
The hull-dimensions of a public *man*.
In throbbing Fleet Street no one seems to care
What Malcolm Sargent measures anywhere.
Through eighty years of excellence and fame
We've had no details of the Churchill frame.
At least, you would imagine, would you not,
They would record what size in heads we've got:
And it would please the masses, I dare say,
To know the map of Bannister or May.
But men are right, of intellect and worth,
Who do not care a cuss about their girth.
If there is any interest in mine,
They're 38 – 33 – and 39.

Punch – January 1, 1957

(2)

I do not find that I am fond
Of this too celebrated blonde,
So photographed, so much discussed
Because of her enormous bust.
The bosom can be passing fair
That apes the apple or the pear:
I do not itch to lay my head
On melons or on loaves of bread.
For Rubens she'd have rung a gong,
But Rubens, I maintain, was wrong.
In love, in Nature, as in Art,
Proportion plays a noble part.
No feature of the female form
Should strikingly exceed the norm.
What famous beauty comes to mind
Who boasted an immense behind?
What poet sings of Clare or Kate
'She has a navel like a plate'?
No, this is *not* the kind of trunk
That I should pin above my bunk.
In dungeon deep I should not get
Much comfort from her silhouette.
I see her, with a dental smile,
Arriving on my desert isle.
I say 'Dear lady, I must own
That I am painfully alone.
Your face is pleasant: I can tell
That we shall manage pretty well
(Though if as useless as you look
I rather doubt if you can cook).
The trouble is, I can't acclaim
The feature which has won you fame.
And in this irritating clime
It would annoy me all the time.

I'm not indifferent to curves
But yours are getting on my nerves!
Frequent my island if you must
But hide the celebrated bust.
If that, you feel, would spoil your stay,
Dear lady, kindly swim away.'

'NO FINE ON FUN'

(1)

On April 30, 1953, at the Royal Academy Dinner, I had the great honour to reply for The Guests and propose the health of the President, Sir Gerald Kelly. Among other things, I said, I think without irrelevance, certainly without shame:

'The Prime Minister had an easy task. He had only to answer for Her Majesty's Ministers. I have to answer for the Opposition as well, and for all the contending eddies of Art and Politics that swirl about this peaceful table. The Prime Minister will know, as First Lord of the Treasury, that this great Exhibition is one of the rare "entertainments" which are exempt from Entertainments Tax. It ranks, in fact, with cricket in the Culture Handicap, and well above the Leicester Galleries. Well, we propose to go farther. We propose to abolish Entertainments Tax entirely.

'NO TAX ON THOUGHT! NO LEVY ON LAUGHTER! NO DUTY ON BEAUTY! WHO TOOK FIFTY MILLIONS OFF THE PEOPLE'S FUN?

'What a cry! What a just and noble cry! All this boasting about "Full Employment"! After 2,000 years of Christianity, and Socialism, and Science, is that the finest carrot we can set before the toiling asses – that all should be able to *work – all the time?* No, Sir, anyone can work – we all like work – and we are rightly taxed for this indulgence. But when we have done, when we go forth to enjoy the finest things that Man can make or do, the things that distinguish us from the savage and the sheep, whether it be fine writing or painting, fine music or singing, or fine riding on a fine horse, then it is barbarous to tax us as if we were enjoying some dangerous narcotic or intoxicant. No, Sir, "Full Enjoyment" is the cry. And that, Sir, is the policy of all the parties, all the arts, all the guests for whom I speak tonight... '

(2)

As I said in the House – as I said at the Royal Academy: 'What are we here for? Full Employment? No – that is but a means. The end is Full Enjoyment, the multifarious blessings of the leisure which is the fruit of good and regular labour. Imagine a world without books, newspapers, music, paintings, concerts and operas, plays – on stage or screen – the manifold delight that we draw from those little boxes in the corner of the room, yes, and all the queer games and gatherings, the feats, the fights, the running and the rowing and the riding, that make the nation a multitude of brothers, delighting in the skill, the swiftness, the fortitude of Man, in the power and beauty of horse and hound. These are the pleasures that distinguish us from the savage and the sheep. Without them, it is true, we should have companionship and friendship and love and marriage, good food and drink, and the joys that Nature provides – but so have the savage and the sheep. (Religion, too, no doubt – but then, where would religion be without the arts and graces that adorn it – the language, the music, the painted window and the sculptured stone?) Without these pleasures, Sir, our lives would be nothing, a daily tramp from the bed to the bench and back again.'

No Fine on Fun – 1957

In 1957 the Entertainments Tax on the living Theatre and Sport was abolished, and in 1960 on the Cinema.

THE WAY OUT

Save, save, they say, and put away
What you would like to spend today!
Don't drink – or smoke – or go abroad,
And all the parties will applaud.
But when the money's in your banks
Expect no more the nation's thanks.
Your earnings now have changed their name:
They're CAPITAL – a cause for shame
While any yield that they may bring
Is DIVIDEND – a filthy thing:
And, what is really quite a bore,
It's UNEARNED INCOME – which pays more.
Give some away to poorer men?
Oh, no – you're DODGING TAXES then.
In short, the patriots who save
Remain in error till the grave:
So die as quickly as you can
And pay DEATH DUTIES like a man.

May 15, 1957

PROTEST

(*From That Man in the Moon*)

You say she does it for the best,
But can your Science never rest?
The Atom, which was nice and small,
You've made the monarch of you all.
You draw explosives from the air,
And alcohol from anywhere.
There's nothing that you can't pervert

To din, destruction, death and dirt.
Since Man was made, he's loved the Moon –
The lovers' kiss, the poets' croon.
But you would change the only face
That pleases all the human race.

October 6, 1957

THE CHRISTMAS STARS

The Christmas stars are back again,
Orion has resumed his reign,
And Sirius, the brightest light,
Is at my window every night.
But foolish Man has got his eye
On rubbish rushing round the sky,
On bits of rockets, parts of cones,
And, I suppose, the puppy's bones.
Nor do they seem to know at all
If rockets fizzle out or fall.
At any moment, through the fog,
There may descend a bit of dog,
Or fragments bigger than a bus
May like a meteor make for *us*.
I may be out-of-date, and odd,
But I prefer the works of God.

December 8, 1957

BALLAD OF BALLISTICS

Beside a glowing gas-fire sat a sturdy artisan.
Said he 'Our sons are growing, Mum. Their future we should
plan.

There's Oxford – there's the ITV – the gates are open wide:
And then, of course, Technology'. The mother thus replied:
> *'Don't put our sons into Science, dear,*
> > *It's not a healthy life, if you ask me.*
> > > *You wouldn't like our Tom*
> > > *To be thinking out a bomb,*
> > *Or inventing things like this here AID.*
> *What with sex, and satellites, and gadding into Space,*
> *Shooting at the Moon and messing up its poor old face,*
> *You can call it Progress, but for me it's a disgrace.*
> > > *You don't want John and Janet*
> > > *Slipping off to some low planet –*
> > *Don't put our sons into Science!'*

'It's very true' the father said 'the things they do are odd,
And many of them seem to think that they're as good as God.
But there, it is a race for Space, they're conquering the sky:
We ought to do our little bit.' The matron answered 'Why?'

> *'Don't put our sons into Science, dear.*
> > *Leave it to the Russians and the Japs.*
> > > *You wouldn't like our boys*
> > > *To invent another noise,*
> > *Unless it was a skiffle group, perhaps.*
> *Making fire from water and explosives from the snow!*
> *Little dogs and bits of litter flying to and fro!*
> *People having babies and the father doesn't know!*
> > > *One ought to think of others:*
> > > *Hands off the Moon, and mothers!*
> > *Don't put our sons into Science!'*

February 9, 1958

WHAT'S MY WHINE?

And now, with terror treading on my tongue,
May I address the Less Contented Young?
I am not one of those who moan and mourn
'It was without our leave that we were born!'
And therefore claim the right to sit and wince
At almost everything that's happened since.
I do not love the literary line
Whose chief motif is, roughly, 'What's My Whine?'
No, no, with all the Bombs they bustle out,
This is a goodly time to be about.
Cheer up, young Tristram, and control your tongue,
For too much anger stupefies the young.
If worldly comforts are a worthy sign
Your generation's miles ahead of mine.
    We had no gramophone. Oh, how you'd laugh
If you could see the early 'phonograph'!
We had no 'wireless'. Almost I forget
Head-phones, cat's whiskers, and the 'crystal set'.
But I remember saying, I admit,
'I do not think that much will come of it'.
No moving pictures, boys. I saw them come,
And then – can you believe it? – they were dumb!
Yes, yes, I swear, they used to print below
'The hero here is saying so-and-so'.
At last the photographs began to speak
And London had hysterics for a week.
But television, Mervyn, even then
Was not conceived by ordinary men:
Nay, though today I regularly 'view',
I don't believe it's possible, do you?
No motor-buses. Horses dragged us round,
And smoke and sulphur filled the Underground.
No flight. I saw brave Blériot come over

(A great mistake, I think) from France to Dover.
It took five weeks to Sydney in a ship:
Today, they tell me, it's a weekend trip.
No radar nursed the steamer in a mess:
No radio could flash the SOS.
No penicillin eased the doctor's toil,
And if you had a boil – you had a boil.
Nor did the dentist send us off so soon
But gassed us with a frightening balloon:
And I don't think that angry little men
Got off with 'local anaesthetics' then.
All sorts of ills are easily dismissed
Which would have put us on the danger list.
The surgeons, with a rare, and recent, knack,
Take any organ out, and put it back:
And marvels move among us, old and young,
With but one kidney or a lonely lung.
Mothers receive such long and loving care
That angry babes are easier to bear.
   You turn a tap, you poor 'frustrated' kid,
And all the Elements do what you bid.
The siren and the sage of every land
Attend your dwelling place at your command.
All these delights you take for granted, rather –
And have the cheek to criticize your father.
When I was young, dear Cyril, one would meet
The beggar and the blind in every street:
Nor could the humblest of the island race
Proceed to Oxford, or the other place.
All these great wonders of the world you scorn
Have happened, little men, since I was born.
How dare you, then, you bunch of bitter weeds,
Affront your fathers and decry their deeds?
No British young, since British young were new,
Have had such boons and benefits as you.

The talk of war 'unsettles' you, I see:
I've served in two, my lads, and suffered three.
We did not whine and whimper at our doom:
We did not cry 'Frustration!' in the womb.
We saw, and shared, some grandeur in the grime.
Cheer up, my lads – you'll understand in time.

Punch – 1958

'DELOUSE THE TREASURY!'

It's an old question: and perhaps there's no answer. But from time to time you might turn it over in the bath. What is to be done about the Treasury? My answer, for many years, has been: 'Purge it. Purge it thoroughly, cruelly, mercilessly. Clean 'em out from top to bottom. Defumigate the place like the bowels of a ship. Let not a bug remain. For the bugs of the Treasury are old and tough, and if you leave one alive it will soon be a nest of mordant error and moral pestilence again.'

But I may be wrong.

I am not thinking now of major affairs. I happen to think – indeed, I know, for I warned them at the time – that the Treasury began the sad story of British inflation by the Budgets of 1947, 1948, etc., when they put new and heavy taxes on all the things that Britons wanted most, in the fond belief that Britons would at once stop buying them. It must be evident now to many thinking men, and even to a professional economist, that the Treasury are the key contributors to British inflation. Well, for example, who but an imbecile would proclaim a crusade against high prices and at the same time maintain a tremendous tax on every sort of oily fuel, which increases almost every price in sight? But such high matters I am content to postpone to another powerful article: and so, I dare say, is our powerful Editor.

What I am concerned with now is the ghastly moral tone, the inhuman malignance, the reptilian lack of principle, the gasteropodic indifference and sloth displayed by the Treasury in small affairs.

Take, for example, the levying of income-tax on the clergyman's Easter offering, about which, by the way, I wrote a rather beautiful hymn, concluding:

> O *Lord, from our unworthy hands*
> *Accept the tribute due,*
> *But kindly pass the appropriate sum*
> *To the Inland Revenue.*

Everybody would like to relieve the poor parson. The Treasury object that it would be 'discriminating', meaning to say that somebody else might cry 'Oy! What about *me?*' If all the big brains in that big building, which can tie the world in knots if they wish, are unable to think of an answer to that it is surprising. 'How many other gifts made in the name of God in a consecrated place are subject to income tax?' is one that occurs to me. It may be no good. But any boss except the Treasury would say 'This is a thing so petty and odious that we will cut it out – and argue afterwards'.

In 1843 our sagacious ancestors passed an Act of Parliament called the Scientific Societies Act. It provided for the exemption from rates of societies 'instituted for the purpose of science, literature or the fine arts exclusively'. For 110 years many modest but excellent societies have been enjoying the benefit of the Statute. Unfortunately, it did not say what it meant by the 'Fine Arts'. Painting, Sculpture, and Architecture qualify without doubt. Music has been admitted, fairly recently, by the courts. But there has been no decision about Drama, Opera, or Ballet. When a Ballet school applied for exemption the Inland Revenue, instructed by the Treasury, no doubt, 'submitted that ballet was not a Fine Art'. This may be right, but it is odd: for the Arts Council, financed by the Treasury, and charged under Royal Charter to foster 'the fine arts exclusively', supports not only Ballet but Opera and Drama. The point was never settled, for the school was defeated on another point concerning the conduct of the society's affairs. The decision in this, or another, case seems to have inflamed the passions of the Inland Revenue and they have been hunting societies right and left, not only new applicants, but innocent old-established bodies. The London Library has lost its exemption upon two technical grounds which had never been raised before. One of them, I believe, is that it is not sufficiently supported by 'voluntary contributions'. The members' subscriptions, it seems, do not count as 'voluntary contributions'. Can you beat it?

'But then', the Hounds of the Inland Revenue may reply, 'we have but one duty, to catch the tax or rate-payer whenever we can. If the benevolent intentions of our ancestors are being thwarted, that is just too bad. If the terms of the statute are out-of-date or obscure – hooray! we take advantage of it.'

Very well. But what of the Master of the Hounds, the Treasury, which in some ways ostentatiously, though punily, supports the Arts? You would think, would you not, that by this time they would have taken note of the Inland Revenue vendetta; introduced a Bill to amend and clarify the old Statute, defined and enumerated 'the Fine Arts exclusively', and generally cleared up the muddle? Well, you would be wrong. The London Library is preparing for a forlorn appeal to some tribunal or other;* no one can say for certain whether the Drama, Ballet, Opera, or even Literature are legally Fine Arts or not; the intentions of our excellent ancestors are being thwarted: but the Inland Revenue are squeezing a few bloody pennies out of some small and innocent lemons; and the Treasury sits still.

That brings us easily to the purchase tax on Musical Instruments, which is a superb example of Treasury parvanimity

---

* It lost.

(new word), imbecility, and meanness. The Treasury, through the Arts Council, subsidize Covent Garden, the British Temple of Music. But they levy purchase tax on every instrument in the orchestra – except one (the piano, Heaven knows why, is exempt). In 1956 the grant to Covent Garden was £270,000, but our clever Treasury gathered about £500,000 from musical instruments. In those days the tax was 60 per cent. In this year's Budget,* in response to the protests of years, it was graciously reduced to 30 per cent; so the yield presumably, will just about repay the grant to Covent Garden. The tax is halved. How generous! But observe what Sir Kingsley Wood said when he instituted the purchase tax in 1940: 'There will be a high rate of tax on the purchase of goods which are either *luxuries* or goods which in the hard circumstance of war we can either do without or of which we can at least postpone the replacement...like furs, articles made with real silks, china and porcelain articles, cut glassware, fancy goods, jewellery... That rate of tax will be at one-third or 33⅓ per cent on the wholesale value.' So, by the gracious concession of 1958, thirteen years after victory, the tax on flute, harp, violin and clarinet stands at the same 'high' rate considered necessary for undoubted 'luxuries' in time of war, when Hitler was at the front door. 30 per cent on a clarinet may be £40. Some instruments have to be bought abroad and pay customs duty as well.

Observe, too, that no other professional man, no craftsman or workman, pays purchase tax on the tools of his trade. There is no tax on the tractor or the electric drill: on the hammer or the saw, on the scalpel or the dental drill, upon the palette, paints or brushes: or even on the typewriter.

Accordingly, in Committee on the Finance Bill, some hon. Members very properly tried to get the Treasury to make a clean job of it and wipe out the mean and silly tax. They were

* 1958.

defeated, by 228 votes to 183. A wretched Minister was put up by the Treasury to say this:

'The basis of the case against the tax was that music making and every instrument was educational and that it was a tax on culture. While it was true it was not wholly true. There was no question that a musical instrument had *a recreational function* in just the same way as cameras and photographic materials. It was right that it should be taxed at the same rate.' (*The Times*).

This was Treasury reasoning at its best. Nobody seems to have said: 'But hammers and saws, palettes and paint and brushes have "a recreational function" too. You don't tax *them*.' Nobody seems to have said: 'Why then do you subsidize Covent Garden? Why then, is your Arts Council charged, with public money, to "foster" the Fine Arts, one of which is Music? Why treat the musician – professional or student – more harshly than the painter? Why, for that matter, tax the camera, which captures beauty and has a claim to art, as if it were a dangerous "luxury"? Is "recreation", in the Welfare State, an undesirable "function"? *Why don't you tax church bells?*' and many other things.

We must not blame the Members. There comes a point when it is useless to go on arguing with the Treasury. The only course is – PURGE 'EM!

Punch – 1958

THE IMMORTAL MEMORY OF BURNS

(From a Speech given at Dumfries Burns Club's 200th Anniversary Dinner)

It would be a wonder indeed, if, after 200 years of due, sincere, and unremitting commemoration there could be found a man who had anything new to say concerning the shining soul, the splendid singer, Robert Burns, who was born 200 years ago. It would be more surprising still if that man were a 'poor wee timorous' English beastie, of Irish extraction.

Yet I see no reason why an Englishman should not be invited to try. It is true that we do not know the poet so intimately and well as the sons of his own soil: yet he is a part, a familiar part, of the life of every Englishman, more so even than any poet of our own. Only the great Kipling, perhaps – another singer – is so often on the lips of the Common Man.

It is not only on New Year's Eve, on Ludgate Hill before St Paul's – nor by Scotsmen only – that 'Auld Lang Syne' is sung. Through all the year, wherever two or three Englishmen are gathered together who wish to express their love of life, their affection for their fellow men, their simple gratitude for simple happiness, how do they do it best? Not with the solemn speeches that begin the feast, but with the friendly Scottish song that sends them home to bed.

And this is not in England only. All round the world, in every ship that flies the British flag; all round the world, wherever the sons of Britain are dwelling or serving, are sweltering or shivering, they sing that song whenever they are in company and have good cheer.

It is safe, I think, to say that there is no moment of any day at which, somewhere under the circling moon, some company of men, in merry or melancholy mood, is not singing 'Auld Lang Syne'. How happy any of us would be if he thought that such a thing would be said about him 162 years after his death.

There is, they say, at the present time, a lump of metal going round the sun.* It cannot be seen, and, thank God, it cannot be heard, so the evidence is not strong. But I am willing to believe it, for it is the kind of crazy thing that Man, in these days, thinks

* Now there are two.

it good and clever to do. I heard the other day some solemn ass describe the despatch of this lump of metal to the regions of the sun – impiously described, at least in my view, as the 'creation of a new planet' – as 'the supreme intellectual achievement of Man'.

My goodness, how much grander is the claim that I have made that, long before these modern marvels of communication were conceived, your poet put a girdle round the earth with a single song – and that song by no means his best – owing nothing to electricity or science, his only instruments the hearts and tongues of ordinary men!

January 27, 1959

I TOLD YOU SO

CLAUSE FOUR (1)

(Written in May, 1959, six months before the General Election)

The Conservatives have won at the last two General Elections. If they win for the third time running it will be one of the most remarkable feats in our history. Something will be seriously wrong with the famous 'pendulum'. The Conservatives' present strength is something of a wonder for those of us who were in the House of Commons in 1945 and saw the Socialists surge in with an enormous majority. They thought then – and many others feared the same – that, like the Liberals before them, the Conservatives were done for. They would never be 'in' again. Labour, by degrees, would build the complete and perfect socialist State. Yet the Conservatives have been 'in' for the last eight years, and may be returned for another five. The fact is that in their busy spell of office between 1945 and 1950 Labour filled too many of their pledges, and now have little left to offer. They nationalized the Bank of England, the Mines, the

Railways, Air Transport, Road Transport, Electricity and Gas. They instituted the National Health Service and put the finishing touches to what we call the Welfare State – which they did not begin. They also, rightly or wrongly, got rid of India and other responsibilities. The Conservatives, always adaptable, have accepted much of this. They took Steel and Road Transport away from the State, but there is not the slightest suggestion anywhere of giving back the Mines, the Railways, the Bank of England, Air Transport, Electricity and Power to private enterprise. They have made small economies in the Health Service, but would not think of scrapping it. They are, in fact, with every appearance of content, administering a semi-Socialist State. By degrees they have made enormous reductions of taxation – everything which the Socialists propose would increase it. They have done well with the pound, with prices, and, on the whole, employment, yet they have removed a mass of unpopular 'controls'. Miraculously, so soon after Suez, they command, I think, more confidence than the other fellows in Foreign Affairs; and for that miracle Mr Macmillan could claim the chief credit. Besides, they can, in relation to the United States, borrow, but amend, that old Socialist boast and say 'Right Speaks To Right'.

The Socialists' logical answer should be to go on with Socialism, which means – or did mean – the Nationalization of the Means of Production, Distribution and Exchange. But Nationalization, they know very well, is a dead dog; it is almost a dirty word. Steel, an efficient, prosperous, contented industry, already subject to some control, is next on the list; but not one in a thousand sees any particular reason why steel should be nationalized. The Socialists themselves are in a muddle – and may be in something worse – about their central doctrine. Mr Gaitskell himself, it is believed, would like the dirty word to be scrapped from the party vocabulary. He has already put about some gentle alternatives like 'public accountability'. He and others of the moderate wing are talking of the State acquiring shares in five or six hundred great firms and industries – whether for the State to assert control or to make money is not quite clear. But such watery stuff is no use to the fiery Leftist, the thorough intellectual. It would be simply supporting the capitalist system. If the State did not acquire control, it would be merely one of those 'functionless shareholders' who are so much abused. If it is to have control, why not acquire it outright and directly?

Mr Aneurin Bevan said last spring: 'Some people are going cold on Socialism… The only answer to modern problems is the expansion of public ownership. If the Labour Party turned its back on public ownership, I would turn my back on the Labour Party.' Even he, however, does not use the dirty word. Mr Gaitskell does. He said last June: 'It is a mistake to suppose that nationalization is identical with Socialism. For us, Socialism is a society in which a number of ultimate ideals are realized such as Social Equality; Full Employment and Industrial Expansion through Economic Planning; Co-operation and Fellowship between the different sections of the community; the complete absence of discrimination on grounds of race, colour or creed, together with the maintenance of political freedom and democracy. A considerable degree of public ownership is one of the means needed to achieve these aims. Nationalization, as usually understood, is one form of public ownership…'

So there we are.

It is as if half the Roman Catholics, to win general popularity, wanted to go slow about the Pope. With such a division, dilemma, such a cancer in its body, I do not see how the Labour party can prevail. Anything can happen before the day; but at the moment I should predict a victory for the Conservatives.

American 'Life' – October 12, 1959

CLAUSE FOUR (2)

'By reason, not ruction,
  We soar to the skies:
The Means of Production
  We nationalize,
While rapture surprising
  We bring within range
By nationalizing
  The Means of Exchange.'

This gay affirmation
  No longer is heard,
For Nationalization
  Is not a nice word.
'Instead' say the singers
  'We'll buy a few shares
And thus have our fingers
  In private affairs.'

O sorrow and schism!
  'You can't take a hand
In Capitalism,
  For that we have banned'.
How unhappy are they
  On the Westminster scene
Who don't mean what they say,
  Or don't say what they mean!

June 7, 1959

MISLEADING CASES

Regina v. Feathers, Furblow, and Philanthropic Pools Ltd

Mr Justice Pheasant began his summing-up to the jury in this lengthy trial today, as follows: 'Members of the Jury. Now and then, from the waste of dreary disputes and offences which occupy Her Majesty's Assizes, there emerges a criminal cause of electric attraction and importance. Such is the case before us now, not only for the novel points of law which it uncovers, but for its social background. Here, for once, it appears, the greater part of the population are interested in the matter of the trial and will rejoice at, or resent, our decision.

'On the material Monday, as you have heard, the accused man Feathers, a plumber, was informed by the accused company Philanthropic Pools, that he, and he alone, had won, with 23 points, a "first dividend" in the football results competition of the preceding Sunday – a sum of £261,214. The man Furblow, a newsvendor, was also told by a kindly emissary that he had won the second dividend, £101,403. These rewards it appears, were exceptional: the drawn matches had been few, and for the most part, unexpected. A Mr Albert Haddock, who had 22 points, was awarded, on a third dividend, the paltry prize of £863.

'Before they had received any money from the company, the defendants Feathers and Furblow were interviewed by the newspapers. Both, as is customary, we understand, began by announcing that money meant nothing to them, that their winnings would make no difference to their simple way of life, and, after a brief visit to the metropolis with their wives, they would return to their usual employment. They then disclosed the secret of their success. Mr Feathers said that he had written on slips of paper the names of all teams beginning with A, B, C, and L, placed them in a lucky hat and desired his niece, aged 11, to extract ten of them. Mr Furblow said that he had asked a stranger in a tavern to choose any twelve numbers between 1 and 54. He added proudly that he had been using this method for the last seven years. Before that his custom was to place the coupon upside-down before him, close his eyes, and make hopeful marks with a pencil.

'One who read this information with especial interest was Mr Haddock. This competitor, as he testified later, had attained his 22 points by a careful study of the "form". He had noted the relative positions of opposing teams in the League Tables, the results of their recent matches, and the corresponding matches in previous years: he had consulted the expert advisers of eight newspapers on the previous Sunday, three evening papers on Tuesday, and a sporting paper on Wednesday and Thursday. He now telegraphed to the Claims Department of Philanthropic Pools:

UNDERSTOOD YOU WERE CONDUCTING COMPETITION IN FORECASTING REPEAT FORECASTING STOP PUBLISHED METHODS OF MESSRS. FEATHERS AND FURBLOW CLEARLY SHOW THEY WERE EMPLOYING METHODS OF AN UNLAWFUL LOTTERY STOP CLAIM THEY SHOULD BE DISQUALIFIED AND FIRST DIVIDEND AWARDED TO ME WHO USED ONLY SKILL AND JUDGMENT ACCORDING TO LAW ALBERT HADDOCK X3 /13.

'To the general astonishment, and the natural annoyance of Feathers and Furblow, the defendant company acceded to this request, and their cheque for £261,214 was duly presented to Mr Haddock by Miss Angel August, an actress. The company, as they have explained to the Court, had long been worried by the number of winning entrants who had publicly attributed their success to practices similar to those of Feathers and Furblow. Some have employed a pin, some, less industrious, an old-fashioned toasting-fork. Some have scattered shot, or brown sugar, on their coupons, and used it as a guide. Others have used the Letter System. These take some message such as God Save The Queen Long May She Reign, and select eight matches in which the first letters of the Home Teams spell out that message. One of the numerous Royal Commissions on Betting and Gaming referred to two winners of very large prizes whose "method of selecting the matches to be included in their forecast was to choose those matches which corresponded with the dates of the birthdays of members of the family". None of these methods, said the company, even when they took the form of a loyal greeting to the Throne, could be dignified with the name of "forecast", a word which is frequent in their Rules. No competitor before Mr Haddock had objected: but when he did, they thought it right to use their discretionary powers of disqualification.

'Feathers and Furblow were unable to sue the company, because of a passage in the Rules providing that nothing in any pool transaction shall be "legally enforceable or the subject of litigation". They then, in an understandable fit of pique, laid an information against the company for conducting an unlawful lottery. The police took over the prosecution and put them in the dock as well for "playing, throwing or drawing" at a lottery. And here we are.

'I must not attempt to influence you in any way: but I have no doubt myself that you will find them guilty. A "forecast" is a mental process. It is described in the Oxford English Dictionary thus "To estimate, conjecture or imagine beforehand (the course of events or future condition of things)". Mr Feathers neither estimated, conjected nor imagined: he used no skill or judgment. He simply drew, with the assistance of his niece, some scraps of paper from a hat. Mr Furblow drew his numbers similarly from a stranger. Now, as one of the Royal Commissions remarked, "The characteristic feature of a lottery is that it is a distribution of prizes by lot or chance". Who can doubt that as far as these two men were concerned that was the character of this transaction, that but for the intervention of Mr Haddock, they would have been large winners in a lottery?

'But in your lively minds, Members of the Jury, I see this question stirring: Does it follow, if these two men are convicted, that you must find the defendant company guilty? I must instruct you to the contrary. The company, you may well conclude, are conducting a *bona fide* competition for persons interested in forecasting the results of football matches. It was, and is, their intention and desire that the prizes shall be won by serious-minded competitors using such skill, judgment and technical information as they may possess or can acquire. This they have sufficiently shown, you may think, by their disqualification of Feathers and Furblow, which was a highly unpopular act. But then, you may inquire, if they are not conducting an unlawful lottery, how can Feathers and Furblow be condemned for taking part in one? That is the kind of question over which the law of our land rides easily and proudly. There are many cases where a guilty act or element can be imported into an innocent enterprise without involving the enterprise itself. A man may write obscene answers to a crossword puzzle or draw lewd pictures in the margin, so as to expose himself to a prosecution; but the newspaper will not be blamed. A man by some trick might continue to consume intoxicating liquor on licensed premises after permitted hours: but the publican, if he had done his best, would not be held responsible. A trespasser may light a dangerous fire, create a public nuisance or start a disorderly house: but the owner of the property will not be charged. In certain matrimonial causes it has been established that A committed adultery with B, but not B with A, though that, I fear, is not so close a parallel. Here again these men have imported evil into an innocent activity. They, and it is feared, a good many others, have done their best to convert a respectable competition into a criminal gamble. If they have to pay any penalty it need not, obviously, be applied to their victims too.

'Do not by the way, pay much attention to the ingenious argument advanced for the defence by Sir Adrian Floss. Sir Adrian observed that in the Treble Chance Pool, for reasons hidden from the Court, the task is to forecast Eight Draws in a single line; that as a rule there are 54 matches in the list; that there are no less than 1,040,465,790 ways in which 8 matches can be selected from 54. Therefore, he said, the use of skill and judgment can not, in fact, greatly affect the result. Indeed, they may be a positive disadvantage: for he who follows "form" will miss the unforeseeable, exceptional results, the "outsiders", as it were, which produce the highest "dividends". Those, he said, can only be caught by a happy chance: so that Feathers and Furblow, though they used no skill, at least showed some judgment. Mr Haddock, on the other hand, said that he always did better when he studied "form" and so on than on the rare occasions when, by way of experiment, he "used a pin". Mr Haddock, I thought, gave his evidence with singular clarity, credibility and charm. All must now be as clear to you as the many miles of mud that lie under the Thames between Westminster and the Nore. Pray retire.'

The jury retired.

Punch – December 1959

IS IT CRICKET?

To the Editor of *The Times*

Sir, – 'Sam Cook', I read, 'carefully rubbed the bail into a dusty ground to remove the shine. Then with his first two deliveries he proceeded to remove Dave Parsons and Dave Gibson.' But is this 'cricket'?

Then there is the inelegant and laughable rubbing of the ball on shirts and trousers by bowlers and fielders to maintain the 'shine'.

Sir, the ball, like the wicket, is for the use of both sides. The wicket may not be improved or tampered with by either side for its own advantage. Should the ball? Evidently not: for 'it is illegal for the bowler to lift the seam of the ball in order to obtain a better hold', and the use of resin by bowlers is also declared 'unfair'.

If the fielding side may alter the natural state of the ball, why should not the batsman capture it between the overs and rub some of the shine off on the soles of his boots? If the college of umpires have no mind in this matter, is there not a case for an amendment of the laws? But I feel rather a killjoy; for the spectacle of a fast bowler rubbing his way into the television screen is one of the funniest things in modern entertainment.

I am, Sir, yours respectfully,

A P HERBERT
August 29, 1959

Sir, – In his letter in your issue of August 29 Sir Alan Herbert appears to regard the polishing of a new ball on shirt or trousers and the deliberate removal of its shine as equally open to criticism. But should not a distinction be drawn between attempts to maintain the original condition of the ball and an expedient that induces premature old age?

Yours faithfully,

A W DOUGLAS
September 1, 1959

Sir, – Mr A W Douglas asks if a distinction should not be drawn between trouser-rubbing, intended 'to maintain the original condition of the ball', and rubbing in the dust that 'induces premature old age'.

No, Sir, or not much: for each is an interference with the course of nature not provided for by the laws of cricket. In general the good cricketer must accept the natural hazards which affect the wicket or 'the implements used'. 'Under no circumstances shall a pitch be watered during a match': nor shall it be mown. The discontented batsmen may not send for a roller, or (it is presumed) pour their lemonades on the pitch. The bowler may not improve the ball with wax or resin, or 'lift the seam'.

But some exceptions are clearly made. After a certain period of wear and tear a new ball may be demanded. 'The batsman may beat the pitch with his bat' (I often wonder why). 'Players may secure their footholds by the use of sawdust'; and 'the bowler may dry the ball when wet on a towel or sawdust.' Nowhere do the laws say that he may rub the ball in the dust when dry to remove the shine, or on his abdomen or bosom to preserve or increase the shine.

The first, no doubt, is morally the worse (it is like deliberately damaging the wicket): but the second is unseemly and ridiculous, and if continued may lead to new excesses. If a shirt, why not a brush – or a velvet pad sewn into the trousers? The batsman, too, may wish to keep the shine on the ball, whether to assist in its passage to the boundary or to outwit the bowler who has rubbed it in the dust. If the umpires and captains have nothing to say, I hope that some aggrieved batsman will bring this question to a head, pick up a dead ball, produce his little polishing set – and see what happens.

Meanwhile, I suggest a simple amendment to law 46: 'The use of resin, wax, &c., by the bowler, *and any attempt by any player to alter the natural condition of the ball when dry, are forbidden*: but a bowler may dry the ball when wet, &c.'

I am, Sir, yours respectfully,

A P HERBERT
September 4, 1959

193

'IS THAT THE FACE…?'

What is the matter with the comic draftsmen?
  They do not seem to like the human race.
They may be funny; they may be good craftsmen:
  But can't they draw an ordinary face?
Each woman now resembles a hyena,
  And all their men are walruses – or worms.
There is no beauty in the whole arena:
  Even the children look a bit like germs.
Our ancestors, who also drew for money,
  Did not see Man so ugly, mad, and mean:
Perhaps they weren't so very, very funny:
  But they were mirrors of the human scene.
They did not only labour for derision:
  Old folk were gracious, and the young were fine.
At all events, we know with some precision
  What men were like in 1869.
Where will they look, in, say, 2000 AD
  To ascertain what kind of folk we were?
Where will they look to find a pretty lady,
  A nice old fellow, or a happy pair?
If this is Man, the Heir of all the Ages,
  Roll on, the Atom-Bomb! What is he worth?
It's only in the advertising pages
  You see that beauty still survives on earth.
Those lovely ladies in elastic undies
  Are one objection to an Atom Bout.
Here is a meaning for a world of Mondays:
  Here is some cause to keep the Russians out.
And here's a mystery, a real surpriser,
  That Man still plays a proud, important part,
Seen by the low commercial advertiser:
  But he's a monkey in the eyes of ART!

Full Enjoyment – June 11, 1950

194

'LET ME GO DOWN THE MINE, DADDY'

A Sad Ballad Of The Future

Beside an old-world slagheap a man and boy reclined;
All round, the silent winders, where there was none to wind.
The father, too, was silent, but soon the stripling sighed,
'Let me go down the mine, Daddy'. His parent thus replied:

> *'They've taken our beautiful coal-mines away,*
> *They won't let us go down the pit.*
> *They're replacing our toil*
> *With new-fangled oil –*
> *And then there's these atoms they split.*
> *Your dad's on the dole,*
> *'Cos they don't need no coal:*
> *They can get what they want from a stone –*
> *Hot water and power*
> *At a penny an hour!*
> *Why can't they leave things alone?'*

'It seems a shame' responded the disappointed heir,
'I've heard from you and grand-dad what fun you had down
    there,
'Far from the roar of traffic, out of the wind and wet.
'Let me go down the mine, Daddy'. Said his father, 'You forget:

> *They've taken our beautiful coal-mines away.*
> *Oh, yes, it was cosy below.*
> *And then, we was top*
> *Of the whole blooming shop,*
> *And they did what we told 'em, you know.*
> *But now all the jobs*
> *Is uranium and knobs,*
> *And the ships get along on their own.*

The oil and the atom
Have ruined us – drat 'em!
Why can't they leave us alone?'

1950

FROM THE RUSSIAN

CONFESSIONAL

'Judges of the People's Court,
  Do not forgive me.
I confess
  My grievous aberrations,
I kneel, I grovel,
  I crawl about
On all fours.
  In my commodious cell
For two years
  I have been well-treated.
I have had the best
  Of everything.
Oysters
  (When in season)
Were brought to me daily
  From the Bay of Lenin.
Heartening extracts
  From the speeches
Of Joseph Stalin,
  The Wise, the Good,
Who discovered
  The Laws of Gravity,
Were played to me
  On the gramophone.

No man ill-used me.
    No drug was administered.
My conscience,
    The eyes of my comrades,
The teachings of Stalin,
    Have illuminated
The dark abysses
    Of my disgusting soul.
Is it not enough?
    I have been guilty
Of criminal self-will
    And bourgeois opinionism.
I told Comrade Ratovsky
    That I was surprised to hear
That Joseph Vissarionovich Stalin
    Had split the first atom
With his own hands,
    Well knowing
This was a Party decision.
    I questioned the assertion
Of Comrade Lavinski
    That Soviet submarines
Are able to fly.
    It is perfectly true
That on March 17, 1946,
    I permitted myself
In a Soviet tram
    To speak to the American Consul,
Well knowing of his conspiracy
    With Bartok, Batsky, Eisenbaum,
And other Imperialist
    Wolves of the West,
To disequilibrize
    The integrationary purpose
Of the Soviet man

In Oblovovosk.
Further proofs
   Of my diversionary trends
And beastly ratiocinationalism
   Are to be found
In my letter
   To the woman Smith
Of England,
   Which I wrote
In Esperanto,
   As I pretended,
For practice in that language,
   But, in truth,
With the childish hope
   Of hiding from justice
My animal opinions
   And sub-human infidelity.
Now, Judges of the People,
   I have but one complaint
(Though even this
   It is not for me to utter),
That my own counsel,
   Comrade Obolsky,
Has presented
   My obscene divagations
In a light less harsh
   Than they deserve.
I have a right
   To the extreme penalty.
I should demand
   A death of boiling oil,
But that, purged and refreshed
   By these proceedings,
I still hope humbly
   To serve more faithfully

LOOK BACK AND LAUGH

The causes I have undermined
    With intellectual tunnelling
And dynamitical distrust.
    So I suggest
That I be cut in pieces
    And sewn together again,
That then, a new man,
    I may continue the glorious struggle
For the Soviet Union,
    For Peace and Brotherhood.'

Full Enjoyment – August 2, 1950

FROM THE CHINESE

THE AMBASSADOR

'In the far, old-fashioned times',
    Said the scribe Ching Fo,
'Every great ruler
    Sent to the court
Of every other ruler
    An ambassador,
Chosen for his discretion,
    His intelligence,
        His charm of manner
And his ability to speak
        The language of the country
The ambassadors dwelt
    In costly state
And were richly rewarded.
    But through their labours
Each ruler
    Was acquainted

With the minds
   Of other rulers,
And could communicate
   A tender greeting
   Or sharp complaint
      Quietly,
Without telling the world,
   Angering a foreign people.
      Or alarming the peasants
   Tending their flocks.
"But secrecy"
   Said the Wise Men,
"Is harmful and wicked.
   How can we trust
The whispering rulers,
   Keeping the peace
      Behind our backs
With ambassadors
   We did not choose?"
So, in these brighter times',
   Said the scribe Ching Fo,
      'The Wise Men
   Of the Four Kings
Gather together
   In the market-place
And publicly
   Abuse each other.
None of the Wise Men
   Is acquainted
With the language
   Of any other,
But hired scholars
   Who know all the tongues
Cleverly divine
   The meaning

Of the principal insults
    And distribute it
(Or something like it)
    To all who can hear.
        But, naturally,
Before the Wise Men meet
    It must be decided
Upon what subjects
    The Wise Men
Are to abuse each other.
    Accordingly,
        With this intent,
Four Lesser Wise Men
    Assemble
In the market-place
    And publicly
Abuse each other
    In many tongues.
Doubt prevails,
    Rancour increases
For a moon or two,
    The peasants,
Hewing their wood,
    Tremble and chatter;
        And it is thought
By the sage Lo Wang
    That Four Inferior Wise Men
Should first assemble
    To decide
Upon what matters
    The Lesser Wise Men
Should abuse each other.
    But all this, evidently,
Is a better way
    To Understanding

And Harmonious Dealing
   Than secret whispers
In the rulers' courts.
Meanwhile the ambassadors
   Still dwell
In foreign cities,
   In costly state,
And are richly rewarded.
   It is to be disputed',
Said the scribe Ching Fo,
   'Just what
An ambassador is for.'

Full Enjoyment – March 21, 1951

THE MISSING SHOW

There is one little thing that I miss
   In all these august Exhibitions:
The surprising lacuna is this –
   A Pavilion of Royal Commissions.

What style, we wonder, should the building be?
   How deep in Britain's story does it go,
The trick of getting information free
   For Governments who really ought to know?
What statesman first said 'What
   Are we to do
(Yes, we should know these things, but we do not)
   About the taverns – or the price of glue?
     Is billiards fit to play
     Upon the seventh day,
   And should a fellow have one wife, or two?
     The people fret,
     They want to bet:

I don't see that it matters much – but still.
    The Bishops mass,
    And some young ass
Is bringing in a Private Member's Bill.
Whatever we decide, we're in the soup:
The Bishops rage, or our supporters droop.
    I tell you what. We'll ask the King
  To summon leading men from every shire:
    They need not know a thing
  About the subject, but they can inquire.
    Fresh minds, and true,
    They'll tell us what to do.
We shall not pay them. But they'll be delighted,
And later one or two, perhaps, be knighted.
    They'll summon witnesses by scores;
    All the Societies, and all the bores,
        Instead of writing to *The Times*
            Or putting questions in the House,
        As loud and regular as chimes,
            Will be as mute as mouse.
Meanwhile, of course – and this is fun –
It's clear that nothing can be done.
The Private Member will withdraw his Bill
And all the fretting populace be still.
            Two years, maybe,
            Or even three,
And they'll produce – or rather they'll abort –
A huge, verbose, but excellent Report,
            Long as a train,
Appendices and diagrams and maps:
And then the Bishops and the betting chaps
            Will start again.
        With any luck, we'll see
        A strong Minority,
        Which will excuse

Our timid views:
For, if they can't agree,
Well, why should we?
And, anyhow, some other set of men
Will be the King's proud Ministers by then.'
Whate'er the statesman's name,
Let it be shown –
Letters of flame,
Praises in stone.
For he devised the perfect English way
Of putting off what we should do today
(Not till tomorrow, dears,
But, say, for twenty years).
Nor do I think of Royal C's alone.
There is that other splendid English thing
The men who work for nothing for the King,
All the Committees,
Tribunals, Boards,
That clutter the cities
Without rewards,
Mayors and Aldermen,
Councillors, Chairmen,
JPs, Trustees –
And, of course, the Lords!
Without all these our wheels would not go round:
The country'd stop like a clock that's not been wound.
These do, or lubricate,
The business of the *State*,
And these, though they are numbered by the million,
Should have a corner in the great Pavilion:
Aye, these, we have no doubt,
Have founded half our fame,
The men who work for nowt,
And die without a name.

But in the centre of the great White Hall
Shall stand the finest specimen of all,
    Charged to record, explore,
        Enumerate,
        Locate,
    The work of those before.
Yes, yes, they say that lost Commissions still,
Somewhere in London, drive a trembling quill,
Not yet unanimous in just what sense
To understand their Terms of Reference,
Or fighting someone of the stubborn sort
Who must have his Minority Report.
Many a worn Commissioner has gone,
But they co-opt another and live on,
Although by whom appointed, and for what,
The oldest Civil Servant has forgot:
    They must be found
    And fed, and crowned.
And someone must assess
How much accrued to human happiness.
    How much was lost,
    And at what cost,
By all these Inquisitions.
        In short, A Report
On Royal Commissions
    By a Royal Commission.

Punch – August 1, 1951

FROM THE CHINESE

CONSOLATION

'I observe sadly,'
    Said the scribe Ching Fo,
'That feeble persons
    Of narrow understanding
Complain of the chance
    That they were begotten
In the present century
    And not in some other.
"We are," they say,
    "Exceptionally deserving.
What have we done
    To merit existence
In the present time
    Of trouble and tumult,
Of rapacious Rulers
    And barbarous taxes?
Nothing is certain,
    We toil without hope,
And no gold pieces
    Are buried in the garden.
We are exhausted by wars
    For which we were unready,
Or by preparation
    For wars which do not come.
The fathers, the mothers,
    Gaze upon the first-born
Doubtfully, wondering
    If they have done well."
All this complaining,
    Said the scribe Ching Fo,
'Is unworthy, vain,

And can be swiftly answered.
It has been calculated
   By men learned in numbers
That in this region
   Of the earth's surface
(None of which is deserving
   Of continual contentment)
The periods of trouble,
   Of tumult and tribulation,
Endure, as a rule,
   For eighty years,
Then, for ten years,
   There is a time of tranquillity.
The present season
   Of tumult and trouble
Has endured, say the Wise Men,
   For fifty years only,
And now there are only
   Thirty years to come.'

Punch – April 2, 1952

FROM THE CHINESE

A WOMAN'S WORK

'I am a tender man,'
   Said the scribe Ching Fo.
'I weep for the women
   When the women weep,
But I do not always
   Understand why they are weeping.
There is loud complaint
   About the labours of the home.

The new word drudgery
  Is heard instead of duty.
The toil is endless,
  Say the sweet sad women.
Always the preparation
  Of rice for the men,
Always the dishes
  Made dirty by the men,
Always the cleaning and mending
  Of raiment for the men,
Always the wood and water
  For the men.
Yes,' said the scribe Ching Fo.
  'For the men alone.
For women, it is well known,
  Left to themselves,
Need no food, water, or fuel,
  Cooking, cleansing, or clothing.
And if by a fortunate pest
  All men were extinguished
The women could recline
  For ever at their ease,
Sucking, now and then,
  A blade of grass
And nibbling a nut
  On the seventh day.
Yet it is difficult
  To understand the weeping
When men with steady mouths
  Endure each day.
Consider the servant
  At the place of the money-changer,
All day, every day,
  Adding the figures,
Counting the gains,

Taking away the debts.
What has he to show
    At the set of sun?
"My Lord," says the woman,
    "What have you done this day?"
"I have added figures," he says,
    "I have taken figures away.
It was a day like the day before.
    And the day that is coming."
But the woman, more blessed,
    Has something to show.
The dishes that were dirty
    Are white and gleaming.
In the pots for cooking
    The man can perceive his face,
Rice could fittingly
    Be served on the floor,
The children, well-washed,
    Recite their verses,
Or show new skill
    At the musical instrument.
All things are better
    Since the dawn of day;
At the money-changer's
    All are the same.
Each day is different
    In the life of woman:
One day the boy-child
    Falls from a tree,
One day the girl-child
    Is bitten by a scorpion,
One day the well is dry,
    But on the next
The cruel rain
    Pours through the roof.
One day an evil spirit

Enters the kitchen,
The fire will not burn,
    And the best dish is broken.
The next day the man-child
    Lies in a fever
And a mad dog
    Mutilates the goat.
Monotony?' said the scribe,
    'The life of woman
Is as monotonous
    As the life of a dog
Tied in a sack
    With an ape and a serpent.
I do not understand
    The weeping and complaining.'

Punch – July 9, 1952

MATRONS AND MOLLS

(*A humble offering to the next American Musical*)

It's a wonderful thing what a dame can do to a guy,
But most I mean the Amurrican Woman – and why?

   She runs her home, and she rules her man, and she governs the
      goddam town,
   We put her on a Pedestal, sir, we give her a golden crown,
   And my, how a guy will fry if he pulls her down!
      For every Amurrican man
      Is a lifelong fan and patron
      Of that pillar of life,
      The Amurrican Wife,
      The Amurrican Maid or Matron.
   But when we git by ourselves a bit
   Where a man can speak without being hit,

Why, ain't it queer to hear such unsuitable names
Like skirts and dolls and janes and molls and broads and floozies
    and dames!

        Don't get me wrahng –
        That don't last lahng,
    It's only a nervous *reflex*,
        Though you might guess
        From the plays and the Press
    That we knew nothing but sex.
        You'd think we wuz nerts
        On dolls and skirts
        And – this is what hurts –
            On floozies,
        And a guy's one aim
        Wuz an undraped dame,
        And one with a name
            For boozes.
    But they're all up there on the Pedestal, sir,
        We boys are just Big Brothers:
    We don't mean dirt when we speak of 'skirt'
        But the League of Amurrican Mothers.

The Queen of Sheba'd a full significant life,
But she wuz a small-town mouse to a Washington wife
    Who's President Ike and the Kremlin boss, Queen Liz and the
        Pope of Rome:
    Her man looks up with a crick in the neck like he looks at a class
        church dome,
    And there ain't no Statue of Liberty in the home.
        For every Amurrican guy
        Has a kind of a shy Mom-worship,
        And if he could choose
        For a two-year cruise
        He'd fight for a berth on her ship.

211

But when he's safe in the smoke-room bar
And the Moms cain't hear what he says that far,
Why, what a queer thing, he'll sing unsuitable verse
About skirts and dolls and janes and molls and frails and floozies
and worse!

Of course, he don't refer to his Mom by such low names,
But who would have guessed he reverenced ALL Amurrican
dames?

Punch – September 8, 1954

THE SCHOOL FOR SAINTS

(From a speech delivered to the Surrey Cricket Club at a Dinner to celebrate, I think, their fourth successive County Championship.)

'I am very proud to be asked to salute the men of Surrey. Nor will I say, as most speakers do, that I cannot imagine why you have chosen me. None could be more suitable. I am a Surrey man, despite my Irish ancestry. I was born at Ashtead, not far from Epsom racecourse. I have made 13 at the Oval – which is more than many of you have – for the Commons against the Lords. I remember to this day the dashing stroke that ended that innings, a drive through the covers that was caught by third man. I once made 53, top score, in a literary match, and to my great surprise hit a 6 over the screen. I was first bowler for my private school, and time and again I used to get my 7 wickets. I bowled very slowly and cunningly in the style afterwards adopted by Laker and Lock. But in my young days things were very different. We did not have all this ritual nonsense about the New Ball. We got along with the old ball till someone hit it over the railway. I once asked the great Ray Lindwall if he was as excited as the radio commentators were when he got a new ball. He said no, he did not really think it made much difference: and the nuisance was that everybody expected him to get a wicket. Nor did we bowlers walk about the field rubbing the ball on our trousers to give it a shine, or rubbing it in the dust to take the shine away. We left the ball as God and the manufacturer made it – and that, I must remind you, is the rule about the wicket.

'I am all for cricket as long as it is not represented to be a superior branch of religion. I cannot accept that it is the nurse of noble character, and the school for saints. It is a tough and terrible, rough, unscrupulous, and ruthless game. No wonder our American friends do not like it. You know how much armour they think it necessary to wear in their special form of football, and even in their rather primitive form of our old beach game – rounders. I wonder what armour they would think it necessary to wear if they emulated the heroes of Britain, fielding naked at silly slip, at damn silly mid-wicket, or lunatic short leg?

'Though, of course, there is another side to that picture. "A bumping pitch and a blinding light" wrote Henry Newbolt "ten to make and the last man in!" In comes some trembling little bowler, paralysed with fear, who, according to the radio commentators, has never held a bat before. (I always wonder, by the way, "Why, in winter time, don't they teach the little bowlers to bat? It is very easily picked up".) But what happens? Do these healthy Christian characters, steeped in the noble traditions of cricket, stand off and let the little fellow collect himself, and have a fair start? Not a bit of it. They crowd round him, the great hulking brutes, crouching like lions, creeping like panthers, breathing down his ears, making rude whistling noises when the ball goes by, and in other words, practising plain intimidation, physical, moral and mental. Is that cricket? Yes, it is.

'The day draws on and the sun sinks low. The Captain of the batting side declares his long innings closed. Is this to give the other side a little fun and rest? No. He knows that at this time of the day the batsman at one end will be looking into the setting sun, and at the other end into the cavernous darkness of the pavilion. Is that cricket? Yes.

'Another scene comes to my mind. I was away in Cornwall listening to a Test Match on the radio – this very year. In the last over of the day one of our fast bowlers – not a Surrey man – was on: and the Captain of the visiting side was in. The new ball was unveiled, consecrated, and brought into action, Jim Swanton almost swooning with excitement. Suddenly, before the very last ball, he said "Hallo – looks like a change of field – May's having a word with X – X is speaking to May. Y has moved into the slips, and W has gone to extra third man. By Jove, there are now 6 slips, 3 third mans, and 2 men in the gully. What do you make of it, Arthur?" "Well, Jim, it looks to me as if he is going to bowl a ball on the offside – what we used to call the off trap". "Arthur, I believe you are right. That is the plan. But I never saw such an elaborate change of field on the last ball of the last over of a Test Match before. I should say it is a record, what do you think, George?" "Yes, Mr Swanton, I think it must be. But there was a similar case in a match against the West Indies in 1946."

'"Well there goes our fast bowler, off on his long march into St John's Wood, black hair, erect, determined, one, two, three, four… And while he is on his lengthy way let us take a look at the scene. It is a beautiful evening; the shadows are lengthening on the grass, which shows that the sun is lower – what do you think, Arthur?"

"That is right, Jim. I suppose there must be thirty or forty thousand people still here, what do you think, Arthur?" "Forty thousand I think is about right, Jim." "Well now X has turned and is ready to bowl. This is the last ball of the last over, it will be very interesting to see if anything comes of this off theory. He turns, he begins to run, one, two, three, four, five, six – he *bowls*! My goodness, he bowls straight at the Captain, and hits him on the elbow. I *say*!"

'And the unfortunate Captain, I believe, was out of action for the rest of the season. Is that cricket? *Yes*.'

1955

THE SIXTIES

NEW YEAR RESOLUTION

I think I shall not take the *Sunday Bosom* any more;
I'm not against the bosom, but it can become a bore:
And Nature is so generous with joys of every kind,
It's possible to weary of the feminine behind.
It isn't only *that*. I watch with wonder every week
The *Bosom*'s wild appearance, its hysterical technique.
The paper looks, somehow, as if it hadn't had a wash,
The printing must be done with a coal-hammer or a cosh.
Erroneous assumptions seem to govern those in charge –
One is that every headline must be ludicrously large
(And, now and then, in case it doesn't magnetize your mind,
They reach the peak of madness with a <u>HEADLINE
UNDERLINED</u>).
These, if they were intended for the old folk's eyes, could pass;
But most of what's below requires a magnifying glass.
Then meaningless 'cross-headings' which insultingly suggest
We cannot read a paragraph without a pause for rest:
And everywhere the editors belabour, beg, and bawl
In piteous apprehension that we *may not* READ AT ALL!
How seldom can you find in this maniacal affair
A simple piece of news in type that doesn't tear its hair.
You grope about and get, between a bosom and an ad,
A tragedy so silly that it isn't even sad,

For bits are in italics, and some other bits in **BLACK**,
While *asterisks* and ARROWS keep the reader ON THE
TRACK,
Or else, if it is high among the scandals and the shocks,
It's penned by wriggly borders in a fascinating 'box'.
In fact, you'll find a glance at this kaleidoscopic page
A strain upon the eyes that may do harm at any age.
You penetrate the make-up and unearth a scrap of news;
But it's in terms no Englishman could properly excuse.
With bogus Yankee verbiage the tiny tale is crammed:
It's 'currently' for 'now' and every goal is 'crashed' or 'slammed'.
If only less were spent upon sub-editors at play,
And more on men and women who had something good to say!
I often sit and speculate what kind of minds are these
That fancy you and I have got some cerebral disease,
Delight to start our Sundays with those bosoms by the sea,
Sensation with our sausages, and SEX beside our tea…?
But then, alas, I meet them with a beer beside the bar,
And, I confess, I find them very much as others are.
What's more, they tell me hotly that they know their business
best,
And many men, I must agree, admire the female chest.
So here remains a mystery that someone should explore.

*　　*　　*　　*　　*

Meanwhile, I *shall not* TAKE the *Sunday Bosom* ANY MORE.

New Statesman –January 2, 1960

THE NEXT STEP

or HARNESSING HELL

(By Our Unscientific Correspondent)

Science, ever-questing, has its nose to the ground – and this is more than a metaphor. With the Other Side of the Moon in the bag, the next target is nothing less than The Inside of the EARTH, a region into which no man has penetrated yet. Jules Verne trifled with the possibility: modern technicology can take it seriously.

Balding, gangling, bespectacled, six-foot three, 41, Professor Fancy stood by a small hole in a large field near London, and modestly breathed his dreams. Three sweating men plied their spades below him, after the ceremonial opening of The Hole.

'Anyone' he said, 'can throw things into Space. This began with the bow and arrow. Besides, Space does not belong to us, and nothing much is there. To pierce the Earth's crust (which is the property of Man) and reach the centre of our own planet, the Piccadilly of the World, is quite another thing. 7,903 miles from here –

OUC Is it as far as that?

PROFESSOR F. The Centre? No. That is the diameter of the Earth. One day – I can give you no particular date – at the other end of this hole, 7,900 miles away, Man will emerge in the garden of Mr Robert Menzies at the Prime Minister's Lodge, Canberra, Australia.

OUC Why not start another hole there, to save time?

PROFESSOR F. Because we do not wish to disturb Mr Menzies prematurely. Besides, the two holes might never meet. In an enterprise of this character many factors have to be considered. That is Project One – a cheap and easy channel of communications between Britain and Australia.

OUC You mean a kind of perglobal Tube railway?

PROFESSOR F. Yes. Nuclear-powered, of course. At 111 m.p.h. the journey would take three days. No seasickness. No airsickness. No stopping. No customs.

OUC And Project Two?

PROFESSOR F. Project One may prove impracticable because of the nature of the Terrestrial Core. The question is – What shall we find at the Earth's Centre?

OUC I haven't the slightest idea.

PROFESSOR F. Nor have we. That is the thrilling point and purpose of our work. Is our planet composed of solid rock? Is the crust comparatively thin, with gas or liquid at the centre? One theory, widely held, is that once we are through the lowest belt of rock, the Permanganates and Palaeoids, we shall find a core of very hard rubber, like the core of a golf ball; which may be a more formidable obstacle to the bore than rock. Others incline to the view that the thick outer shell – about 1,000 miles – is composed of silicate rock, and after that depth we shall find a core of metallic iron.

OUC Metallic iron? But that will be a tiresome obstacle.

PROFESSOR F. Ah, but it is probably in the liquid state.

OUC Oh? Liquid? They used to say that it was one vast furnace there – hence the volcanoes.

PROFESSOR F. That is a hypothesis not to be lightly set aside. It is not without significance that through all ages Hell has been imagined as a place of perennial fire, and burning the principal torment. On a planet which contains so much water, so many perilous seas, one might have expected continual drowning to be the ultimate penalty. It may be that before the Earth settled into its final form, primitive Man, through some vast fissure or funnel, may have set eyes on some fiery, terrible scene in the bowels of the Earth.

OUC But if this theory is right, it will be difficult to get to Mr Menzies

PROFESSOR F. That is so. But that leads me to Project Two. Access to this vast meso-global furnace will yield a source of power and heat superior to anything that has hitherto been imagined. Nuclear power – even energy from the sun's rays – will be nothing to it. Moreover, if some of the clergy are to be believed, it is a source which would still continue if our Sun should ever cool significantly, as many fear.

OUC You mean that the heat etc. would come up a little pipe to the Earth's surface?

PROFESSOR F. Exactly. After all, it has been done with oil – and gas from coal. The forces now uneconomically expended on volcanoes, and occasional earthquakes, would be channelled and controlled for the use and comfort of Man. The volcanoes would be sealed off and go out of business.

OUC In effect, you would be harnessing Hell?

PROFESSOR F. That is a somewhat unscientific expression: but for the moment I accept it. It is, I confess, in line with much modern thought and experience. All that old-fashioned fission-and-fusion stuff was once regarded as evil, because it was the father of horrible bombs of one kind or another. But when my clever brothers in Science announced that the same methods – especially those that produced the Hydrogen Bomb – would be directed to peaceful purposes in civil life, the whole thing became respectable at once. How much more splendid if the next generation learn to think of the fires of Hell, not with fear, but gratefully, as the source of their hot water and electric light!

OUC But will you not regret the failure of Project One?

PROFESSOR F. I think that a difficult question. I am a great admirer of Mr Menzies and should like to meet him again. But Project Two has tremendous attractions too. Think of the excitement as, at last, we break through the outer shell – the first men to see – and photograph – the Inside of the Earth!

OUC I hope that your pictures will be more exciting than the Backside of the Moon. That snap-shot served only to confirm the ancient theory that the Moon is just a lump of cheese.

PROFESSOR F. They may be much more exciting. Who knows? All previous theories may be proved erroneous. The interior may be one enormous hollow – no fire, no liquid, no gas – just a colossal cave.

OUC The biggest air-raid-shelter in the world?

PROFESSOR F. Yes. This may be the answer to the Hydrogen Bomb.

OUC Unless, of course, they drop one down the hole.

PROFESSOR F. It is not beyond the bounds of possibility that we may find some form of life down there – some primitive Troglodytic race which has learned to exist on a minimum of air. We may look down on an enormous ocean, slowly circling as the Earth circles, and inhabited by unimaginable monsters.

OUC I think the furnace theory is more fun. But won't it be warm work installing your Tube?

PROFESSOR F. That is arranged for: there will be many tubes. One will carry down the Shepley frigorific system which, as you know, extracts cold, by modern molecular reaction processes, from heat itself. As for the personnel, hundreds are being conditioned already.

OUC Who, do you think, will go first?

PROFESSOR F. Moles.

OUC Moles?

PROFESSOR F. Moles. We have one thousand in training. They are kept in ovens which gradually get warmer and warmer. They love it.

February, 1960

BIRDS DON'T WANT WINGS

OR, *A Note on the Scientist's Passion for Good Plain English*

The two great Universities have recently been debating, nay, boiling, about 'compulsory Latin'. They disagree: and it is not quite clear what either has decided, so we won't go into the general question now. But one of the favourite arguments may well be considered alone.

I read in a leading article – one of our 'popular' papers – '*Latin is not much use to the young scientist*': and a few of the professors have said the same thing in different words – most of them of Latin birth. It is the most astonishing argument of the lot. You might as well say 'Water is not much use to swimmers'. For the scientist (a Latin and Greek word) can hardly open his mouth without using Latin and Greek: and whenever he invents or discovers a new thing it is given a Greek or Latin name. What name do the go-ahead Americans give to the gallant youths who are going to travel in space (L) – 'astronauts': astron, a star (G) and nauta (L), a sailor. It is not precise, for they have not the slightest hope or intention of reaching a star: but there it is.

The same tough, progressive race have sensibly divided the world of 'radio' (L) into 'audio' (I hear – L) for what we call 'sound broadcasting' and 'video' (I see – L) for what we call 'television' (G & L).

Never were the dead languages so alive and kicking. You may hear one taxi-driver say to another 'Jim's queer, but he's better. It's a wonder what they can do with them anti-biotics'. You and I might have thought of better words – anti-bacteria, or anti-bug: but don't tell me that Latin and Greek are not much use to the medical student.

You and I may talk of cleaners and cleansing, but the scientist must have 'detergents'. You and I get along with bone-setters and would settle for doctors of the mind: both, perhaps, are inexact, and so we must go to the 'useless' languages for 'osteopath' and 'psychiatrist'. Almost everything in the medicine (L) cupboard, in the chemist's shop, in the healer's armoury, comes from the useless languages – acetic acid, adrenalin, ammonia, anaesthetic, analgesic, anodyne, antidote, antiseptic, anti-toxin, aperient, appendectomy, arsenic, astringent, bicarbonate, boracic, caesarian section, calomel, carbolic, catheter, caustic, chloroform, deodorant, diagnosis, digitalis, disinfectant, diuretic, embrocation, emetic, emulsion, enema, ether, eucalyptus, expectorant, farinaceous, fomentation, gentian, germicide, homeopathy, hygiene, hypnotism, hypodermic, inhaler, injection, inoculation, intravenous, laudanum, leucocyte, linctus, liniment, lotion, magnesia, mercury, morphia, narcotic, nux vomica, opium, opthalmoscope, pathology, pepsin, pharmacopeia, post mortem, prophylactic, purgatives, salicylic acid, saline, sal volatile, sedative, strychnine, suppository, syringe, stethoscope, tablet, thermometer, tincture, tonic, toxic, vaccination, vis medicatrix naturae, vomit, etcetera.

Then almost every patient (L) has something Latin or Greek the matter with him – not through his fault but because of some 'scientist' – abscess, adenoids, ague, anaemia, anthrax, aneurism, aphasia, apoplexy, arthritis, asphyxia, asthma, astigmatism, angina pectoris, bacteria, bile, bronchitis, botulism, bubo, cancer, carbuncle, carcinoma, catarrh, cerebral (thrombosis), cholera, cirrhosis, colic, colitis, coma, concussion, congestion, conjunctivitis, constipation, consumption, contagion, contusion, convulsions, coronary, corpulence, cystitis, debility, delirium tremens, diabetes, diarrhoea, diphtheria, dipsomania, dislocation, dysentery, dyspepsia, eczema, elephantiasis, emaciation, embolism, emphysema, empyema, encephalitis, enteric, enteritis, epidemic, epilepsy, eructation, erysipelas, erythema, exhaustion, fatal casualty, fibrositis, fissure, fistula, flatulence, fracture, ganglion, gangrene, gastro-enteritis, germs, gestation, gonorrhoea, haemophilia, haemorrhage, haemorrhoids, hernia, herpes, hydrocephalus, hydrophobia, hydropsy, hyperthyroid, hypertrophy, hypochondria, hysteria, incontinence, insanity, indigestion, inertia, infection, inflammation, insomnia, intemperance, intestines, jaundice (yes – from L galbinus – yellow), juvenile delinquency, laryngitis, leprosy, lethargy, libido, lumbago, lupus vulgaris, mania, muscles (L musculus – little mouse), melancholia, menstruation, monomania, morbidity, morphinomania, nausea, nephritis, neuralgia, neurasthenia, neuritis, neurosis, obesity, oedema, ophthalmia, osteomyelitis, otitis, pain, pallor, palpitation, paralysis, peritonitis, phlebitis, phthisis, phobia, plethora, pleurisy, pneumonia, podagra (gout), polypus, puberty, pus, pyaemia, pyrexia, quartan fever, quinsy, rheumatism, rheumatic arthritis, rigor mortis, rodent ulcer, rupture, scabies, schizophrenia, sciatica, sclerosis, somnambulism, syncope, suicide, synovitis, tetanus, thrombosis, tonsillitis, tuberculosis, typhoid, ulcer, uraemia, urethra, uric acid, urticaria, not forgetting the unobtrusive uvula, valetudinarianism (ha!), varicose veins, vermiform appendix, vertigo, virus, and, of course, dear old zoster (shingles).

So many things, on the other hand, that God or Science has created to instruct or enrich the mind of Man have labels from one of these ridiculous (L) languages – the Solar System itself, Nature and the Universe, the Ecliptic, the Equator, the Firmament, the Planets, the Signs of the Zodiac, the Ocean, the Horizon, the Celestial and the Magnetic Pole, the Prime Meridian, which runs through Greenwich, Latitude and Longitude, Hemisphere and Equinox, Astronomy and Atlas, the Right Ascension and the Declination of the stars, History, Geography, Navigation and Exploration, Comet and Satellite, Atmosphere and Orbit – School and Education – Art, Poet and Author, Music and Pictures, the Drama, the Opera, Comedy and Tragedy, the Theatre, the Script, the Scene and the Act, the Proscenium, the Orchestra, the Auditorium, the Photograph, the Gramophone, the Cinema, Radio and Television *etcetera*.

I should not presume to interrupt the dons in their lofty arguments. Far back in 1945 I prepared an Education (Latin and Greek) Bill. It provided that every pupil in every school should spend at least an hour a week on the 'dead' languages, not anatomizing the irregular verbs, or even muttering *amo – amas – amat*, but learning enough to read the news of the day with understanding and satisfaction – if it is only interim, agenda, alibi and quid pro quo, and what is the point of putting -ize or -itis at the end of words. Not long ago an educated matron of 36 rang me up at breakfast-time and said that before her little Willie went back to school he had to know the meaning of 'a.m.' and 'p.m.'. I said, 'But you can tell him that!' 'No', she said, 'I haven't the faintest notion'. If that was the law, if everybody had a compulsory smattering from the beginning the Universities need not have all this trouble. Every man, at this stage, could choose for himself. Perhaps I am wrong; perhaps it is a waste of time for 'ordinary people' to learn why antibiotics and appendectomy, flatulence, gramophone and television received those names. But if the Scientist, who invents and labels them, can do very well without the slightest knowledge of L or G, I will willingly devour my beautiful grey top-hat, the only hat I have. Let others off, if you will, but for the scientist they should be compulsory.

1960

ODE

CONCERNING THE AMERICAN CONSTITUTION

O the great American Constitution,
 On which the wise men worked so many hours!
O the great American Constitution!
 But how much better if they'd copied ours!

O the great – but space does not permit,
And hereinafter let us call it IT.
    Good constitutions grow, like ships,
        The present pinching from the past:
    Each voyage gives a vessel tips –
        None is exactly like the last.
          Thus, unlike IT,
        The British Constitution
          Grew bit by bit,
        A gentle evolution,
Not gentle always, no, for now and then
Rough things were done by rude, indignant men,
But on the whole the change was soft and slow:
We move like glaciers – and hardly know.
What is 'the Cabinet'? What Act
Decreed it? None. It's just a fact.
No man can open any single book
And say 'The British Constitution! Look!'
        It's everywhere,
        In cellars, in the air;
    Old cases, half-forgotten laws
    Will always give the rebel pause,
Some dusty clause he didn't know was there.
    And yet if change is wanted in the land
    Our castle is as supple as the sand,
    And all the liberties we love the best,
        The institutions too,
    Could be by Parliament itself suppressed
        In a week or two.

    But IT was built, a solid block,
    Of hard unmalleable rock
        To stand for ever –
    A pity, for what man can see
    Exactly all that is to be?

We're not so clever:
A pity, for some changes would,
If you will pardon me, be good.
About American politics, a man can easily blunder,
But the Elephant comes in somewhere, and I, for one, don't
    wonder.
For the Elephant takes – with some excuse –
A couple of years to reproduce,
And that's the rate of spate of the great
    American Constitution.

And so – no fault of the brave Marines –
They tend to reach the relevant scenes
    A coupla years too late,
        Though then, I agree,
        O Gee!
    They do some execution.
Nobody knows – no question's stiffer –
    Exactly what a Democrat's got
And how the Republicans differ.
(They might as well, it seems to me,
Be Party A and Party B)
    But it seems to matter
        A lot
    From the way they natter.
And that's what makes me laugh like a drover
Sometimes, when the loud election's over.
    At the end of the fray
        What do we see?
    A President who's A
        With a Congress run by B.
So when the President says 'Hi! we wanna grow wheat',
And the Congress answers 'Maize is the thing to eat',
'Wheat! I repeat', says the President, but all he gets is Noes –
Does the President go? Does Congress go? No, nobody goes.

(And this, at the risk of some estrangement,
I must describe as an odd arrangement.)

And then I have some personal objections
To all the palaver of Presidential Elections.
Gee, what a goddam complicated way
To find a fellah 100 per cent OK!
Two years before (the Elephant once more)
We hear the first of this quadrennial bore –
  Distant mutters
  From Senator Sutters,
  Long reports
  On Governor Schwarz –
  Then there's Attorney Blow,
  Dark horse of Idaho:
Eggheim may stand, if Muckelbaum is squared;
Schmoot favours Rumpeldump (as if we cared!).
 Then suddenly, it seems, it's *on*:
 Wackhauffer's won in Oregon,
Sol Rumpeldump is sweeping Cincinnati,
And Botch has knocked the stuffing out of Gatti.
But when you think 'They hate each other hearty'
You find they all belong to the same damn party!
It's Eccles calling Amory a villain,
And Butler at the polls against Macmillan.
  Then in both camps
 There's a rough house called a Convention:
  They act like tramps
 And it's all too silly to mention.
  Now Schwarz is kissing Schmoot,
  And Rumpeldump loves Root,
They close their ranks for the big campaign,
And the darn thing seems to start all over again.
Meanwhile, Washington goes into a kind of coma
For fear of offending the people of Oklahoma,

Daren't open its mouth
Because of the South,
Daren't say Boo to a Gyppy
For fear of Mississippi,
And the world must wait for the great
            American Constitution.
Two years in every four they suffer this petrifaction,
So half the time the United States is practically out of action.
        But we're a slick, swift-working nation:
        We gave two days to the Abdication.
        If things look sinister,
            If the people press,
        We get a new Prime Minister
            In a month or less.
            If the guy at the White House
            Turns out to be a louse,
            It takes four years – or murder:
            And what could be absurder?

'OLD IRON'

or, WHAT ABOUT THE TIDES?

I often sit and think – don't you? – with quiet satisfaction, of all
the bits of man-made metal that are charging about, here and
there, hither and thither, in that thrilling part of the Universe
called Space. Far back in November 1958 that enthusiastic
person Professor Lovell of Jodrell Bank, said (or so the
Guardian – née *Manchester* – reported):

'When I think of the enormous scientific and
technological problems which had to be solved, I still
stand in awe when I reflect that, this evening, at least four

objects launched by Man are relentlessly circling this earth.'

Does that thought often get you to your feet in awe? It does me. Oh, it does! I used to stand in awe when I thought of some of the works of Shakespeare, Milton, Dickens, and others (who also faced a few technical problems), some of the speeches of Pericles, Lincoln and Churchill, some of the music of Tschaikowsky, Wagner, Beethoven and Co, some of the ships that Man has made, for sea and sky, of photography and penicillin, of records and radio and radar and poor old-fashioned television. But now I sit stolid and still in my chair unless I chance to think of the invisible, inaudible, man-made objects relentlessly circling the sky.

But one trouble is that I have lost count of them. Recently it was reported, or surmised, that the American 'paddle wheel' satellite had disappeared (if a thing invisible can be said to disappear). That ruined the month for me. But what remains? I confess that I have not the slightest notion how many circlers are still at their relentless work. Nor could I tell you off-hand about their cargo. Do they carry dogs, frogs, cats, rats, monkeys or pregnant waterfleas? Fleet Street, surely, should be keeping me in proper touch with awe.

We know, at least, that any bits of metal still flying about are either Russian or American. There are some who fret because there are no British man-launched objects up there. This does not upset me much. I am quite un-insular, non-jingo, in this affair. As long as there are plenty of metal eggs in the sky I do not care who hatched them. I look forward to a great augmentation of awe when Egypt launches her first gay sputnik from the Nile, when China follows with two, when France and Germany, Italy, Japan, Greece and Ghana all have two or three. If every Member of the United Nations has three, that, I reckon, will make about 240 circlers. What fun! What awe!

Long ago, it seems, when the first sputnik appeared (but, my goodness, it was only October 1957) a foolish poet wrote:

Lord, what a mess the firmament will be
When all the nations boast of two or three!

And some of the serious folk had the same unworthy fears. A United States Congress Select Committee concluded that 'the technically advanced nations could some day obliterate themselves purely by accident – by throwing the automatic war switch in the mistaken belief that an attack was being made... ' What did they think might cause the mistake? The promiscuous, unadvertised creation of sputniks or 'satellites'. Dr Hagen, 'director of the Vanguard project', had testified before the USCSN:

'The distinction, upon a quick look, between a satellite going overhead or coming at you, and a missile or meteor, is not very great. It will take a careful look to determine in a very short time whether the object you see coming is *some old satellite*, an intercontinental ballistic missile coming from across the water, or a stray meteor coming into the earth'.

And the *Washington Star* said:

'Without advance notice of the firing (of a satellite), a Russian radar man might misinterpret the object on his screen as a missile headed towards the Ural Mountains industrial area... '

I call all this rather fanciful, don't you? And then there was some absurd stuff about sputniks, or parts of sputniks, returning dangerously to Mother Earth. The poet already mentioned wrote:

> '*Nor do they seem to know at all*
> *If rockets fizzle out or fall.*
> *At any moment, through the fog*
> *There may descend a bit of dog…*'

But those apprehensive Americans on the Select Committee went much further (according to the *Guardian* – née *Manchester*):

> 'The Congress report declares that the evidence derived from the experience of the Russian sputniks suggests that the heavier pieces do not entirely burn up or disintegrate… The heavy carrier of the second sputnik, which had a 1,100 lb. load, re-entered the atmosphere in spectacular fashion over the Caribbean. Large chunks of it were still visible at an altitude of no more than 50 miles.
>
> 'The carrier of the third sputnik…was a vehicle the size of a Pullman car, about 92 ft. long and weighing somewhere between two and five tons. In each case it is strongly believed that some pieces survived the plunge and landed, meteor-like, on earth…'

The report says that the damage falling chunks of satellite debris could do would be enormous. 'A large one might wipe out the better part of a city block.'

If this nonsense means anything it means that any one of us, at any hour, may receive a chunk of satellite in the chimney. What a pity to put such thoughts into people's heads! I am sure that everyone in charge of satellites will be most careful.

Then, of course, there are even greater opportunities for awe than the casual celestial litter of satellites and sputniks. I bet you have forgotten all about them, but there are two bits of old iron going round and round the sun. Or so they say. These – you remember now? – are not mere satellites, but *new planets*. The first was sent up by the Russians on January 2, 1959. At first, according to the Press, it was aimed at the moon. 'ROCKET SHOULD GET THERE TOMORROW' 'The Russians are completely confident that they will hit the moon.' Then it was going to go round the moon. Then it cleverly missed the moon, and we were told 'DESTINATION SUN – Rocket Will Become A New Planet Says Moscow'. This, by the way, was not a new idea. On December 6, 1958, we had heard that an American rocket, due to leave next day, would be 'aimed at the moon!' But the 'gold plated cone' might 'travel on into outer space to become a tiny artificial planet of the sun'. That particular fellow (Juno II, I think it was) failed. But later, after the Russians, the Americans did create a 'new planet' too.

They cannot be seen. They very rarely 'bleep'. But there they are, it seems, for ever, and I often give them a reverent thought. More treats are to come. On November 10, 1959, an American said that they hope to put a rocket (or part of one) 'in continuous orbit around the Moon'. That will be New Planet Number 3. No doubt, in due time all the great nations will create a planet or two.

I wish I could close on that note of quiet content. But once again, the serious fellows have upset me. Before the first NP took station, the gay and excited 'Scientific Correspondent' of a Sunday paper wrote:

> 'If the rocket goes into orbit round the sun *it will snowball into a full-sized planet through collecting the cosmic dust in outer space, and may well alter the complex gravitational fields of the solar system.'*

A high astronomer, the writer said, agreed with him, but thought it would take 'a very long time'.
The editor of the same paper wrote enthusiastically:

> 'Man has now the power to throw a spanner into the unimaginably complex machinery of the Universe. He can upset the cosmic clock'.

These two assertions may, for all I know, be nonsense: but, I must say, they sadly diminished my awe, and I wish that Science and the Rocketmongers would say something to soothe me. I am perfectly satisfied with the cosmic clock as it is, and doubt if it would be a good thing to upset it. For example, what about the tides?

There are still some old-fashioned folk who believe that 'the tides are caused by the attraction of the Moon for the waters of the Earth, while a similar but smaller effect is due to the Sun' (Whitaker's Almanack). For a very long time Man has confidently assumed that the present celestial arrangements will continue, and he cleverly predicts, to the nearest inch, the height of High Water and Low Water at points all over the globe, for months and years ahead. He has built his ships and his harbours to fit those predictions, and such is his confidence that he has drawn things rather fine. The big ships, creeping into our estuaries on the top of the flood, have only a few feet of water under them. Even a small permanent alteration in the water levels would be a tremendous nuisance: a big one would be disaster to every tidal port and city.

Now I suppose that if there were 1,000 awe-inspiring satellites instead of two or three they would make no difference. But 'full-sized planets' (the size of Venus, say) circling the sun and moon, might be important. Is it fanciful to ask if a number of them, all flying somebody's flag, might not greatly increase the pull of the heavenly bodies on the waters of the earth? You would then alternately have your harbours dry and your maritime cities swept by destructive floods. One week the *Queen Elizabeth* would be unable to get out of Southampton at all: the next she would be submerged at her moorings. Man, very carelessly, has built many of his finest cities near the sea; and in the end perhaps he would have to abandon them and retire to the mountains.

You may say 'Oh well, it couldn't happen for many thousands of years. By that time, ships may be out of date. And anyway, we can't abandon Progress because of Posterity'.

Oh, I say! Not bother about Posterity? Why then, do we go on paying off the National Debt? Are we really entitled to put a spanner in the cosmic clock (or whatever that editor said), to muck up, not only our own planet, but the solar system we inherited in good order and condition?

But I am not interested in what you say. I want a soothing word from Science. *Could* such things happen or not? If they could, are they taking any steps to stop them? Oh, let them speak quickly, that I may go back to my contented awe!

1960

ANNUAL DINNER

The Animals' Annual Banquet began as a brave affair:
There were Lion and Lamb and Lizard, with an Elephant in the
    Chair:
There were Tiger and Tern and Tunny, and Salmon and Swan
    and Snail.
They ate by a sandy sea-shore, for the sake of the Shrimp and
    Whale.
The Fish bubbled up by the million, and boiled in the blue
    lagoon,
The Birds flew down like a snowfall, and darkened the tropic
    Moon –

With a rumpus of roars and bellows and cackles and grunts and screeches:
The gist of the din was doubtful – but a Crocodile said 'No speeches!'.

Now, when they had done with dining, they lay on the hot red sand,
Sweet Silence fell on the Ocean and slept on the scented land:
Till slowly arose the Chairman, and he trumpeted 'Birds! Fish! Beasts!
We do not arrange for orations at the Animals' Annual Feasts.
But this is the first occasion on which we have had the Birds,
And therefore I feel it fitting to trumpet a few brief words – '
O Lord! what a storm of roaring, and hisses and howls and screeches!
The gist of the din was doubtful – but it seemed to refer to speeches.

Then roared a revered old Lion: 'Experience shows it's best,
When one has a full fat belly, to recline, to digest at rest.
You don't see, after his dinner, a Lion arise and roar,
Unless, and it's not the case now, we feel that we want some more.
So let us preserve our customs – but, since I am on my paws,
I suggest that the health of The Ladies is always a worthy cause – '
But then was a storm of roaring, and bellows and caws and screeches:
The gist of the din was doubtful – but the Elephant said 'No speeches!'.

Next rose a distinguished Sturgeon, and 'Briefly' he said 'I wish
To make an emphatical protest on behalf of United Fish.
We only, of all God's creatures, are proud that we make no Noise,
Nor, frankly, do we regard it as one of the Earth's great joys.

But, since we can make no speeches – what's more, I must
   add, can't hear –
It must be unfair if others – I hope that the point is clear – '
O Lord! what a storm of roaring, of bellows and grunts and
   screeches:
The gist of the din was doubtful – but the general theme was
   speeches.

Then down came a beautiful Blackbird, and he said 'It's a sad
   strange thing
There isn't a Toad or Tiger, there isn't a Fish can *sing*.
No wonder that none of you itches to sit at the close of day
And listen to Lions roaring, or attend to the Asses' bray.
But if at the end of the Banquet, instead of the stuff they do,
You would care for some soft rich music, from a vocalist or
   two – ?'
Ah, then was a storm of roaring, of cackles and caws and screeches:
The gist of the din was doubtful – but the gist of it was 'No
   speeches!'.

But the Chairman said 'Carry on, Sir', the pretty Bird called his
   clan,
And five and seventy Blackbirds sang as sweetly as Blackbirds
   can.
A fond hush fell on the feasters, and even the Fish could hear,
Old Lion alone was grunting, and a Crocodile wept one tear.
But then the unfortunate Chairman said 'After the songs we've
   heard
I have to propose, very briefly, the health of the gifted Bird – '
Then the Animals (Fish included) cried angrily 'Hey! no
speeches!'
The company hurried off homeward with bellows and grunts
and screeches,
   And Silence uneasily settled on the sea and the hot red beaches.
                                                    Punch – 1960

THE BLUE SEA

or, THE PERILS OF PARODY

I should have known better. I had been warned – twice.

I have always been against 'practical jokes'. But long ago I was on the rude Atlantic on April 1, returning to Britain in a 'banana boat' from Jamaica. The usual meagre meal of 'Radio News' was provided every morning, and one of the officers suggested that on All Fools Day I should concoct some special news to brighten the lives of the passengers. I did: and the officer pinned it on the board. Health is a big subject at sea – there is so little else to talk about: and among my political and general news I inserted two startling health stories. A new disease called *inertia praecox* was raging in England (especially in the West Country, to which we were bound). The Oxford and Cambridge Boat Race might well be postponed, for there were three or four cases in each of the crews. The disease was of foreign origin, and every ship arriving in England had to do two days in 'quarantine'. There was a lot more corroborative detail about *inertia praecox* which I forget, but one of the symptoms was 'an invincible aversion to normal tasks and duties', and another was 'an overpowering lassitude after the midday meal'. Then there was Professor Somebody who in an address to the Royal Hypochondriacal Society had deprecated the modern craze for vitamins. 'The latest researches show' he said 'that an excessive vitamin intake, especially in the form of fruit, may be dangerous to health.'

All the morning I listened, rather guiltily, to my fellow-passengers gravely discussing the news. The two small health-stories disturbed them very much more than the revolutions, earthquakes, fallen governments and tidal waves that I had invented in South America and elsewhere. They were worried, naturally, about *inertia praecox*, and the probable delay at Avonmouth. They drafted careful cables to hotels and relatives.

239

Many of them shrewdly connected the Professor's pronouncement on vitamins with this alarming new disease; and there were animated but inconclusive debates on the 'vitamin-intake' of the average man. The green sea of bananas in the hold was inspected every four hours. Any bunch that showed a tiny tinge of yellow was hauled out (for ripening it seems, is contagious) and hung on deck. There the fruit ripened rapidly and the passengers helped themselves as they passed. But on this morning I heard one old lady after another say 'My dear, no bananas today. You read the news, didn't you – about the fruit and this new disease? Just fancy! Two days in quarantine!'

At noon, according to custom, we began to confess our foolery, myself with alacrity, for I was sorry for our victims. One by one, I took them aside, and told them that *inertia praecox* was a myth, that vitamins could do no harm. But very soon I desisted: for they would not believe me. 'Don't be silly' they said, 'I saw it myself – in the *news*– this morning'. I told them that I had written the news myself, and they laughed – loudly, some of them, for they thought that I was trying to be funny, unkindly, others, for they thought me conceited. 'Nobody' they said 'could have invented *that*'. 'Great is Truth' no doubt 'and it will prevail' as the Roman said. But it will have a tough gallop to catch anything that has appeared in print – or even type. It is not for anyone who lives by pen and press to make a mock of Credulity, the principal prop and purpose of our craft: but it disturbed me then. Three or four days later old ladies were still obstinately refusing their morning bananas.

Many years later, I had cause to deplore all 'practical jokes' again. I went to Copenhagen, not long after the war, to 'lecture' to the Anglo-Danish Society, a fine friendly body whose members speak English at their meetings, even if no Englishman is there. The 'lecture' went pretty well, and the next day, rather pleased with myself, I was lunching with the Secretary in a delightful grill room. He showed me a newspaper with my name at the top of a column and, having no Danish, I said 'What does it say?' 'Well' he said, rather coolly, 'It seems you're a bit of a practical joker, Mr Haddock.' 'Never!' I said hotly. 'Well, listen to this' he said 'It was Mr Haddock who, with a friend, roped off an area in Piccadilly, dug a hole and for some days diverted the traffic with imaginary repairs.' '*What?*' I yelled, 'It was Mr Haddock' he continued smoothly, 'who, in Piccadilly again, bet Sir John Simon that he could not run a hundred yards in under 12 seconds. When Sir John said 'But how shall we *know?*' Mr Haddock said, 'Here, take my stopwatch', and when Sir John had run twenty yards, he said 'Stop thief! He's got my watch.' 'Sir John Simon!' I gasped. 'It was Mr Haddock who stopped a man in St James' Street and said 'Would you mind holding the end of this tape for a minute. We're surveying'. Then he went round the corner, gave the other end to another stranger, walked away and left the helpful citizens to themselves. It was Mr Haddock – '

Every single one of the late Horace Cole's misadventures were put down to poor Haddock. What a reputation for a man on a Goodwill Mission! I left the country at once.

Ocean travel can corrupt the best of us. Years later, after the war, I was in the Red Sea, returning from Australia in the good ship ORCHID. It was a Gala Night. The oldest gentlemen wore funny hats, and took a glass of wine. But it was not beer but beauty that led me astray – the beauty of the scene. Steaming North, we had passed Perim, and enjoyed a day that justified the poster pictures; a blue satin sea, a stage blue sky, with enough small clouds to make an arty sunset. The night put up a still more splendid show. Two planets escorted us, Mars to port and Jupiter (cuddling up to the Heavenly Twins) to starboard. Astern or above us, far better than the phoney planets, were all the senior stars, Sirius, Canopus, Orion, Capella, Aldebaran and Co. Ahead, at last, on the starboard bow, we could see the North Star, and Britain's own Great Bear still guarding the distant Suez Canal. Later that night I saw, on the port quarter, the

Southern Cross as well. Few passengers believed me, but the 'double' is quite possible if you stay up late enough – or get up early enough.

Thus, with sober elation, I surveyed the wondrous scene, of which the 'note' was indomitably blue – the sea, the sky, were Oxford blue, Sirius and Canopus, and a few others, Cambridge. Suddenly, it occurred to me – 'The *Red* Sea!' What a ridiculous – and what a repellent name!'

It was the work of a few minutes only to found the Blue Sea Club.

Here are some extracts from the minutes of the first meeting:

'(2) The Purser, Mr E W String, was elected permanent President.

(3) The following Rules were then adopted:
   (i) All members shall invariably refer to the relevant stretch of water as the BLUE Sea.
   (ii) Any member who hears another person refer to the RED Sea shall correct him with the words "You mean the BLUE Sea".
   (iii) There shall be no other rules.

(4) A telegram was then sent to Sir Winston Churchill. His reply will be circulated later.'

A few days later I sent the members the following cable 'as from' (for once, used correctly) the Right Honourable Sir Winston Churchill:

STRING PRESIDENT BLUE SEA CLUB RMS ORCHID BLUE SEA
I WAS VERY GLAD TO HEAR OF THE FORMATION OF THE BLUE SEA CLUB IN FAMOUS ORCHID STOP AS A SCHOOLBOY IT OCCURRED TO ME THAT THE RED WAS A FOOLISH AND UNFITTING APPELLATION FOR ANY PORTION OF THE SEAS AND OCEANS STOP TODAY THERE ARE STILL MORE

POWERFUL REASONS FOR THE CHANGE THAT YOU PROPOSE STOP THE COLOUR RED COMMA IT IS TRUE COMMA IS A GRAND INGREDIENT OF THE UNION FLAG AND THAT GLORIOUS ENSIGN WHICH IS WORN BY THE MERCHANT VESSELS OF BRITAIN IN ALL THE WATERS OF THE WORLD COLON IT ALSO DISTINGUISHES THE VEHICLES AND RECEPTACLES OF HER MAJESTY'S MAILS STOP BUT IN THE FIELD OF POLITICAL AND INTERNATIONAL AFFAIRS IT HAS ACQUIRED IN RECENT YEARS AN ODIOUS AND PERILOUS SIGNIFICANCE STOP AT THE SOUND OF THE WORD RED THERE IS AN INSTINCTIVE STIR OF REPUGNANCE IN THE HEART OP EVERY DECENT CITIZEN OF THE WORLD COLON AND IN THE LANDS UPHAPPILY ADJACENT TO THE DOMAINS OF MOSCOW ALARM COMMA WELL FOUNDED COMMA IS ADDED TO DISGUST STOP HOW INAPPROPRIATE COMMA THEN COMMA AS YOU SAY COMMA MR PRESIDENT COMMA THAT THIS NOTORIOUS TITLE OF STUPIDITY AND TERROR SHOULD BE ALLOWED TO DISHONOUR THE BLUE AND PLACID WATERS THROUGH WHICH YOU STEAM TODAY STOP IN THE GREAT LAND MASSES ON EITHER SIDE OF YOU THE WHOLESOME DEEDS Of BRITAIN ARE KNOWN AND NUMEROUS STOP UP AND DOWN THESE WATERS THERE PASS IN CONTINUAL PROCESSION THE PROUD AND PEACEFUL SHIPS OF OUR NATION COMMA CARRYING PROM HEMISPHERE TO HEMISPHERE NOT ONLY THE BLESSINGS OP TRADE BUT THE LAMPS OF LIBERTY COMMA ENLIGHTENED LIVING COMMA KINDLY GOVERNMENT STOP WHETHER ON LAND OR WATER COMMA WHAT COMPARABLE CLAIM CAN BE MADE IN THOSE REGIONS BY THAT COMMITTEE OF MORONS AND MONSTERS WHO

RULE IN THE RUSSIAN CAPITAL QUERY YET COMMA AS WE KNOW COMMA THEIR AMBITION IS AS BOUNDLESS AS THEIR IGNORANCE AND INHUMANITY STOP IF THEIR VAST AND WICKED DESIGNS WERE EVER FULFILLED THEY WOULD NOT STOP COMMA YOU MAY BE SURE COMMA AT THE RED SEA COLON RED OCEANS COMMA RED CONTINENTS COMMA WOULD DISFIGURE THE CHARTS AND MAPS OF THE EARTH STOP GOD FORBID THAT THIS OLD AND DECENT PLANET SHOULD EVER COME TO SUCH A PASS EXCLAMATION BUT COMMA MEANWHILE COMMA THE MERE EXISTENCE OF A STRETCH OF WATER WITH THAT ILL OMENED AND DETESTED NAME MAY COMMA AS WE SAY COMMA PUT IDEAS INTO THOSE CHILDISH MINDS STOP LET US THEREFORE COMMA BY ALL MEANS COMMA EXPEL THAT NAME FROM THE MAPS COMMA THE MOUTHS COMMA THE VERY MINDS OF CIVILIZED MEN STOP THIS COMMA I THINK COMMA WOULD BE A GOOD JOB FOR THAT QUEER BODY UNESCO STOP BUT IT MAY WELL BE TOO MUCH FOR THE CUMBROUS MACHINERY OF INTERNATIONAL DIPLOMACY COMMA SO EASILY PUT OUT OF ACTION BY THE SAND OF JEALOUSY OR THE SPANNER OF INTRIGUE STOP THIS MAY WELL BE A CASE WHERE MORE CAN BE DONE BY A MOVEMENT OF ORDINARY MEN COMMA ESPECIALLY THE MARINERS WHO HAVE THEIR BUSINESS IN THOSE WATERS AND CAN CARRY SOUND DOCTRINE TO ALL PORTS OF THE WORLD STOP THEREFORE COMMA MR PRESIDENT COMMA I AM PROUD THAT YOU HAVE MADE ME A FOUNDATION MEMBER OF YOUR CLUB COMMA AND I WISH YOU WELL IN YOUR WORK STOP LET

ME KNOW FROM TIME TO TIME HOW IT GOES STOP
SAIL ON AND PROSPER STOP
WINSTON CHURCHILL
TREASURER BLUE SEA CLUB ORCHID COLLECT

The small word 'collect' which means, children, that the recipient is to pay the charges, was put in to amuse the Purser. But the document, by accident, reached the Captain of the Orchid, who was heard saying rather crossly: 'Now see, what you've done with your silly jokes! £39! And who's going to pay it?'

Punch – 1960

A P HERBERT

A.P.H. HIS LIFE AND TIMES

In 1970 the inimitable A P Herbert turned eighty and celebrated becoming the latest octogenarian by publishing his autobiography. Already much admired and loved for his numerous articles, essays, books, plays, poetry and musicals and his satirical outlook on the world, this time he turns his gaze to his own life and examines the events that brought him to his eightieth birthday – Winchester and Oxford, Gallipoli and France, and then, in 1924, to the staff of *Punch* where he remained for sixty years delighting readers with his regular column.

Alan Herbert was very much an Englishman and a gentleman – outspoken patriot, defender of the good and denouncer of injustice – and, in everything, he retained his sense of fun. And this zest for life that saw him through so much will delight readers as they delve into the life of this great man.

HONEYBUBBLE & CO.

Mr Honeybubble proved to be one of A P Herbert's most popular creations and avid readers followed his progress through life in A P H's column in *Punch* where he first appeared. Here his exploits are collected together with a cast of other colourful characters from the riches of their creator's imagination. *Honeybubble & Co* is a delightful series of sketches revealing some of the more humorous aspects of the human nature.

A P Herbert

Light Articles Only

In this amusing collection of articles and essays, A P Herbert ponders the world around him in his own inimitable style. Witty, droll and a respecter of no man, the admirable APH provides a series of hilarious and unique sketches – and gently points the finger at one or two of our own idiosyncrasies. Such comic dexterity and inspired versatility is beautifully enhanced by a string of ingenious illustrations.

Number Nine

Admiral of the Fleet the Earl of Caraway and Stoke is, as one might expect being an Admiral, a man of the sea. In fact, so much so that for him, all the world's a ship, and all the men and women merely sailors…

The Admiral's dedication to King and country could never be questioned – but surely it was a bit much expecting him to give up his ancestral home for the psychological testing of candidates for the Civil Service. Tired of the constant intrusion, and aided and abetted by his son Anthony and the lovely Peach, he embarks upon a battle of wits against the political hopefuls. The result is a hilarious tale of double-crossing, eavesdropping – and total mayhem.

A P Herbert

The Old Flame

Robin Moon finds Phyllis rather a distraction in the Sunday morning service – after all her golden hair does seem to shine rather more brightly than the Angel Gabriel's heavenly locks. His wife, Angela, on the other hand, is more preoccupied with the cavalier Major Trevor than perhaps she should be during the Litany. Relations between the Moons head towards an unhappy crescendo, and when, after an admirable pot-luck Sunday lunch, Robin descends to the depths of mentioning what happened on their honeymoon, the result is inevitable – they must embark on one of their enforced separations. Finding his independence once more, Robin feels free to link up with Phyllis and her friends, and begins to dabble in some far from innocent matchmaking.

This ingenious work brilliantly addresses that oh so perplexing a problem – that of 'the old flame'.

The Thames

A P Herbert lived by the Thames for many years and was a fervent campaigner for its preservation and up-keep. Here, in this beautifully descriptive history, he uses his love and knowledge of the mighty river to tell its story from every aspect – from its dangerous currents to its tranquil inlets, and from its cities and bridges to its people and businesses. Adding his renowned wisdom and wit to his vast knowledge, A P Herbert creates a fascinating and entertaining guided tour of the Thames, and offers his own plans for the river's future. This is the perfect companion for lovers of both London and her waterways.

OTHER TITLES BY A P HERBERT AVAILABLE DIRECT
FROM HOUSE OF STRATUS

Quantity		£	$(US)	$(CAN)	€
	A.P.H. His Life and Times	9.99	16.50	24.95	16.50
	General Cargo	7.99	12.99	17.49	13.00
	Honeybubble & Co.	7.99	12.99	17.49	13.00
	The House by the River	7.99	12.99	17.49	13.00
	Light Articles Only	7.99	12.99	17.49	13.00
	Made For Man	7.99	12.99	17.49	13.00
	The Man About Town	7.99	12.99	17.49	13.00
	Mild and Bitter	7.99	12.99	17.49	13.00
	More Uncommon Law	8.99	14.99	22.50	15.00
	Number Nine	7.99	12.99	17.49	13.00
	The Old Flame	7.99	12.99	17.49	13.00
	The Secret Battle	7.99	12.99	17.49	13.00
	Sip! Swallow!	7.99	12.99	17.49	13.00
	The Thames	10.99	17.99	26.95	18.00
	Topsy MP	7.99	12.99	17.49	13.00
	Topsy Turvy	7.99	12.99	17.49	13.00
	Trials of Topsy	7.99	12.99	17.49	13.00
	Uncommon Law	9.99	16.50	24.95	16.50
	The Water Gipsies	8.99	14.99	22.50	15.00
	What a Word!	7.99	12.99	17.49	13.00

ALL HOUSE OF STRATUS BOOKS ARE AVAILABLE FROM GOOD BOOKSHOPS
OR DIRECT FROM THE PUBLISHER:

Internet: www.houseofstratus.com including author interviews, reviews, features.

Email: sales@houseofstratus.com please quote author, title and credit card details.

Hotline: UK ONLY: 0800 169 1780, please quote author, title and credit card details.
INTERNATIONAL: +44 (0) 20 7494 6400, please quote author, title and credit card details.

Send to: **House of Stratus Sales Department**
24c Old Burlington Street
London
W1X 1RL
UK

Please allow for postage costs charged per order plus an amount per book as set out in the tables below:

	£(Sterling)	$(US)	$(CAN)	€(Euros)
Cost per order				
UK	1.50	2.25	3.50	2.50
Europe	3.00	4.50	6.75	5.00
North America	3.00	4.50	6.75	5.00
Rest of World	3.00	4.50	6.75	5.00
Additional cost per book				
UK	0.50	0.75	1.15	0.85
Europe	1.00	1.50	2.30	1.70
North America	2.00	3.00	4.60	3.40
Rest of World	2.50	3.75	5.75	4.25

PLEASE SEND CHEQUE, POSTAL ORDER (STERLING ONLY), EUROCHEQUE, OR INTERNATIONAL MONEY ORDER (PLEASE CIRCLE METHOD OF PAYMENT YOU WISH TO USE)
MAKE PAYABLE TO: STRATUS HOLDINGS plc

Cost of book(s): —————————— Example: 3 x books at £6.99 each: £20.97

Cost of order: —————————— Example: £2.00 (Delivery to UK address)

Additional cost per book: —————— Example: 3 x £0.50: £1.50

Order total including postage: ———— Example: £24.47

Please tick currency you wish to use and add total amount of order:

☐ £ (Sterling)　　☐ $ (US)　　☐ $ (CAN)　　☐ € (EUROS)

VISA, MASTERCARD, SWITCH, AMEX, SOLO, JCB:

☐☐☐☐☐☐☐☐☐☐☐☐☐☐☐☐☐☐☐☐

Issue number (Switch only):

☐☐☐

Start Date:　　　　　　　　**Expiry Date:**

☐☐ / ☐☐　　　　　　　　☐☐ / ☐☐

Signature: ————————————

NAME: ————————————————————

ADDRESS: ————————————————————

————————————————————

POSTCODE: ——————

Please allow 28 days for delivery.

Prices subject to change without notice.
Please tick box if you do not wish to receive any additional information. ☐

House of Stratus publishes many other titles in this genre; please check our website (**www.houseofstratus.com**) for more details.